T0146453

Devil's
GAMBLE

∽◦ Tarnished Billionaires ◦∽

MICHELE ARRIS

Crimson Romance
New York London Toronto Sydney New Delhi

To my family. You all continue to be my inspiration.

CRIMSON
ROMANCE
Crimson Romance
An Imprint of Simon & Schuster, Inc.
1230 Avenue of the Americas
New York, NY 10020

First Crimson Romance ebook edition NOVEMBER 2017.

CRIMSON ROMANCE and colophon are trademarks of Simon and Schuster.

For information about special discounts for bulk purchases, please contact Simon & Schuster Special Sales at 1-866-506-1949 or business@simonandschuster.com.

The Simon & Schuster Speakers Bureau can bring authors to your live event. For more information or to book an event contact the Simon & Schuster Speakers Bureau at 1-866-248-3049 or visit our website at www.simonspeakers.com.

Manufactured in the United States of America

ISBN 978-1-5072-0807-6
ISBN 978-1-5072-0704-8 (ebook)

Praise for Michele Arris

Devil's Deal

"Arris brings a fun voice to romance. Her men are wildly successful, but they are also nice guys. The sparks that fly whenever the couple is together create a story that is fast-paced and full of humor and real emotion. Lucas and Bailey form a strong and believable bond that bodes well for the promised stories about their friends. The women are accomplished and talented and are equal partners in the relationships that develop — the Tarnished Billionaires series opener will put a smile in readers' hearts!" —RT Book Reviews

Chapter One

This is frickin' fantastic!

Sienna Keller stood just outside the door of the small office she'd been assigned by the director of the L.A. Municipal Art Gallery, marveling over the many art enthusiasts in attendance. Within the well-lit exhibition space, several stood before her pieces with heads angled, a few with brows pinched in deep concentration, and those with cheeks palmed, all studying, admiring, and looking to purchase her work.

Numerous orders had been placed at her New York exhibit last week. Now in L.A., so many orders had come in, estimated delivery on her pieces was pushing into the beginning of next summer. At this rate, she'd be elbow deep in watercolors, oils, acrylics, clay molds, and hammered metals virtually around the clock.

Following tonight's event, the staff hired for the art tour—thanks to her sponsor, Marx Venture Capital—would skillfully pack up the displays and ship them off to Vegas for the final three-day exhibit. She had one day to prep and another to rest before the doors opened in two days.

Sienna was happily exhausted. Never in her wildest dreams would she have imagined winning the D.C. National Art Gallery's Artist of the Year contest. The prize had been a viewing room at the gallery designated to display her artwork for one year along with an art showcase tour in New York, Los Angeles, and Vegas.

She'd hoped, wished, and prayed aplenty for a chance like this, and on occasion, had to pinch herself that winning the art contest hadn't been another one of her many fanciful daydreams.

The ring of her cell phone in the office gave her a start. She came out of her relaxed lounge against the wall and poked her head inside the room to read the display. Her heart fluttered like that of an eager child as she scooped it up. "Hi, Mom." She paused for a moment, waiting with anxious hope, but only received a low, distinctive exhale from undoubtedly a Marlboro Light Menthol. "Glad you called. I was hoping to see you last week at my art show in New York. I had a great turnout. It—"

"You had a great turnout, huh?" Another stretched exhale. "I would've been there, but you know it costs an arm and a leg to get into the city. I can't be throwing money away on cab rides. And sometimes life happens, Sienna. It doesn't just revolve around your little art show schedule."

Sienna bit her lip and swallowed hard to stifle the familiar ache crawling into her throat. "Yes, mom, I know a cab ride into Manhattan from the Bronx can get pricey. I told you I would've taken care of the fare. I understand that life happens. I didn't mean—"

"I know what you meant," she huffed.

"Mom, I only meant that you'd promised to come out that Wednesday because—"

"I tried to use my card yesterday at Micky's, but it was declined. That cheap bastard wouldn't even give me an I.O.U. for one measly pack."

"Sorry, I forgot to make the deposit to your account yesterday. I've been super busy. I took care of it this morning. The money should be there. I added a little extra for you this month. My art shows have been going better than I could've imagined. My goodness, mom, it has been fantastic. I've had so many—"

"It's late. You can tell me about it another time. I'm up well past my bedtime. I better take my medicine and get to bed."

"Uh, okay, sure, we'll catch up another time."

The line disconnected. Sienna set the phone on the desk, then resumed her pose outside the office against the wall. Weariness suddenly weighed heavier upon her shoulders.

Even at twenty-five, it would have been nice to hear the woman say the words, happy birthday. Just once. Whoever said you don't miss what you've never had was a liar.

People like us aren't granted wishes, child. You have to give up something to get something in this world. From the looks of you, you won't ever have much worth giving. You can blame that on your sorry excuse of a father.

Her mother's verbal assault was usually followed by a hard, bruising pinch on the shoulder just to be certain her words had sunk in. Oh, it had sunk in . . . crater deep.

Sienna supposed looking into the face of the child that reminded you of the person you despised most would cause disdain, even though she'd tried her hardest to be a good girl—kept her grades up, cleaned the apartment, stayed out of trouble, stayed in the shadows. Nothing had ever been good enough.

Her father had always been a trigger button Sienna knew not to push, even on her mother's good days, which were few and far between. It wasn't her fault that her genealogy compass spun a wide circle. She only knew that the man may have been Asian American. That was a big maybe.

It also hadn't been her fault her genes had spit out a long, narrow, toffee-brown frame and pencil stick arms and legs. Unlucky for her, that didn't stop her mother's lecherous asshole companions' unprovoked advances. A tightness coiled in her belly as old memories she didn't like to confront flooded into her happy space.

Shaking herself loose from that haunting period in her life, she looked around at her artwork showcased on crisp white walls and her sculptures perched atop white marble plinths. Her mother's words held no truth anymore. She didn't have to sell her soul to achieve her dream. And, as it turned out, she'd only had to wait another twelve years to sprout enough breasts and ass to balance out her five-ten, model-angle stature. *So there.*

"You keep scowling at the patrons like that, you're going to scare them off from handing over their credit card info."

Sienna's head turned to her sponsoring rep, Gavin Crane, Mr. tall, blond, blue-eyed, handsome, and massively irritating at the moment.

"Why are you back here holding up the wall instead of out mingling? You're not still salty over that order I placed for you earlier, are you? How hard could it be for you to paint the woman's dead cockatoo?"

Salty? Seriously, he didn't just go there. Damn right, she was annoyed about the cockatoo, but the current grooves in her forehead had nothing to do with his overbearing ass.

"Gavin, you fired my curator this morning without my permission. Then you placed that order without my consent."

"I didn't like how he arranged things. As for painting the woman's dead bird, judging by what I now know of your work, you could probably complete the project in your sleep."

Sienna took a quiet breath for restraint. It was either that or choke him. "I'll say again, it's not about the order being difficult to fulfill. I don't want you making promises to clients without checking with me first. As for why I'm back here, I'm resting . . . *was* resting my voice. I've been talking for six hours straight."

"You should be working the room, flashing that beautiful smile that I rarely get the pleasure to bask in."

He smiled, a slight baring of gleaming white, just enough to be cocky. The side compliment only made her bristle. She'd watched him most of the damn night flirt with every pretty face he came upon, cockatoo lady included.

"I think you've been working the room tonight enough for the both of us. That redhead with the Bichon Frise nestled in her Chanel handbag managed to hold your limited attention." A small jab. She'd also been taking a reprieve from him. His overt flirtatious behavior with the female patrons had become irritating to watch. She wasn't sure why tonight's performance pricked at a nerve; his antics had been no different back in New York. "When the two of you exited together, I'd assumed I wouldn't see you until we departed for Vegas tomorrow afternoon."

He reared back with a soft flutter of blond lashes, then his expression returned to a wealth of white-teeth charm once more. "You assumed wrong. I saw the lady to her car after she gave me this." He slipped a hand into the inside pocket of his perfectly tailored, charcoal gray suit coat, pulled out an order receipt, and snapped the paper in front of her face. "Madam, this is how it's done."

Sienna's eyes widened. She snatched the slip from his hand and studied it like one would a counterfeit bill. "Oh my god, these pieces combined are priced at about twelve grand."

"Twenty-five." He winked on a corner-lip whisper. "I marked up the price on each item. The woman didn't bat a lash."

She gasped. "Gavin, you can't do that."

"Why not? These people came here tonight to spend money. You're a new name with superb talent. They want to be the first to have you, but they don't want to pay what you're worth."

She flinched with a chilling streak of déjà vu. He was unaware how heavy those words were, having come so soon after the memory of her past had invaded and consumed her quiet, happy, Zen corner of the room.

"You're sporting that frown again. What's wrong?" he asked, concern in his blue gaze.

He took a broad step, impeding in her personal space, something she didn't allow people to do, even if she had to express physical force to get her point across. Her mom would have told her to take advantage of the opportunity. Sienna had vowed a long time ago to make damn certain that the apple *would* fall far from the tree. To that end, most only needed to be told once, but over the course of her tour, Gavin Crane had never respected her boundaries. He'd been the only man she could recall that she'd let cross the line without popping off to her back-the-fuck-up aggressive attack. And she was not sure why. Maybe it was his boyish, dimpled smile that always washed over his face when he looked at her. Who knows.

"What's on your mind, Sienna? You can talk to me."

His hand came up, and she was sure he'd offer up a comforting touch on her arm, her shoulder, her cheek, something, but that hand veered to his hair, fingers combing back the thick waves. He may intrude into her personal space, but he'd never touched her, not even a bump on the arm in passing or an accidental brush of fingers when handing over a pen. On occasion, she wondered what his touch would feel like. Rough and aggressive or soothing and caressing? Then she'd snap back to her senses. He was a problem she didn't need.

"It's nothing."

He cut a side-eye at her, studying. "I'm a scholar at reading people, and those lovely brown eyes of yours are telling. I'm only going to keep asking until you spill it."

My birthday was last Wednesday, and once again, my mother didn't bother to acknowledge my existence in the world because I'm a stark reminder of the man she hates, who I have never met. Her only concern is that I fund her account each month. And it all frickin' hurts.

She schooled her expression to put an end to his scrutiny. Discussing her nightmarish past with him wasn't going to happen. She'd suck up the disappointment like she'd done her entire twenty-five years.

"Just tired . . . and my feet hurt."

"I understand. It's been a long week. Another hour to go, then we'll grab dinner. Afterward, you'll kick back and relax. Maybe have a glass of wine. I could rub your feet and massage your calves. How does that sound?" Wearing a broad grin that lit up his blatant good looks, he brought his hands up and wiggled his fingers. "These can work miracles. I haven't had any complaints so far."

He'd have to touch her to do that. Why did her heart suddenly punch against her breastbone over the thought of his big, strong hands on her, a vivid picture of him stroking and caressing? What followed was a slideshow of his flirtatious conduct with many of the women the entire damn night. Not that she had been left out. He'd been dropping subtle *I'd like to screw you* hints from the day after her contest win where they'd shared a cup of coffee and he'd told her that he would be accompanying her on the tour.

"Thanks, but I'm good." Her reply was intentionally frigid. She didn't need the headache.

He inclined his head and eased back a step with cautious understanding. "As I said earlier, you're extremely talented. Quite honestly, I've been astounded by your catalog of work, and I've told you before that you've underpriced most of it. As your sponsor rep, I'm here to help you with the business aspect of all of this. Yet you insist on battling with me at every turn, when all I'm trying to do here is see that you get the best deal for your hard work."

Sienna didn't like being undermined, even if it had been in her favor. They'd been butting heads because of it from day one. Just the night before, he'd taken it upon himself to have the staff move her black and white paintings to the rear of the gallery because he felt the colorful artwork would draw more attention up front. They'd locked horns tight over that. It was well-known among artists that the opposite was in fact true.

He'd also rearranged the floor sculptures from smallest to largest merely for esthetics, he'd said, as though he was the foremost authority on the matter. Granted, she was new to this whole art exhibit tour thing, but she'd worked as a docent and knew how to set up a gallery, for damn sake. He could be infuriatingly officious, yet exceptionally attentive within the same breath. That irked her the most about him.

Too tired to argue, she let him have this round . . . somewhat. "Next time ask me before you go making changes and placing orders. This is my work, and this is my exhibit," she told him with calm authority. "Lucas Marx will get his money's worth of advertising for Marx Venture Capital, if that's your concern here. I've made sure his logo plaque is staged right at the door. It's the first thing people see when they enter. Heck, they almost trip over the damn thing."

He gave a dismissive wave of his hand. "Lucas's company is shelling out the bucks for this tour, yes, but he only cares that his wife is happy. You're Bailey's best friend, so he wants to ensure that you're looked after. Mostly, he wants to see a profit. As MVC's GM, I'm here to make certain that happens. Striking deals is what I do. I won't allow these moochers to take advantage of your talent. Now go praise your great work. That should be easy to do." Slipping his hands into the front pockets of his slacks, he strolled off, but turned, and walked backward. "That redhead with the dog . . . not my type." His gaze did a slow roll from the top of her cropped, spiky dark hair to the pointy toe of her black patent leather stilettos. A wicked smile split his mouth before he slipped in among the fray of bodies.

Sienna smoothed both hands down the hip-hugging, sleeveless black sheath dress that hit just above the knee. She couldn't help soaking up his not so subtle flirtation. Even so, the redhead, *not his type, my ass.*

Chapter Two

Sienna gave a glance over at Gavin beside her as they ambled down the brightly lit corridor and came to a stop before her suite's double doors. They'd been given top-notch accommodations at the Grant Royal Hotel and Resort; another perk of the tour. Both Gavin and Lucas Marx were BFFs with Sean Grant, the hotel mogul himself.

Each night after the exhibit, they'd have a glass of wine after dinner to relax, and he'd make her laugh by cracking jokes about some of the patrons that attended her showings. He actually had a great sense of humor. They'd talk politics—he took a progressive stance. Surprisingly, he'd appeared rapt when she'd talk endlessly about her love of art, and he even asked questions, which showed he hadn't been pretending to listen to her. When they weren't arguing, their conversations came easy, comfortable. She'd even go so far as to say, enjoyable. Go figure.

Exhaustion had her leaning back against the heavy oak surface to stay upright. "Dinner was delicious. I must admit, you've been spot-on about the best places to eat out here. Even that little rundown, crypt looking hole in the wall you took me to yesterday turned out to be really good. How do you even know about these places? Some of the locations where we've gone—" She paused, giving him a once over in his tailored designer suit, silk tie, and buffed black shoes. "Let's just say a mom and pop locale doesn't seem like it would be your speed."

His features tightened slightly, his stare intense. "Don't assume to know me, Miss Keller." Just as quick, his laidback, buoyant expression smoothed back into place. "Ready for that drink?"

"I'm pretty worn out." At five-ten, rarely did she have to look up at a man. He was easily six-four, all chiseled angles and fierce strength.

She'd never been the sort to get all googly-eyed over a handsome face, but whenever she took the time to study him, really look at Gavin Crane, there was something about the man's exceptionally attractive features and cerulean gaze that tended to arrest her. He definitely fell into what she and her girlfriend, Bailey, coined as the *hottie column*.

"We had a great week, wouldn't you agree?" he commented, breaking into her thoughts as he peeled out of his suit coat and draped it neatly over his forearm.

She gave a subtle study of the broad expanse of his shoulders in the well-fitted, pale blue button down, then met his eyes. "Yes, it was. My goodness, those guys had my work packed up in minutes. The same can be said for New York. Not one item had been damaged when it arrived here. Let's see if that holds true when it reaches Vegas."

"It had better if they want to get paid. I don't want to see so much as a chip in a frame."

His expression was stern for a moment before he replaced it with a small smile and came in close, close enough she felt his heat, but maintained just enough distance to hold the control. And he smelled good, awfully good, even after a full day of mingling and brushing elbows. A forearm came to rest against the door at her left shoulder—personal space effectively invaded. Why didn't it ever kick-start her barrier's alarm? Whatever the reason, a hottie he may be, she didn't have time for it. If ever she needed a reminder on where his sort of distraction could lead, all she had to do was turn to her mother.

I'd been hand-picked by my instructor out of twenty girls to study at the Ailey School. Alvin Ailey, himself, saw me dance. Then you happened, and that father of yours disappeared along with my full scholarship getting yanked right from under me. It should've been my face up there on that studio window display.

Sienna's stomach flipped suddenly. She couldn't walk past the Alvin Ailey American Dance Theater without wincing with a sea of guilt for being born.

Shaking herself loose from another of her mother's little lullaby antidotes, she took a quiet breath to let the tension within uncoil and forced the thought back behind her heavy safety barrier. "Thanks for handling the arrangement to get everything shipped off."

"You're welcome. Have I told you tonight how stunning you look in that dress?" His eyes dipped to the conservative V of her cleavage, then slowly tracked upward, returning his cool gaze to her face. "My offer still stands to rub your feet." He wiggled his fingers then, with a thumb gesture over his shoulder at the rich mahogany double doors across the wide hall, he grinned, that charming-cheek grin. "Your place or mine? I don't live very far. I promise to have you home at a decent hour."

Though her heart punched against her ribs as before, she maintained her detachment. "Nah, I'm going to take a hot shower and crawl into bed."

He came out of his relaxed pose, stepped back, and sighed with expressed disappointment. "I'll have to let my imagination run with that, I suppose. You have your room keycard?"

She pulled it from her black leather clutch purse. He took it from her, and with a quick swipe at the lock, opened, and stood just inside the room with his back braced flush against the door, giving her a wide area to pass without them making contact.

Just then her cell phone rang. She took it from her purse to view the display and quickly connected. "Hey. Hold on a moment." Pressing the phone at her chest, she looked at Gavin, whose attention was laser focused on the phone in her hand. "I have to take this."

"I'll see you in the morning," he said with little inflection as he reached to his right and set the keycard on the entry table, then his steady stare held hers briefly. "Sleep well." He stepped out. The door closed quietly behind him.

Sienna waited for the resounding clank of the door across the hall before she let go a breath, and her pulse managed to calm. *Wow.* She'd expected he'd ask to come inside. A small part of her, that perverse side of her, wanted him to, only so she could turn him away. Turning down his invitation wouldn't have been just because she felt he was a player or a pain in the ass on occasion, it was something else, some kind of deeply embedded feeling that her mind fought against.

Judging from the scrapbook articles from various local papers, her mother had once been a spectacular dancer, and had things been different, she may have even become renowned. Sadly, she'd never know. All the more important why Sienna needed to stay focused, not become distracted by a handsome face. She refused to become a scrapbook page cut-out. That being said, whatever it was about Gavin Crane, it didn't trigger the alarm whenever he came near. And that scared the hell out of her.

Remembering her call, she brought the phone to her ear. "Hey, Faith. Are you back home in Cape Cod?" They'd been friends since freshman year at Georgetown and recently had a falling out over Faith's attempts to hook up with Bailey's then boyfriend turned husband, Lucas Marx. Apologies had been made, but Bailey and Faith's friendship had pretty much severed over it. However, Sienna tried to maintain a friendship with Faith. Faith felt responsible for the death of her mother and was convinced her father still blamed her for it; Sienna understood why the girl was so messed up, why she tended to make really dumb choices.

"Uh, soon. I wanted to wish you a belated happy birthday. I'm sorry I didn't call last week."

"It's fine, and thanks." Hearing a rustle of sniffles on the line, Sienna grew concerned. "Are you okay?" She slipped out of her heels and dropped down on the couch, propping her feet upon the glass inlayed white marble coffee table.

"I . . . I'm good. No worries." A soft chuckle. "Well, it's late. I better get off. Best of luck on your art tour."

"Thanks. Faith, are you sure you're okay? We can talk. What is it?"

"I'm fine. I need to get some sleep. We'll catch up soon. Good night."

The line disconnected. Sienna frowned. "What the hell?" An uneasiness had her thumb prepped to hit redial, but she refrained. It was always hard to gauge her friend's mood. Faith tended to ride an emotional seesaw. Rest usually got her back on track.

Deciding she'd check on her friend in the morning, she rose to her feet and headed off to bed.

Sleep. That was what she needed herself.

• • •

Gavin tossed his suit coat onto the couch and tugged loose his tie on his way across the room to the bar caddy. He picked up a bottle. *Maker's Mark.* Not his first choice, but it would serve its purpose. He poured a small amount and tossed it back while pulling from his pocket the scrap of paper with the redhead, Courtney's, cell number scribbled on it. He filled the glass again about a fourth and carried it over to the couch to retrieve his cell from his suit coat pocket. The phone chimed before he could even pull it out. *Sean.* He read the text:

How are the rooms?
Free

Gavin texted back.

Lol, cheap motherfucker.
Presidential suites. At $1,200 a night, damn right.
Let me know if Sienna needs anything. Your ass can sleep outside.

As Gavin searched for the middle finger emoji, the phone rang. Ignoring his buddy, he took the call from Lucas. "What's doing?"

"Just wanted to see how things were going. I was reviewing the expense sheet you sent over yesterday from the tour so far. Do you have Sienna eating peanut butter sandwiches or something? Cost is substantially lower then I'd expected."

"You can blame or thank Sienna for that. Among other things, she came up with this ridiculous daily budget. The woman is excruciatingly frugal. As for her art work, man, the orders for her pieces are coming in left and right."

"That's no surprise to me. She has an exceptional skill. Make sure she has everything she needs outside of her self-imposed budget."

"I got it covered." Gavin set his whiskey on the table in front of him and relaxed back against the couch, releasing a deep sigh. "Dude, she gets pissed at me over just about everything. I can't do anything right according to her."

"Well, I'm sure you make that easy to do…the pissing off part. I heard you fired her curator."

"You know about that?" Gavin grunted, but it was no surprise. Lucas had a direct pipeline to the goings-on through his wife. "Damn right, I fired his ass. If he'd spent more time doing what he'd been hired to do, instead of staring at Sienna all starry-eyed most of the damn day, he'd still have his job."

"But of course, you're not staring at her starry-eyed."

Gavin dismissed the remark as he studied the slip of paper with Courtney's number. "One thing is certain. She needs me here to deal with these vultures, whether she'd admit it or not. She'd priced her pieces far below what I felt they were worth. Hell, far below market in this industry. Even that became a battle with her. Lucas, man, she's… Her work is incredible. She has this oil painting in her collection that blows me away. Every time I look at it, I find something new that I like about it."

"You're a lover of art now, is that it?" Lucas chuckled lightly.

"I wouldn't go that far. I admire her contemporary style. What's wrong with that?"

"So, you took off work for three and a half weeks merely out of the goodness of your heart to help her on her tour and because you appreciate her work. You have no ulterior motive?"

Gavin retrieved his glass from the table and took a swallow. "Dude, you already know that I was feeling her."

"You wanted to sleep with her," Lucas said dryly.

"Okay, I'll own that. But I see it's not something she's into. It's cool. My purpose now is to help her. I don't think she realizes just how much money she's made and can potentially make on her work. I'm talking fucking ridiculous money, man, if she'd let me guide this tour."

"I'm aware. I have the report. Well, I'll catch up with you at the end of the week."

"Sure thing. Later."

"Oh, what did you all do for her birthday?" Lucas asked.

Gavin blinked. "Sienna had a birthday? When?"

"Last week. Wednesday. I only know because while we were lying in bed, Bailey called her to wish her a happy birthday. Bailey mentioned that they call one another at the precise time of their birth every year."

"I didn't know it was her birthday. She didn't mention it."

"Bailey also said Sienna's mother was supposed to attend her exhibit that day but was a no show. The woman hasn't been a solid figure in Sienna's life. Hey, keep that info to yourself."

"Got it."

"Later."

Gavin hung up. He'd thought he and Sienna had become at the very least friends, if only in the barest sense enough to share birthday news. *Damn. Talk about keeping your guarded gloves up.* The woman was seriously closed off.

His attention shifted back to the scrap of paper in his hand. There had been no question Courtney wanted to play tonight. When he'd walked her to her car, she'd extended him an invitation to her place.

She had a terrific set of breasts and a body that offered up all sorts of promises. He needed to work off some energy; it had been damn near two months without sex. Why, then, was he hesitant to call her?

Sienna Keller.

Exaggeratedly cropped dark hair, slant-angled ebony eyes, full suckable lips, a perfect ass, legs that went on for days and all set on smooth summer-wheat-brown skin.

She'd been tumbling around in his head from the very night he'd met her at the art competition in D.C. He'd been awed by her talent, by her intellect, by her no nonsense attitude, by the woman as a whole.

When she wasn't battling with him over every damn thing, which he actually found kind of hot, she hardly gave him a second glance. It was probably for the best. It wasn't like he'd let anything grow beyond the physical between them anyway, and he'd learned rather quickly that she wasn't the sort for just a hookup.

The moment she'd want to know more about him, he'd have to cut things off, so what would be the point? Courtney was the sort he was used to. It was easy. No strings. Hit it and move on. A grimace of distaste flooded over him at the thought.

Sienna.

He finished his whiskey and headed off to the bedroom, but not before tossing the scrap of paper into the wastebasket.

Chapter Three

The final three-day exhibit would be held at the Grant Royal Hotel and Resort, located in the pulse of the Vegas Strip. The fact that Sienna would be staying at the hotel made it very convenient.

The elegant ballroom had been prepped to receive her work. Easels and pedestals, both in rich mahogany, were staged about the ecru marble floor.

Sienna walked around the room, examining and cataloging each of her pieces. Not a single scratch. That relieved a ton of stress. She'd been sure something would end up broken or damaged in transport, but to her surprise, every piece arrived intact.

"All good over here."

She turned in the direction of Gavin's call from across the room. Crouched over several of her oil paintings that lay flat upon the floor, he closely checked the canvases, running his fingers over the corners of the frames. She'd come to learn that he was partial to the brightly colored pieces.

He'd given quite a bit of his time to help her. When asked if being away from his duties at MVC for such a long period would put a strain on his position, he'd replied, "It's not an issue." She still found it odd that a man in his position would assist her. Surely there had to be someone he could have assigned to the task.

MVC was footing the bill for all of this. Perhaps he wanted to be up close and personal to ensure the company got its money's worth. That was precisely why she'd been such a stickler. It was important to be taken seriously. She may not have much going for her, like a Chanel handbag and a pooch to carry it in, but one thing was certain: she was a damn good artist, and a successful exhibit tour would broaden her art career.

"How's it looking over there?" he called out, breaking into her thoughts and the echoed silence of the large space.

"Same over here. Everything looks good." She strolled over to him.

He glanced up from his crouch over one of her oil on canvas. "I think this one is my favorite." He pulled out the title tag from the frame's corner edge. "Rustling Rainy Night." Meeting her gaze again, he gave a soft smile and returned his attention to the painting. "Right here," he pointed, "I like how you have the street lights reflecting the tree leaves onto the pavement in a multitude of colors. And how the couple sharing the umbrella are walking along the path arm and arm with their shadows blending into the wet pavement. I can't explain it in that artsy way I've watched you do it with buyers, but you get what I'm trying to say." His focus remained locked on the painting as he came to his feet. Then, he turned to her and stared wide-eyed as though he'd found some newly discovered wonder. "It's the most beautiful painting I've ever seen. You have an amazing gift."

He slipped into an intense stare, knocking her off guard. He'd never spoken or looked at her like that before, that look of pure warmth, no flirty undertone.

"Thank you. It's one of my favorites as well." She was too startled by his expressed sincerity to maintain her detached, all-business persona. A sudden, irrational yearning washed over her, the desire to want more, share more, but she pushed the feelings down, sealing them under a tightly closed lid. "I've made a sketch of the room's layout and put coordinating numbers in the squares where I'd like the staff to place each piece." She angled the paper for him to view.

He blinked once, warmth dispersed, cool blue eyes back to normal. "I'll see that it gets done. You go rest up." He glanced at his watch. "It's twenty past two. The exhibit opens at 5:00 p.m. sharp. When I'm done here, I'll get a quick shower and pop over to your room around 4:45."

Before Sienna could respond, he took the paper from her hand and started barking out orders to a young man attempting to situate one of her rather large metal abstract sculptures.

Mr. Pushy. That said, she appreciated all he'd done for her.

Out of nowhere, a yawn built momentum and stretched her cheeks wide. She hadn't gotten much sleep over the past several weeks. It was starting to catch up with her. A quick nap sounded heavenly.

She made another circle around the room, giving everything one last check. Catching a glance from Gavin, he shooed her with his hand and mouthed silently, *go.* Offering a smile, she left without objection.

Chapter Four

The hard pounding against the door woke Sienna with a start. She looked at the clock on the nightstand and leaped out of bed on a cursed breath. It was four thirty. The rumble of knocks came again as she hurriedly tied her robe, crossed to the door, and yanked it open.

Gavin rushed in, circling and scanning the room. "Woman, I was about to kick in the door. I've been knocking and calling your cell for damn near ten minutes. Are you okay?" He came up to her, studying with anxious eyes.

"I overslept. My cell—" She looked around for her phone. "It's in my purse." She went over to the couch and pulled it out to find several missed calls and text messages from him. "I didn't hear it. I'm sorry. I took a shower, then lay down. I was more tired than I realized. I'm so late." She sprinted toward the bedroom, but then came to an abrupt halt, and pivoted on her bare insteps, facing him across the room. "Why are you wearing a tuxedo?"

"It's opening night of the final stretch of your exhibit. We're going to do it up in style." He beamed. "I made a few calls. It's a black-tie affair. Invitation only. We will have a select crowd, one with deep, deep pockets."

Sienna frowned with quick mounting frustration and heightened anxiety. "I didn't tell you to do that." She stalked the distance to him, her gaze flickering over his clean-shaven features before taking note of that cool, confident grin. "You had no right arranging this without my approval. I had a load of followers on my Facebook page looking forward to this show. How dare you go and do something like this. Now I'll likely have no one show up, and I'll become a laughing—"

"I received fifty-three confirms, and twenty or so solid maybes," he cut in.

She blinked, fists still balled tightly at her sides to keep from choking him. "What do you mean fifty-three confirms?" His grin was as inflexible as his confidence that this whole thing he'd concocted wouldn't blow up in his . . . her face.

"You heard me correctly." He came up to her. Gentle hands held her upper arms, unmoving at first, then his thumbs caressed, an astoundingly soothing touch. Her pulse catapulted, her breath catching in her throat. Her knees surprisingly weakened, but she fought against it. "Sie-Sie, relax." Soft, compellingly soft was his tone. "Would you just trust me for once? As for your Facebook followers, they have tomorrow and the next day to visit the exhibit. I can guarantee what you'll make off three, maybe four of your pieces tonight, will cover the next two days' sales combined."

Sienna's temper dropped to a low simmer, and a warm shudder rushed through her that she hoped he hadn't noticed. The feel of his strong hands finally upon her—even if it was merely through the sleeves of her thick cotton robe—sent a spiral of sensation rocketing throughout her body.

He'd never used her nickname, Sie—another first—but he'd added a little twist to it, Sie-Sie. She kind of liked it.

"That's all well and good, but I didn't pack anything that would come close to passing as formal attire."

"No worries." He went to the door and opened it. In walked a hotel attendant pushing a rack of gowns enveloped within heavy, clear plastic garment bags. He pressed folded cash into the man's hand on a handshake, saw him out, and then turned to her. "I had him wait outside until I was sure you wouldn't take off my head. I didn't want the poor guy to get caught in the crossfire should your aim have been off."

"The night's still young, and I'm a good shot," Sienna muttered, and he chuckled. She wanted to wipe that arrogant grin of his off with a kiss. *What the hell?* Her eyelids fluttered in stark surprise. Yet, instead of fighting against the feeling, she relaxed within the buffet of her emotions. Still, she narrowed her eyes to stake her position. "You shouldn't have done any of this without consulting with me first. How many times do I have to tell you that?"

"Every chance you get, apparently," he mocked under his breath, while dragging his fingers through his neatly combed hair. "You get dressed, and I'll head downstairs. Guests will start arriving any minute. Enter through the kitchen. That way, you'll slip in without being noticed." Without another word, he turned, and strolled out of the suite.

If it wouldn't affect her reviews, she'd not show up at all. *Damn you, Gavin Crane.* Stepping before the rack, she jerked the garment bags, sifting through the array of designer gowns that were all a size four. *Think you know me, do you? Such an aggravating, arrogant, bossy, looks smoking hot in a tux . . .* She unzipped the plastic and took from it a gorgeous, red, one-shoulder body hugging number with a slit high up the right thigh . . . *Considerate man.*

She carried the dress over to the full-length, tri-fold mirror, viewing it from all angles. "Oh yes."

• • •

Gavin paced the kitchen, dodging waiters carrying trays of hors d'oeuvres and champagne-filled glasses. Cursing low, he checked his watch a third time. Twenty after five. How hard could it be to put on a dress?

He pulled out his cell and texted:

Where are you?

"Behind you."

He spun around. The sight of her stalled the air in his lungs. Her smooth, flawless brown coloring against the red shimmery fabric, lips painted a rich ruby-red, short, dark hair slicked down at the sides and boldly spiked up top, the woman looked fierce— tall and lean with curves hitting in just the right places.

He'd always found her stunningly attractive, but damn, the look of her standing before him nearly buckled his knees. In that moment, she could have asked for the moon, and he would have called NASA to hitch a ride up to get it for her.

She held up her phone with his text displayed, then put it in her purse. With a shy smile, she ran a hand along the back of her hair. "The dress, what do you think? It's not too much, is it?

I want to lick every inch of you.

Sticking his phone in his pocket, Gavin pushed aside the many images he had of them tangled together between cool sheets. "No, you'll fit right in. Here…" He reached to his left to retrieve the jewelry box on the table and opened it to show her the crushed diamond choker. "I figured whatever dress you chose, this would work."

She gasped; her eyes stretched and stared at the jewels. "Gavin, they're…" Her awed gaze met his eyes, and she shook her head. "I-I can't—"

"You have to look the part." It was a birthday gift, but he couldn't tell her that. He took the necklace from the box and circled behind her to fasten it around her neck. His fingers took liberties, the tips skating along her warm skin, gliding across the ridge of her collarbone. Soft as new spun silk. He closed his eyes for a moment and inhaled the sweet floral fragrance of her perfume.

She looked over her shoulder, and their stares held as her delicate fingers brushed his at the angle of her shoulder. "Thank you."

Gavin could have stood there staring at her forever, but her brows lifted, and she turned away, breaking his trance.

"Music? Why is there music playing?" She took a quick side-step to dodge a waiter carrying a well-prepared tray out the door. "Was that caviar?"

"It's a party."

"It's not a party. It's an art exhibit." She strutted out of the kitchen, purpose in her steps.

He followed, yet allowed a generous gap to appreciate the way her hips and ass worked that dress. She pivoted into the small office and dropped her clutch purse into the desk drawer, then stepped out onto the gallery floor. Gavin came up beside her as she looked out at the crowd. Waiters circled the room, and guests mingled and perused her work.

"See. What did I tell you? A full house. As we are in Vegas, pun intended." He looked into her fathomless dark eyes and smiled. Their gazes held. "Sie-Sie, I have your back. You just have to trust me."

Her brows puckered with a look of confusion. "You did this," slender fingers brushed along the jewels circling her throat, "all of this for me?" He nodded, and a slow smile brightened her exquisite features. She threw her arms around his neck and drew him into a tight breasts-to-chest embrace.

Gavin froze, completely caught off guard. He pinned himself in place, drawing on firm self-control as he wrapped his arms around her narrow waist and took in her warmth through the layers of fabric that impeded skin-on-skin contact. Within the tenderness of her hug, he relaxed into the warmth of her body, his hands subtly exploring the supple, lean angle of her back. Damn, she felt good in his arms, fitting perfectly along the length of his tall frame, as if she were created just for him. As swift and shocking as the hug came, she broke the connection and stepped back.

"Thank you for all of this, for everything."

I want you. It was as plain as that. In that moment, he wished he was just a simple, regular guy. No demons, no secrets. He'd gambled and lost enough times to know that revealing things about himself, about his family, that murky side of his world, never went over well. "Like I said, I got you."

"We better go mingle." She smiled, excitement gleaming in her eyes as she sauntered off.

Gavin sighed. "Yeah, let's do that."

Chapter Five

"We'll make a quick stop in Silicon Valley, I'll check in with the office, and then we'll head back to D.C. together." Gavin walked Sienna to her door. The tour was complete. Now they would go their separate ways. He wasn't ready.

He held up her black spiky heels. "I believe these are for you."

She took the shoes and slipped them on her feet, now nearly meeting him eye to eye, then leaned back against the door, eyes closing briefly on a sigh. It was approaching midnight. They'd gone out to dinner and celebrated the tour's success over two bottles of Dom Perignon. No doubt she was exhausted. He, however, was wired as hell. Champagne always did that to him.

"What do you say, Sie-Sie, will you join me in California? We made a pretty good team these past weeks, wouldn't you agree?"

"You do realize everyone usually calls me Sie."

He grinned. "I'm not everyone."

Her stare held his. "No, Mr. Crane, you're definitely not like everyone else. Winning the contest was wonderful and exciting, but a bit scary, too. The tour, all of it, had been what I'd always dreamed of, but I never thought I'd get an opportunity like this. When you weren't working on my last nerve," a small smile brimmed her lips, "you made it all not so terrifying. Thank you for that."

"You don't have to thank me. I've been exactly where I've wanted to be . . . here with you." Her expression changed—forehead furrowed slightly before she looked away. Guarded. He realized his words expressed a fraction too much sentiment. He'd have to be more careful.

"So, will you come with me to Silicon Valley? A couple of days there, you could relax in one of the Grant Royal suites and get pampered, while I attend my meetings. The tour has been nonstop, no doubt you could use the break." It was said casually to try to draw her back out from behind the steel guardrail she'd thrown up.

"There's that magazine interview I have to do about how the tour went, remember? And I need to get started on my painting. If I don't get on it soon, it'll begin to pile up. We'll connect in D.C. when you get back from California." Turning away, she pulled out her keycard from her purse. Before she could swipe the lock, he caught her wrist, unable to stand being so close without touching her. Her eyes widened, then leveled, studying him as she backed away within the narrow space between him and the door.

"Sienna, I, uh." Gavin didn't know what he wanted to say. Or was it that he did know, but was too afraid of what her reaction would be?

It went against his nature, against who he was as an individual to not speak his mind, always voicing what he felt no matter what. She spoke her mind, took no prisoners as well. It was one of the many things he found appealing about her.

"You okay?" she asked with a quizzical stare as he firmly held her wrist.

He nodded. There was so much he wanted to say, but was pretty sure she wouldn't want to hear it.

"I should head in." She pulled her arm back to dislodge his hand, but he jerked her against his chest, not sure what possessed him to do it, he just knew he had to. It was now or never. His gaze didn't waver from hers as he circled an arm at her waist, and a hand at her nape, holding her captive as his mouth crushed hers, tasting her for the first time. Sweet. So incredibly sweet, he had to fight back a whimper.

He arched into her, allowing the solid form of him to feel the long, lush contours of her, and could feel the tension in the full column of her frame, yet she didn't pull away, not at first.

A whisper of his name was felt against his lips as her head angled, lips parting, allowing his tongue to explore deeper.

From their first embrace, he'd since drummed up images in his head of how she'd felt in his arms and imagined how she'd taste on his lips and how he'd greedily lap up every ounce of her.

Her hand slid down to his chest and pushed, drawing back with much effort. "Gavin," she breathed, her eyes meeting his in full awareness. "I don't think we . . . this—"

"I want you, Sienna." Surprise flared in her eyes, then softened as he drew her to him once more, fingers snaking into her hair, feathering the short locks. Some days it was styled in spiky disarray on top and tamely smoothed down on the sides. Other days like today, it was arranged in cropped curly tresses that he relished in running his fingers through while savoring her unhurriedly, nibbling her lips as he rode the ebb and flow of her rapid breaths.

He dragged a hand down her back, over the curve of her buttocks, squeezing before gliding it underneath her dress as his mouth trailed a path down the delicate length of her neck, his tongue tasting her soft flesh, and then drawing back up, taking possession of her mouth, kissing greedily.

Again, his name breached her lips, but with more authority. She pushed away his exploring hand from between her legs and broke away from his fevered kiss, snatching short breaths, eyes wide, looking almost panicked. "Gavin," she panted heavily, "stop."

Her voice was a hoarse whisper at the outer corners of his passion-clouded mind, the soothing tone drugging. "You want me to stop?" Damn, how he didn't want to stop, but he didn't want to spook her any more than he had already. "Is it really what you want?" he asked, his breathing just as labored, the rawness of his need apparent.

She gave him a long look, then delivered a faint shake of her head before she grabbed hold of his shoulders and yanked him down to conquer her mouth, tongues dueling in a deliciously wet, open mouth assault. Aggressive and hungry, then slow and astoundingly tender. Her arms circled his neck and drew him in, kissing him with a startling thoroughness.

Pressing her back against the door, he rocked his hips, the jut of his erection stroking against her abdomen, while his hands took on an urgent exploration of her body, moving over firm breasts, slightly flared hips, and slender thighs.

Her hands met his chest once more, adding pressure, pushing until he drew back just enough to meet her gaze. "We," catching quick breaths, "we should get out of the hall. My place or yours?"

Hell yes! Gavin thought of the condoms packed away in his shaving bag.

Kissing the side of her neck, trekking upward, his tongue rimmed her ear. "Both. We'll start out at my place and end at yours." He pulled his keycard from his pants pocket. A slip of paper came out with it and fluttered to the floor. Before he could grab it, she picked it up and studied it. Something flickered across her face, then she drew back and nodded, sucking her teeth. "Stacey Palmer. Which one was she?" Her expression went from desire to disgust in a hot second. "I have to hand it to you, you do put your time in."

Gavin frowned over the grossly misunderstood intent. "You have it wrong." He scratched across his forehead, trying to quickly think of something to say that would erase the scowl she sported. "I'd forgotten it was in my pocket. I had no intentions of calling her. I haven't contacted any of the others," he rushed out. Her frown wedged crater deep. *Fuck, why did I say that?* Her unforgiving glare had him flustered. "Look, let's rewind."

Tossing the paper at his chest, she came out of her rigid pose, took out her keycard from her purse, swiped it at the lock, and yanked down aggressively on the door handle. "Thanks for the offer, but I'll pass," she said with take-no-shit certainty, strode in, and closed the door in his face.

Gavin stared blankly. He should have trashed the paper the moment the woman signed the damn sales slip. Talk about royally screwing himself over.

You idiot.

Chapter Six

Sienna's finger hovered over the keypad of her phone. Had she been irrational about the woman? What guarantee did she have other than Gavin's word that he hadn't hooked up with her or any of the other women that she'd witnessed fawn over him?

She'd checked out of the hotel well before dawn to catch her flight without a word to him. It had been wrong of her to be so harsh, so cold toward him after everything he'd done for her over the past weeks. But something had flared and struck deep inside her at seeing that woman's name and number. Jealousy. A huge coil of possessiveness had risen and punched her in the chest. Then to say there had been others as well... Though he claimed that he hadn't been with any of them, all she had to go on was his word. Could she trust him?

She typed: *We should talk about . . .* Her thumb paused, hovered. Talk about what? Her mad exodus from Vegas like a thief in the night? Stacey? His kiss?

Damn you, Gavin Crane, for crossing over my emotional steely blockade.

But she'd allowed it, so who should she really blame?

To even consider getting involved with him was bordering on lunacy. The last thing she needed was drama, be it emotional or with all the quivering touchy-feely bits. Why did he have to complicate things with his kiss?

Oh, how the man could kiss. That hot, scorch-you-down-to-your-bones kiss, accompanied by the feel of that hard, protruding part of his body against her belly, it all carried with it a ton of unnecessary problems she could live without, thank you very much. *But his kiss* . . . Eyes shuttered, she licked her lips, remembering the delicious feel of his soft lips crushed to hers and the taste of his warm tongue that she'd greedily sucked on like a woman in heat. Heck, that was pretty spot-on. It was almost nine months without sex. Being enveloped in his tall, bold, blond presence over the past several weeks had been an excruciating feat for her.

She'd secretly watched him, and oftentimes, had to snap herself out of picturing what he'd look like underneath his designer suits, sketching in her head the sharp, angled muscles and lean planes of his body. On occasion, he'd caught her looking his way and smiled as if they shared a closely guarded secret.

With that smile and his easy good looks, women gravitated to him. She would have sworn several returned to her showings simply because of his presence. Obviously, Stacey had been interested in getting her claws in him. Sienna's stomach took on a quivering tightness of possessiveness just as it had the night before when she'd stared at the woman's number. She released a quiet breath to calm the sudden surge and moistened her lips once more, recalling his kiss and his strong hands holding her captive as he devoured her mouth.

"Miss?"

"Umm, yes."

"Uh…"

Sienna's eyes sprung open. She stared at the Uber driver, who grinned a bit sheepishly. "I-I'm sorry, what was that?"

"I said, we're here. This is the address you provided."

She looked out the window at her apartment building. Absorbed in her thoughts of Gavin and his kiss, and his glorious tongue, imagining all the deliciously wicked things it could do to her, she hadn't realized that she'd made it home. Deciding not to send the text, she deleted it, stuck her phone in the back pocket of her jeans, climbed out with her suitcases, and headed up the walk.

There will be no more thinking about Mr. Gavin Crane from here forward, she told herself firmly as she grabbed hold of the knob. The door set open, just within the frame. She took a cautious step inside and drew up short at the sight of Faith cowering on the floor, her hands up, shielding her swollen face, her blue eyes wide in abject fear. Sienna's gaze flickered to the man hovering over her, meeting his severe scowl that blanketed his rough-worn features. *Dale Carter.*

Her mind flashed back to the night nearly three years earlier when she and Bailey were awakened by a police canine unit that barged into their apartment looking for a Faith Sullivan and Dale Carter. She and Bailey sat handcuffed while the officers turned their apartment upside down in search of contraband. Following that incident, they'd kicked Faith out. Faith was absolved of any charges, but Dale went to prison. It was discovered that he had been maintaining a large drug operation.

Though Sienna and Bailey had been furious with Faith following the whole search and seizure incident, they remained her friend. Well, Sienna couldn't speak for Bailey. Faith slept with Bailey's ex back in college, and then attempted to do the same with Lucas. It had sliced a severe fissure in their friendship.

Sienna often cut Faith some slack. The girl wasn't a bad person, she just had extremely poor judgment, a challenging home life, and evidently awful taste in men.

"What in the world . . . get your hands off her!" She dropped her carry-on and did a mad dash at the man, slamming him so hard in the chest, that he fell back onto the heavy oak coffee table. "What the hell do you think you're doing?" She looked around at the overturned armchair and papers strewn about, then back at the man working to gain his footing. "Your ass should still be counting down your stint in Jessup Correctional. Faith claims they let you out for good behavior. Good behavior, my ass." His glare narrowed, lips thinned, and she shot the look right back at him on her crouch down to examine the bruises on her friend's face. "What are you still doing with him? I thought you said you were going back home to Cape Cod." Snatching a tissue from the box laying haphazardly on her right, she used it to dab at the blood streaming from the slash on Faith's lower lip. "That bastard did this to you?" Sienna sent a venomous look up at the scumbag. Apparently, those years spent in jail hadn't been good to him. His skin appeared sallow and weathered, even more now that the judicial system's diet plan had gotten a hold of him. His brown eyes were dulled out, most likely from excessive drinking, smoking, and who knows what else. His dirty blond hair was matted and sweat-soaked. She didn't know what Faith had ever found appealing in the asshole. Perhaps it was some sort of twisted parental defiance. She could only imagine the look on the Sullivans' faces, especially Faith's father, Judge Sullivan, at the sight of his daughter entering the private country club with Dale on her arm.

Coming to her feet, she took a protective stance in front of Faith and faced the bastard before her. "Get the hell out of my place. How many times do I have to tell you you're not welcome here?"

"Sienna, I'm sorry. I didn't want to do it. I'm sorry." Faith cried into her palms, shaking, her pleading voice strained from her choking sobs.

"Yes, you should regret getting mixed up with this loser again." She helped her friend to her feet and over to the one cushion that remained on the couch, then faced Dale. "Do you have a hearing problem? I said get out!" When he merely smiled, flashing tobacco-stained teeth, she stepped over to him, meeting him eye to eye. "Assholes like you prey on those they can bully and control. Try that shit with me, and I'll kick your ass."

"Oh, you think so?" His lips twisted in cocky amusement. "Man, how I detest you, you smart-mouthed bitch. If I had more time, I'd enjoy seeing you try."

Sienna whipped out her cell phone from her back pocket. "I'm not wasting my time with you. I'll let the police deal with your ass." She looked at Faith. "You're going to press charges on this fuck-face . . . send his ass back to jail where he belongs."

"Oh god, Sienna!" Faith shrieked and pointed at Dale.

Sienna jerked her head around and was met with a gun pointed squarely between her eyes.

"Put the phone down. Bitch, I said drop it," he snarled through a malicious growl.

Alarm and fear stalled the breath in her lungs. With her heart pulsing rapidly in her chest, she eased the cell phone onto the table. "It's down. Now, Dale, put the gun down."

Visibly shaking, cautiously, slowly, Faith stood up. "Dale, please stop this. You've had too much to drink, that's all. You're not yourself. Put the gun down. We'll find another way."

"Shut the fuck up! We had another way, but you managed to fuck it up!" he shouted, his bloodshot, russet-brown eyes eerily flat. He swung his gun over to her, and Faith whimpered, hands up, shielding her face, and shrank back. "That fucking aunt of yours didn't come through. What the fuck am I supposed to do with three grand?" He glowered. "All you had to do was fuck him, and you couldn't even do that. This shit would be over if you'd done what I told you to do," he barked, then leveled his aim back at Sienna, jabbing the gun in the air. "I see your ass ain't talking smack now." He cupped his ear and leaned in. "What? Got nothing to say? That's what I thought. Now here's what's gonna happen. You're gonna take out your checkbook and write a check out to me for fifty large from that IRA you got."

"What?" Listening to the fool's jabbering, Sienna turned her head to Faith, who looked away. "What is he talking about?" No reply came as the picture was slowly coming together. "Faith, is this why you showed up at my door several weeks ago? Because of him? He's referring to you trying to hook up with Lucas, isn't he?"

Sienna clamped her lips tight, heart-crushing realization nearly paralyzing her. "You were to sleep with Lucas, then what, you'd threaten to tell Bailey, bribe him to keep quiet? Did I get it right?"

"He made me do it," Faith rushed out through tears.

Looking around her ransacked apartment, Sienna shook her head in shock, hurt, and utter betrayal. "You and your piece of shit boyfriend also came here to rob me." Caught off guard, her head swung sideways, and her body hit the floor hard from the thunderous blow of both Dale's fist and the butt of the gun in his hand. A gash opened above her left eye. "You son of a bitch." Dazed, she shook her head to quiet the ringing in her ears while crawling away from him stalking toward her.

"Bitch, you're asking me to put a bullet in your fucking head." His brutal hand grabbed her by the throat, squeezing, squeezing, squeezing. "Where's your checkbook to that IRA? Faith told me all about that insurance money you got when your grandma died."

"Fuck you!" Sienna shrilled and swung out. Her nails caught him across the left side of his face. At that same moment, Faith screeched and jumped on Dale's back, wildly punching and scratching, causing him to release his suffocating hold. Dizzy, with blood blurring her vision in her left eye, Sienna sucked in much needed air, latching on to consciousness by a pure, primal desire to survive.

She managed to see through the growing fogginess that Dale still held the gun aimed at her, unwavering as he reached back with his free hand, and seized Faith's hair. Faith screamed as a clump was yanked out of her scalp.

Seeing Dale shift his attention to getting Faith off him by repeatedly slamming his back against the wall, Sienna used the opportunity to scramble across the floor for her phone. Before she could dial for help, Dale had shaken Faith loose with her dropping to the floor. He stalked forward. Sienna armed herself with the figurine lying on its side upon the table and swung out, shattering the weighty ceramic against his knee. He let loose a blood-curdling howl, stumbled, and fell back on his ass. She was aiming for his gun hand, but her equilibrium was grossly askew—seeing double out of her good eye. He was more than pissed at her now as he pointed the gun at her chest.

"Bitch, oh, you're gonna pay for that." A growl ripped out, low, rumbling.

This was how she would die. He was going to kill her. She saw it in his dark, soulless eyes as his arm stretched taut, his intention precise. She scrambled backward, desperately trying to get out of the way of his aim.

Everything seemed to slow down. Behind Dale, she watched as Faith came to her feet, let out a feral cry on a running leap, and tackled her at the resounding click. A stinging heat rippled up Sienna's left side to her chest, seizing all breath from her. She felt herself slipping into darkness before she hit the carpet.

Chapter Seven

Gavin came awake to the sound of his cell phone ringing on the nightstand. With his face buried in the pillow, he snatched it up and cracked open an eye to view the display. *Lucas.* Giving a look at the digital clock on the nightstand, he tapped the phone, and brought it to his ear. "What?"

"Get to the plane."

"Do you know what time it is?" He pinched his tired eyes.

"It's Sienna."

Stretching his limbs, he rolled to his back, and yawned out, "What about Sienna?"

"She's been shot."

Gavin sprung upright. "What! What happened? Is she all right?" His heart raced like a speeding train, his distress instantly choking his throat.

"Bailey's friend, Kevin, called me. It was Faith's boyfriend, a guy named Dale Carter. Kevin said the shooting happened yesterday in Sienna's apartment. He found them unconscious.

"Sienna has been moved from the ICU. Faith's injury wasn't severe. According to Kevin, the bullet passed through her shoulder and into Sienna, cracking one of her ribs. It's what prevented Sienna from suffering more internal injuries. Kevin was told by the doctor that had the bullet been a few centimeters higher, it would have hit Sienna's heart.

Gavin sucked a quick intake of breath. "Damn."

"We'll meet you at the plane."

He was already shoving his legs into his jeans. "I'll be there."

Chapter Eight

"I'm aware you didn't have to take my call." Gavin palmed his forehead, fingers scratching agitatedly back and forth. "And I'm very much aware that you didn't have to help me out." He let out a heavy sigh. How many times did he have to hear that he was an ungrateful son? Apparently a thousand times wasn't the magic number.

Thinking of Sienna laid up in the hospital from a gunshot wound and fighting a concussion—he'd learned that she'd also been struck in the head during the assault—it was worth the sacrifice of listening to Murtagh Kavanagh drone on. Contacting him wasn't a smart move, but Gavin had acted on blind impulse, fearing for Sienna's safety. Now, as long as the man's security watched over her, he'd happily sit back and take the verbal beat-down. That fool, Dale, that shot her could come for her. The probability was high, since he still hadn't been apprehended.

His jaw clenched, fury filling him as he imagined the many ways he intended to maim that asshole that hurt his lady. Okay, she wasn't his lady. Still, it terrified him how easily he could have lost her. Dale would discover that hurting her was his grandest mistake.

"Do you understand your importance, son?"

Gavin blinked, torn from his thoughts. A good fifteen seconds had been missed of the convo. "If you say so," he answered, not sure about what exactly, but assumed it likely had to do with the debt he now owed his father for the use of his men. They'd settled on three assignments, and he'd be at the man's beck and call to carry them out. Fucking fantastic. *Not.*

"This is a perfect opportunity for you to learn the intricacies of the organization, get a feel for how tasks are handed down, and the repercussions when my orders aren't followed to the letter," Murtagh said.

If that merely meant ordering the wrong office supplies, Gavin would shake it off, dismiss it. Instead, the true meaning of those words chilled the blood in his veins. "I have to go. I'll come by the house when things settle down."

"Do I need to remind you of our agreement?"

As if he would ever forget. "I said I'd be by after I get a handle on things. Later." He closed the line, and then closed his eyes. Seated at the conference table aboard Lucas's private jet, he reared back in his chair to collect himself. Talking to his father always made him edgy. The man didn't deal in simple acts of kindness. Everything came at a price.

He got up and joined Lucas and Bailey seated at the opposite end of the cabin, slouching down in the chair across from the couple.

"Hey, should I be congratulating you?" Bailey asked and then turned her head to Lucas. "You know about this?" He merely relaxed back with an arm draped along the spine of the leather couch. "You do, don't you?" Lucas winked at her, and her lips twisted in a smirk, while giving him a playful slap on the thigh. She then turned back and said, "Kevin mentioned you told the hospital that you're Sienna's husband. They'll only release information on her condition to a Mr. Gavin Crane. You also had guards stationed outside Sienna and Faith's rooms. Thank you for that. I was worried Dale might show up, since they can identify him."

"I see we think alike. That's precisely why I did it. What can you tell me about that chump, Dale?"

"You have a security staff at your beck and call. I thought you were general manager of Marx Venture Capital. What is it exactly that you do for Lucas?" was her question instead. "Should I be concerned for my husband's safety?" It was said with a smile, yet her inquisitive gaze shifted back and forth between him and her husband.

"Kevin mentioned that Dale is involved with some pretty hard hitters in the drug scene," Lucas put in. He and Gavin exchanged knowing looks in his obvious attempt to redirect the conversation away from her question. They'd been friends since the age of six, and his buddy helped to guard his secret.

"Dale was released from prison a few months ago on *good behavior*." Bailey made hard air quotes. "He'd been incarcerated because of some drug-related offense that he and Faith had been mixed up in years ago. By the way, I called Faith's father and stepmother. They're on their way. The only number I had for Sienna's mother had been disconnected." She looked at Gavin. "Did you and my best friend get married while in Vegas or not?"

"Trust me, if we were married, Sienna would've been in California with me, instead of leaving without a word." He forced a grin. "I suppose, three and a half weeks of me hanging around was her limit." Reading Bailey's pitying gaze—ladies apparently talk—he went on. "I gave the hospital instruction that your friends, Kevin and Diego, are the only individuals allowed in Sienna's room. No one else," he said firmly. "I don't want anyone near her other than the hospital staff until I get there. That bastard that shot her will know that she's heavily protected. He should pray the police locate his ass before I do. He will pay for this shit. Does he think he can attack her and continue to breathe?" Across from him, Bailey's green eyes widened. Irritation had roughened his tone. He didn't mean to show it, but the mere thought of that asshole brought the fury in him to the surface. Gavin took a breath to level out. "I just need to see for myself that Sienna's okay."

"Me too. Kevin said according to the doctor, there was evidence that she'd tried to fight back. What Dale did . . . if I'd lost Sienna..." Bailey pressed fingers to her lips to stifle the slight quiver, eyes glistening with unshed tears. "She's like my sister." Her husband took her hand and placed a kiss in her palm to help settle her distress. Their gazes met, sharing a momentary exchange of affection.

"Try not to worry. You don't want to stress yourself," Lucas cautioned and caressed a hand across the slight roundness of her pregnant belly in the fitted white T-shirt.

Bailey nodded. "I knew Faith was up to something. She showed up out of the blue after two years without a peep from her."

Lucas leaned forward and rested his elbows on his knees. "When Faith came to my office," he glimpsed over his shoulder at his wife, whose stare was trained on him, "Faith told me her boyfriend was in some sort of trouble, and that he forced her to try to seduce me into sleeping with her." He gave another glance at his wife. She offered a supportive nod and tenderly stroked his back. "Faith intended to blackmail me into giving her money. She tried to tell me something else, but I'd become so angry over what she'd tried to do, I threw her out. Maybe this was it. Dale may have threatened to hurt her if she didn't follow through. Or maybe he threatened to harm Sienna and Bailey. Had I just given her the damn money, this wouldn't have happened. Sienna wouldn't have been nearly killed."

"Bro, you and I know that shit never ends there. That chump would've kept coming back. It's not your fault," Gavin told him.

"He's right, babe. Dale is bad news, always have been." Bailey told a story about a police raid that took place at her and Sienna's apartment several years ago. The canine unit searched their place for drug contraband, all thanks to Faith and her involvement with Dale.

"It sickens me that Sienna was caught in the middle of Dale and Faith's mess."

"Yeah—" Gavin paused to listen to the pilot over the intercom informing them that the plane was about to land. "It will be this Dale asshole's life regret. Believe that."

Chapter Nine

"Excuse me, we're looking for Sienna Keller's room."

Hospital staff busied about within the narrow administration area, tripping over feet. Gavin's address had been to whoever would bite first.

Three individuals—two ladies and a man—looked up. The stocky redhead closest to him tilted her head to her computer screen. Her fingers tapped on a few keys.

The man seated at the far end rose from his chair and came forward. "Janet, she's the one with the guards posted. Sir, I'm afraid she's under restriction. Your name?"

It was good to see someone on the ball. "Gavin Crane, her husband." He flipped his driver's license before the man, who checked it against the information on Nurse Redhead's computer. The hospital had been informed that Sienna went by her maiden name. Gavin didn't expect there to be any issue.

"Mr. Crane, I'm Owen, the one you spoke to earlier. Your wife was moved to a private room as you requested. I made my rounds an hour ago. She was resting." Owen flipped through papers on a clipboard. "Um, I have here the doctor should be in to see her around eight o'clock."

Simultaneously, Gavin, Bailey, and Lucas checked their watches. It was 7:40 a.m. "Good to know. Which way?" Gavin asked.

Owen pointed left. "Down the hall there, then make your first right. You'll see the two men standing outside her door at the end of the hall."

"Thanks."

Spotting the guards, Bailey rushed ahead but was stalled at the door by a hand planted solidly on her shoulder.

Lucas shot forward, brows creased. "Take your hand off her before I break it off."

Gavin came up, towering over the broad-shouldered guard that mocked his glare. "You heard him. What the hell is wrong with you?"

The guard dropped his hand but boldly stood his ground. "No one is to enter." His tone was direct and decisive. "Unless . . . are you a cop?"

"Do I look like a damn cop?" Gavin snarled. His attention shifted, recognizing the other man. "Mike, who's this chump?"

"Mr. Crane, this here is Danny Lafferty." Beside him, Danny sucked in a breath, apparently realizing his grave mistake.

Eyeing the young punk that had more muscles than brain, Gavin realized that good ol' Pop had sent a whelp as penance for his not wanting any part in the family business. Gavin preferred to live his life free of the DEA, ATF, FBI, etc., while his father and most of his family worked daily at ducking and dodging the feds—except for his mother, who was smart to opt out via divorce.

Like the Italian mafia, the Irish had their fair share of organized crime, and *not so lucky me happens to be the second born son to the Northeast's top man in charge.*

"Where's Ian?" Gavin asked.

Mike shifted his weight from one foot to the other, back and forth, as if relieving the pressure from shoes that were a size too small. "He's stuck on an assignment. Your father had me take Danny here in his place, you know, to give 'im some exposure." Mike glimpsed over at Danny's ghost-sheet complexion now looking in need of medical attention. "I had 'im stationed at the other lady's room, but her people showed up and took her away, so I got 'im here with me."

"Sor-sorry, Mr. Crane, just doing my job," Danny uttered, eyelids low.

"He's Maggie's boy. I don't know if you remember her. I should've told 'im it was you, sir. I take full responsibility." Mike opened the door and stepped aside. "All's been quiet here, apart from the hospital workers coming and going."

"It's good to see you, Mike." They shook hands.

"You, too, Mr. Crane."

They entered the room, and Kevin stood up from the couch.

Bailey approached Sienna's sleeping form and lightly placed a kiss above the bandage that stretched from her left brow to her temple, then moved to Kevin and gave him a hug.

Gavin cut a look at Lucas, whose blue eyes were laser focused on Bailey nestled within her ex's arms. The two men had once come to fisticuffs over the woman. The fact that his wife maintained a friendship with her ex, knowing Lucas the way that Gavin did, it had to be difficult for his buddy. That said, the couple was madly in love, and they were going to have a baby. There really weren't any issues from what Gavin could see.

"How is she?" Bailey whispered and came out of Kevin's embrace.

Kevin looked past Bailey to Lucas and acknowledged him with a nod. The same stiff greeting was given to Gavin now seated in the chair at Sienna's bedside, holding her hand. Looking down at Bailey, Kevin's eyes softened. Unadulterated affection for the woman flooded his bold, dark features. "She's in and out. She'll be glad to see you."

"Faith's gone?" Bailey asked.

"Her father arranged for her to get treatment at a psych facility near his home. Faith kept screaming that she'd killed Sienna just like she'd killed her mother. They had to sedate her." Kevin shook his head. "She killed her own mother. That's some wild shit."

"It was an accident. Her mother had been drinking and grabbed the wheel," Bailey said in quick defense.

"I can't get more on Sienna's condition," Kevin made a gesture with his chin in Gavin's direction, "because your boy over there told them that he's her husband. They'll only speak with him."

Gavin looked up from studying the bandage on Sienna's face. "It was for her safety. It was the only way I could have my men guard her until I arrived."

Kevin's glower was scalding. "Do you think I would've let anyone get near her? I haven't left her side."

Gavin tensed as a huge boulder of possessiveness rose in his chest. "I don't know, Kevin, one might think this is more than you merely being neighborly."

"Your type would think that," Kevin shot back. "Not that it's any of your business, but Sienna and Bailey are good *friends* of mine. I've always looked out for the both of them. And Diego watched over Faith until her parents arrived. In other words, we got this. Sienna didn't need you saying that you're her husband, bringing in all of this drama with guards and shit."

"Precautions." Satisfied that the man didn't have a thing for Sienna, with his aggressive tide calm again, Gavin centered his attention on caressing the back of his fingers tenderly down her left cheek. As soft as sun-warmed rose petals. "I wasn't taking any chances with my lady's welfare."

"Your lady?" Kevin released a tight cheek chuckle and shifted narrow dark eyes between Gavin and Lucas. "What is it with you white boys always trying to control shit?"

"Kevin!" Bailey gasped.

"White boys?" Both Gavin and Lucas repeated in concert.

His small smile mocking, Gavin stood up, and strode over to Kevin. "Is there something you wish to get off your chest?"

Kevin held his ground firm. "You heard me. Like I said, I've been watching out for these ladies long before you two came into the picture."

"Guys, enough." Bailey stood between them with her palms braced on their chests, looking from one rigid frown to the other.

Lucas tugged his pregnant wife out of the way. She sighed her irritation. "This is crazy ridiculous at a time like this."

"I second that."

Hearing Sienna's weak voice, everyone's full attention flew to the bed. Bailey rushed over. Their cheeks pressed fondly. "Oh, Sie." She drew back. "I was so worried. How are you feeling?"

"All things considered, I'm good. Is there water?"

Gavin quickly rounded to the opposite side of the bed. He grabbed the plastic pitcher from the side-table, filled the cup, and brought it to her lips. After a few sips, she rested back on the pillow. He placed the cup on the table, then sat in the chair, and took her hand in his, caressing her cool, delicate skin.

"Hey, you." He smiled and stroked the back of his fingers lightly down her cheek. "Long time, no see."

"Maybe going with you to California would've been the smart choice," she said, her voice a hoarse whisper.

"Oh, you think? That's right, you should have, you stubborn woman. Instead, you ghosted me." An intentionally soft reprimand. She'd been through enough.

"You came to me." A hint of wonderment was detected, her doe-brown eyes filling with warmth.

"What do you mean, I came to you? Of course I came. Where else would I be?" He leaned in, taking advantage of the opportunity to press his lips to her soft cheek, then gently brushed back the wisp of hair at her temples as he studied the bandage partially covering her left eye, trailing a finger along the thick gauze. "He did this to you?"

"The bastard caught me by surprise." She winced from his light touch, and he jerked his hand away.

"He will pay heavily for that," Gavin gritted as he looked over at the I.V. tethered to the back of her other hand. "How are you really? Are you in any pain?"

"A little, but I'll manage."

"What was Faith doing with Dale?" Bailey asked Sienna. "I thought she told you she was going back home."

"The dude tried to rob Sie with Faith's help. He wanted her to write a check for fifty grand," Kevin supplied with a nod to Sienna.

"Yes, but Faith actually tried to stop him from hurting me. She saved my life. How is Faith? I need to know that she's okay. I wouldn't be alive if it weren't for her."

"Her father took her home for treatment," Bailey answered, then glanced up at Lucas, and he met her gaze as she said, "That day Faith went to Lucas's office, she had intended to blackmail him for money to give to Dale."

"I would've given her the money if I'd known it would end with you getting hurt," Lucas said, his solemn tone openly filled with guilt.

Sienna gave a light shake of her head. "No, I'm glad you didn't give that dipshit a dime. As for Faith, the girl should have known that your nose was opened wide only for Bailey." She tried to laugh but coughed and grunted instead.

The door opened. "Knock, knock. Wow, a full house today. Good morning, I'm Dr. Burton."

"Good timing, Doc. She needs something for the pain," Gavin said in an almost directive.

"Let's first see where we are." Dr. Burton smiled warmly at her patient. "Should we clear the room?"

Sienna looked around at them all. "Not necessary."

"I'll just draw the curtain." Everyone, except Gavin, stepped back from the bed. He grilled Dr. Burton with questions in between Sienna's faint hisses and groans. Short minutes later, the doctor drew back the curtain and jotted down her notes.

Sienna shifted to sit up. "Oh, shhh…" She hissed a sharp breath.

Concerned, Gavin stroked her hand while speaking to the doctor. "She's obviously uncomfortable here. You have to give her something."

"Mr. Crane, your wife is coming along nicely."

Ignoring Sienna's questioning look over the term wife, he said, "That's great to hear, but she's in pain. What about the meds?"

"I'll prescribe a muscle relaxant and something for her headache." Dr. Burton looked between them. "That was a pretty nasty blow you received." She addressed Gavin. "I want to check in on her for a couple of days. If all goes well, you can take your wife home and see to her care. She'll need to be monitored closely. We want to ensure that there is no residual damage from the concussion she suffered." Dr. Burton gave a delicate pat on Sienna's arm. "I'll be back to check on you again later."

Gavin shook the doctor's hand, and then she left the room. He turned to Sienna with a slight smile. "I told the hospital that we were married."

"I see that." Sienna looked out at their audience. "I guess I'll need to find a place to stay. I can't go back to the apartment."

"You'll stay with us." Bailey looked at Lucas. "Right, babe?"

"Of course," Lucas said.

"No, she'll stay with me." It was a gruff command, Gavin realized. Everyone's eyes were solidly pinned on him.

Kevin went to the side of the bed and took Sienna's hand. "I should get home and get some sleep."

"Kev, thank you. If you hadn't shown up—" She reached out for him and drew him into a hug.

"I only wish I'd gone over there sooner than I did."

"No. That fool may have shot you, too."

"If you need anything, you know to call me anytime." Kevin turned to Bailey. "That also goes for you." He hugged and kissed her on the cheek. "Stay sweet, dollface. You know where to find me." He then turned to Gavin and Lucas, his features stone firm. "Take care of these ladies."

"Thanks for everything," Lucas said, and they shook hands.

Gavin extended his hand. "I appreciate you being here for her. Are we cool?"

A short hesitation. Kevin nodded and grasped hold. "We're good." He turned back to Sienna. "I'll check in on you tomorrow." He headed out.

Gavin resumed his seat next to the bed. "After you get the all-clear from Doc Burton, I'll take you to my place."

"Gavin, I can't ask you to do that. You've given up so much of your time helping me with my tour. What about your job?"

"He can take as much time off as he needs," Lucas put in. "There's Skype for manager meetings, and he can send work electronically whenever necessary."

Gavin threw both hands up with a grin. "The perks of working for your best friend. See, it's all good. I got this." He took her hand in his and placed a kiss on the back of it. "Let me take care of you."

"Lucas and I will go to the apartment to get some of your things. I'll get the place packed up as well. Don't worry about a thing," Bailey assured her.

There was another knock on the door. Mike poked his head inside. "Mr. Crane, there's a cop here that wants to see the lady."

Gavin stood up and answered with a nod.

The man entered. "Good morning, I'm Agent Carl Bryant." He showed his ATF Badge. "I'd like to ask you a few questions if I could. Do you feel up to it, Miss Keller, or is it Mrs. Crane? Or, perhaps it's Mrs. Kavanagh? You tell me." He eyed Gavin as he spoke, lips curving upward.

"When my D.C. contact phoned with information that Kavanagh's men were on duty here protecting Gavin Crane's wife, a shooting victim, I had to come check it out. And as sure as a Seattle rain, Daddy's boys are here to greet me." His cold grin remained dead-set on Gavin.

"Crane, I've always admired you for keeping your nose clean." Agent Bryant shook his head, a look of disparagement creasing his brows. "I suppose it was only a matter of time. What's the

Kavanagh's connection in this? It's a shame your lovely wife got caught in the dirty crosshairs of . . . what was it, payback for a deal gone sour? We know about that recent shipment that arrived stateside. Is there a connection here? We are also aware that Kavanagh Whiskey Distillery has increased the number of shipments over the past three months. Now would be a good time to share what you know."

"Gavin, what is he talking about?" Sienna looked between him and the agent.

"Either ask your questions, Agent Bryant, or get the hell out." Gavin glowered.

Agent Bryant shifted his attention to Bailey and Lucas who were now seated on the couch. "Lucas Marx of Marx Venture Capital. You and Crane are still an item, I see. I thought the Marxes only dealt in white collar misdeeds."

Appearing unfazed, Lucas said nothing, maintaining his composure. However, his wife held an unwavering, serrated-edged stare on the short, stocky man, perched, her spine erect, looking prepped to defend her husband if it came to that.

"So, Mrs. Crane, can you tell me if this incident has anything to do with the Kavanaghs in any way?"

Sienna frowned and sent a questioning glance at Gavin, then looked back over at Agent Bryant. "The Kavanaghs? What do you mean? Who are the Kavanaghs?"

A broader grin brightened Agent Bryant's pink, pudgy cheeks as he looked over at Gavin. "Well, now, Mr. Crane, aren't you full of surprises." He turned back to Sienna. "Mrs. Crane, do you have any idea who you're married to here?" She blinked once, her stare pinned on the agent, but no other reply came from the bed. "Let me enlighten you."

Gavin remained silent as the man laid out every dirty element of his family tree. When it was over, he forced himself to look at Sienna and wished he hadn't.

Chapter Ten

"Oh my god, Bailey, you heard what that agent said. Gavin is part of the mob!" Sienna whispered her fear, aware that Lucas and Gavin were likely standing just outside the door. Both had followed Agent Bryant out of the room after the man had explained to her in vivid detail the Kavanaghs involvement in organized crime. "This is the Irish mob were talking about."

Bailey's nose crinkled. "Is the I.R.A. really still a thing?"

"Uh, apparently! You heard what that agent said."

"Sie, Gavin isn't part of his family's world. And wasn't it you who said that you wouldn't want to be blamed for the sins of your mother?"

"Yes, but we're talking the mob here, not a strung-out, alcoholic, comatose mother. The mafia is next-level shit. I've had enough drama in my life to last me a lifetime. I don't need to add organized crime to the crazy."

Warm green eyes met hers. "I know, sweetie, but Gavin obviously cares for you. He had guards stationed at your door to watch over you."

"That agent said they were Kavanagh's men. And using the name Crane to hide that he's really Gavin Kavanagh..." Sienna rapidly shook her throbbing head. "Nope, not for me. I can't—"

"The man deserves a chance to explain himself." It was a firm chiding. "At least give him that. And you heard what Agent Bryant said. Gavin uses his mother's maiden name to disassociate himself from the Kavanaghs. Agent Bryant doesn't believe that that's the case now because of the shooting. He assumed that Gavin and the mob are mixed up in it. But you and I know Gavin had nothing to do with Dale shooting you." Bailey paused. "If you don't want to stay with him—"

"I do." In that startling moment of honesty, Sienna held her best friend's gaze as the reality of her feelings sunk in deep. "I do, Bails, but I don't want any part of this Kavanagh gun running, drug smuggling, and all the other crazy shit that Agent Bryant mentioned."

"Gavin's name is Crane, not Kavanagh. And he works for Lucas." Her tone was soft, yet uncompromising. "He has made a life for himself away from all of that. I feel everyone deserves a fair shake, don't you?" She sighed. "Sie, just talk to him."

Sienna took in a breath and exhaled slowly, allowing her nerves to settle, processing it all. Learning that the man she'd spent the past several weeks with was related to an organized crime family was quite a lot to digest.

"Fine, I'll hear him out." She brought up a hand at the smile that blanketed her friend's tawny-brown features. "If I'm not satisfied with what I hear, if I wake up with a horse's head in my bed, it'll be your fault." Laughter bubbled up and spilled out between them. A wide yawn broke her amusement. "I think those muscle relaxers are starting to kick in."

"Good."

• • •

"Did you see the look on her face? Repulsed. Shit, I thought she'd throw up from the gory stench Agent Bryant happily described." Gavin raked his fingers through his hair and paced in a narrow circle before the closed door. "I wanted to give us some time together before I told her about my family. Now she'll likely want nothing to do with me. Fuck, *I'd* leave me if I'd found out what she'd just discovered."

"Sienna knows you're my GM. You've been legit—not part of your family's organization," Lucas said.

"Yes, well…" Gavin paused. "Do you hear that? They're laughing. That's a good sign, right?"

Lucas nodded. "You're overthinking all of this."

"Maybe. I don't know." He stroked the knot of tension at the back of his neck. "When you told me she'd been shot, man," a harsh breath left him as he relived that heart-stopping moment, "I thought I'd lost her. That woman has become important to me. Can't even explain it. She's stubborn, imperious—"

Lucas gave him a broad smile and gripped his shoulder. "So you've met your match?

Gavin returned a sheepish grin. "Maybe I have."

"That's great, my man."

"Now I just have to show her that I'm for real, serious about us. She's closed, cagey."

"Wouldn't you be if you'd lived the life she has? She practically had to raise herself for a time. Sienna shared with me a small glimpse into her life."

As Gavin listened to the things Lucas told him about Sienna's past, the way she'd suffered as a child, he wanted to reverse time, find those that hurt her, and strike them down. Dale Carter floated from the outer corners of his focus, back to front and center. He frowned, anger swelling. That shithead was another asshole that tried to violate her.

"Had I traveled home with Sienna, she wouldn't have been assaulted and nearly killed. "Things would've ended a lot differently for Dale. He'd better pray the cops catch him before Kavanagh's men do, believe that."

"Dude, you need to call off the hounds. Let the police deal with him. Sienna is okay, that's what's most important."

"I want that motherfucker's head. I can't let this shit slide, Lucas, you know that. If it had been Bailey stretched out in that hospital bed with her face all swollen, a bullet wound near her heart and suffering a major concussion, you'd want to take the head of the one who put her there."

Lucas's brow puckered, then leveled back into a smooth plane of reasoning. "I would, but I'd hope you, Dax, or Sean would talk me off the ledge before I did something that I'd regret." His head tilted, looking past Gavin. "Speaking of."

Gavin turned to see his buddies approaching. Sean Grant and Daxton Pattarozzi completed their brotherhood. They'd all met in boarding school around the age of six and had been best friends ever since. Like Gavin's role as GM at MVC, Dax worked in a similar capacity at Sean's company, Grant Enterprises.

"Sean, Dax, it's good to see you." Palms met with bro hugs. "I thought you two were working in London all week."

"I called them. I figured your ass would want to do something stupid," Lucas drawled.

"I canceled my meetings and had my plane in the air as soon as we heard about your lady," Sean said. "How is she?"

"She's as good as to be expected after what she went through. Bailey's in there with her now. Let me check on her." Gavin eased the door open and poked his head inside. Bailey was seated on the couch, looking at her phone, and Sienna was asleep. He mouthed silently, "How is she?"

With a smile, Bailey raised a thumb.

He nodded and closed the door, then beckoned the guys over to the secluded corner of the hall. "She's asleep."

"Don't disturb her. So, you're using Kavanagh's men to find the guy that did this," Sean remarked. "No doubt, it comes at a price."

Gavin glanced upward in growing irritation. "Look, I know what you're going to say. You three just don't get it."

"I won't even attempt to say I know what you're feeling. Your lady was assaulted—" Dax started.

"Pistol whipped and shot," Gavin made clear with a rigid stare at them all. "That motherfucker tried to kill her. Did you all miss that part? And she's not my lady," he said awkwardly. "We're . . . She's…" He sighed and shook his head. "It doesn't matter. I'm going to look after her. I won't let anyone hurt her again, starting with that fuck-nut."

Sean stepped in a bit closer and whispered, "I know you want the guy to pay, but you have to think rationally here. I'm not saying she doesn't deserve retribution, but if it's discovered that you had anything to do with that asshole's demise, it—"

"You're right," Gavin interrupted, aware of where Sean was headed, and wanted to put an end to the counseling. "You're right, all of you. Sienna is okay. That's what matters. I'll let it be." His buddies' unblinking scrutiny said they weren't buying the bullshit. "I'm serious. I'll leave it to the authorities to handle the guy," he attempted to assure them. Their readable stares didn't let up.

He thought back to when the four of them were in boarding school. Everyone knew his father was Murtagh Kavanagh, the Irish mob boss. Most parents forbade their sons and daughters from associating with him. But Lucas Marx, Daxton Pattarozzi, and Sean Grant were the only guys not afraid to befriend him. He valued their friendship.

"Thanks for always being there, for always looking out."

"We got your back, you know that," Sean replied. "To that end, you can't cut ties with the Kavanaghs, then nine-one-one them for help."

At that hard-hitting admonishment, Gavin released a sigh of mounting frustration. "Are you and Lucas swapping notes in class? I said I get it; I shouldn't have called him. I was thinking of Sienna, thought that fucker might try something."

"I'm with Gav on this one. I'd want to cap the motherfucker, too." Dax dropped a supportive hand down on Gavin's shoulder. "What is it your father wants you to do to settle the debt for the use of his men and for the track you placed on Dale?"

There was an expectation. They all knew how things operated in his father's inner workings. "I'll be handed down assignments that involve watching Dylan's back. Three was the agreed upon number. To refuse the man would be worse than getting my limbs gnawed off by wolves." They stared back in clear understanding.

"What are the assignments, exactly? And while you're watching your brother's back, who's got yours? Just say the word, and I'm there," Dax said, his nearly colorless, pale gray eyes locked firmly upon him, and the hand on his shoulder squeezed lightly. "I got you, bro."

There was a unified nod among them all.

Gavin's chest filled full of love and deep appreciation for the guys. Though he loved his brothers, Dylan and Edwin, the men standing before him were his family. Their bond was solid. No judgment among them, which is why the last thing he would do is get them mixed up in foul Kavanagh shit.

"This is my mess. I'll deal with it."

"Stress that it was one favor you'd asked of him," Lucas advised. "You needed to protect your lady from her friend's drug-dealing boyfriend, plain and simple. Even I know how your father feels about family."

"Yeah, but business outweighs family," Gavin countered. "Especially if there's something to gain. Me working for him is what he's always wanted."

"I can relate to that," Sean put in. Considering that the man's father had taken him from his mother when he was five, and then shipped him off to boarding school, both Harris Grant and Murtagh Kavanagh battled for top honors in the shitty father department.

"Complete the assignments, then find a way to cut things off for good," Lucas said.

The nods were in unison.

"True that," Gavin agreed.

Chapter Eleven

The car held Gavin's scent, a mix of premium leather and expensive cologne.

Sienna watched him work the gear shift as the car slowly pulled away from the hospital.

Merging onto the Capital Beltway, she braced herself, expecting he'd open up the engine, and let the baby purr. She excitedly anticipated it, but he drove as though he was hauling his ailing grandmother. Driving in and around D.C., Maryland, and Virginia, even the slow lanes along the DMV corridors roared above sixty miles per hour. The speedometer hardly skimmed forty.

His relaxed bearing belied the tension that seemed to stretch between them. Their interaction had been tenuous from the moment the ATF agent supplied her with a storm of information about him two days ago. He hadn't spoke about it and neither had she.

Sienna looked at him. "Gavin?"

"You have questions, I suspect," he said, eyes staring straight ahead.

Would he talk about the elephant squeezing between them in the limited space of the car's cabin? Heck yes, her mind was overflowing with questions that needed answers, but for now, she'd only ask one. "Why are you coaxing along like a student driver? I know this bad boy would sing at eighty." She ran a palm over the buttery soft, camel-colored leather seat. "Beautiful, by the way."

His head turned; his clear blue gaze roamed over her face. "I know." He winked.

"I meant the car."

"I won it in a poker game."

Her eyes widened. "Someone gave you their Lamborghini?"

He looked at her, and a dimpled grin flickered for a fraction on his smooth-shaven face. "Nobody *gave* me anything. I won it from my buddy, Sean." His attention went back to the road.

"So you like to gamble, is that it?"

"What fun is life if you don't take chances?" Silence stretched, then he looked between her and the road. "Trust me, he doesn't miss it. He ordered himself a Bugatti the very next day. He belongs to the Monticello Motor Club."

"Am I supposed to know what that is?"

He glanced over again, and she shrugged. "They pretty much just race cars for fun."

"Oh." Still, she couldn't imagine handing over a car worth upwards of two-hundred grand as payment in a card game. To a man such as Sean Grant, billionaire of the Grant Royal Resorts fortune, perhaps it was just another day in the life. "You can pick up the pace, you know. At this rate, my injuries will have mended by the time we make it to your place."

He sped up, but not by much.

They rode along quietly. Sienna wanted him to initiate the issue about his family, open up on his own without her having to prod it out of him. He looked over, and she held her breath in preparation to hear all of the down-and-dirty details.

"Sean, and another buddy of mine, Daxton, came to the hospital, but you were asleep."

Nope, he wasn't going to talk about it. She sighed low. "Really? That was nice. I would've liked to meet them." His head swung to her again, giving her a strange look. "What? If they're your friends, I'd like to get to know them. I know Lucas, of course. And you and I stayed at the Grant Royal throughout my art tour, but I haven't met Sean. And now there's Daxton."

"They're my brothers . . . not blood, more than that. Each can sometimes be a pain in the ass like a brother, too."

Sienna laughed. "I feel the same way about Bailey . . . pain in the ass and all. And even Faith, with her wackadoodle self. I love those girls."

He scowled. "Even after what she did to you? That woman tried to rob you and nearly got you killed."

"It wasn't on her. It was Dale. Faith said he made her do it, and I believe her. She's had it rough. When she was sixteen, while driving her mother home, her car hit a utility pole, and her mother was killed. It wasn't her fault. Her mother was drunk and grabbed the wheel. But Faith believes her father still blames her for the death." She paused, pressing a hand at her side. "Faith stopped that asshole from hurting me. When Dale was choking me, she—"

His head jerked over, eyes wide, then narrowed. "He choked you, too?"

Sienna nodded and zeroed in on the smooth angles of his face; his jaw formed into a solid wall of steel. "Yes, but Faith jumped on his back to try and stop him. I owe my life to her."

"That bastard will pay for what he did to you, believe that," he all but growled.

"Hope so . . . if they catch him, that is." No response came, but the lines between his brows etched deeper, and that vein in his neck pulsed more rapidly under the severe tension of his clenched jaw.

About twenty minutes later, the car parked beneath a luxury high-rise apartment building in the heart of Georgetown.

Sienna pushed open the passenger door and twisted to exit. "Shhh," she wheezed through her teeth at the shooting pain that stabbed her side, stalling the air in her lungs.

"Stay put." He quickly got out and rounded the rear of the vehicle. Carefully, he took her hand and helped her to her feet. "I have your prescription up in the apartment."

"Nah, I'm good." A speculative look surfaced across his features, studying her. "Really, the discomfort isn't anything I can't handle. I don't need it." Again, his narrowed stare said, *bullshit*. He'd be right. It hurt to complete a full breath, not to mention the pounding going on in her head.

Sienna avoided taking pharmaceuticals of any kind. She had too many memories of seeing her mother in a comatose state after taking whatever she could get her hands on. Though her mother's ailment was mostly emotional pain, it was pain, nonetheless, and she had a very low tolerance threshold. Sienna wasn't interested in finding out if addiction was a family trait. In the hospital, there hadn't been much of a choice. Now, she'd tolerate the knife-like stabs and consistent throbbing head.

"Gavin, I'm fine, really." She forced a smile for reassurance. "I just need to rest."

His attention shifted, giving a scan of the garage. "He should be here by now."

"Who should be—" Sienna paused as a black van came barreling down the aisle toward them and came to a stop behind the car. She tensed at the sight of the side door sliding open. A man in a black suit, shirt, and tie combo stepped out. He pulled a wheelchair from the van's interior. A quiet breath of relief left her. For a moment, she'd pictured getting sprayed with bullets like in the movies. Her imagination was getting the best of her. Damn, Gavin and she really needed to have that talk.

"Sorry, I'm late. Here you go, Mr. Crane." The man propped open the chair.

"It's about damn time! I expected you here when I arrived. Where the hell have you—"

"Gavin?" His head turned to her with eyes hard that gradually softened. "It's fine. Say thank you." The low spoken dictate must have penetrated. Gentle fingers brushed along the outline of her chin, then he turned back.

"Thanks, Mac, but in the future, when I ask you to be here, be here, got it?"

"No problem, Mr. Crane. Anything you need, just say the word." There seemed to be an eager need to please Gavin, undercut by a keenness not to anger him as well.

Mac climbed back into the van, slid the door closed, and it sped away.

Gavin brought the wheelchair forward and helped ease Sienna into the seat, then rolled her to the elevator. It was extremely kind of him to see to her care and comfort. As they made their way up, not a peep was spoken. She gave a look up over her shoulder and found his eyes dead-set on her. In that moment, the doors parted, and he rolled her just across the hall.

Entering his place, the afternoon sun streamed in through the bare windows, painting the room in brilliant light.

A rectangle, knotted-wood table was positioned between a black leather sofa and two loveseats. The furniture pieces were staged before an enormous flat screen—about seventy inches easy. It took up a significant portion of the exposed red brick wall it hung upon. Below it stretched a narrow gas fireplace that set flush within the wall. Across the room, a gray marble island and metal barstools separated the living room and kitchen. To the right, four high-back, black leather chairs surrounded a dark oak dining table. It was situated within an intimate alcove in front the same style of floor to ceiling windows. Dark hardwood floors were carried throughout the space.

"Your place gets terrific light."

"Yeah, I guess. I got you something." He rolled her chair toward the windows.

Sienna gasped upon spotting the easel, crisp white canvases in varying sizes that rested against the windowpane, oil and acrylic paints in every color imaginable, and several brush kits—practically an entire art studio worth of supplies.

"When you're feeling better, I thought you might like to wet a brush or something. I didn't know what to get, so I picked up a few things that I thought might be useful."

She looked up at him in amazement, but much more than that was a feeling of deep appreciation welling up to tighten her throat. "You call this a few things? Gavin, you really didn't need to do all of this."

"Woman, you keep telling me what I didn't need to do. Does seeing the art supplies make you happy?"

"Yes. Very much so." Sienna smiled, wishing she had the strength to dive into all of it.

"Then I succeeded at what I aimed to do. Say thank you." He grinned.

"Thank you." She mirrored his grin, unable to help it.

He pivoted the chair and wheeled her out of the room. They passed several closed doors along a wide hallway and entered a bedroom through a set of dark oak double doors at the end of the hall. The same style of windows as in the living room offered the room a burst of natural light. Wheeling her to the middle of the space, he gestured a hand over at the doors to her right.

"That's the bathroom. Next to it is the closet. Bailey dropped off some of your things. I cleared out a few drawers and put everything away. I didn't have time to remove all my things. I'll get around to it."

Sienna's breath caught as she stared up at the painting on the wall above the king-size bed. "Rustling Raining Night. That's my painting."

"I bought it."

"You really like it?" She looked up over her shoulder in complete awe that he'd purchased her painting and hung it over his bed, no less. No guy had ever shown that genuine level of appreciation for her work. And to actually display it where he'd see it at the start of each day and before he closed his eyes each night. . . Overwhelmed by the sentiment, she didn't know how to handle the sudden flood of emotions that rushed through her, so she pushed the feelings behind the safety of that comfortable wall of steel.

"I liked it, so I bought it. It's as simple as that."

"This is your room."

"How'd you figure that out?"

There was a play of amusement in his eyes. "Gavin," she took his hand in hers, "thank you. It means a lot."

"This is your room now for however long you want it."

"Where will you sleep?" Her attention moved back to the large bed, easily imagining them curled up together beneath that thick, black comforter . . . and the horse's head. She shuddered at the last thought.

"I'll crash in one of the bedrooms down the hall."

"Gavin, you didn't have—" She caught herself. "Thanks." A heart-stopping smile was sent her way.

"Do you mind if I freshen up? The hospital shower didn't give me a confident clean. I haven't had a decent shower in three days." He wheeled her into the bathroom. Seeing the oversize, jetted tub, she could already feel the soothing bubbles licking away the aches in her body. "On second thought, I think I'll take a bath."

"Whatever you want. Here, let me start it for you." He stepped over to the tub. "I'll set the jets on low."

Perfect. Sienna eased out of the chair. Each step sent a shooting pain up her left side, and oddly, it kept on pulse with the throbbing in her head. He turned back just in time to catch her as she swayed on her feet, nearly falling face forward.

"Whoa, easy there. Maybe you should lie down for a while."

Strong arms cradled her around the waist, their bodies lightly touching, their gazes locked. Her eyes dipped to his mouth, and her tongue slipped across her lower lip, still feeling the mark of his kiss, remembering his taste. She wanted to curl up in his comforting warmth and security, but knew she shouldn't. The things she'd learned about him . . . his family . . . it scared her. And she didn't scare easily. But her purpose of staying in his home was to learn all there was to know about him before casting judgment.

Feeling the light stroke of his hand up and down her spine, the gesture so thought-provokingly tender, a warm shiver streaked through her. "The dizziness seems to only happen when I stand," she voiced softly, unable to pull her gaze away from him.

"Then we'll do this a different way." Taking a seat on the edge of the tub, he brought her to his lap, and began unbuttoning her blouse.

Sienna stiffened, tightly fisting her shirt. "What are you doing?"

"Well you can't take a bath in your clothes, now can you?"

"No, but—"

His eyes rolled upward. "Come on now, I've seen plenty of naked women."

A jolt of jealousy shot through her. Of course, he'd seen plenty of naked women. Look at him—tall—blond—blue-eyed—devilishly handsome.

"I can manage a bath on my own," she said with bite. His comment bothered her; though it was stupid, irrational jealousy, she couldn't help the sudden feeling of possessiveness that he was hers and no one else's . . . ever.

"You just said you're dizzy."

"Only when I stand. I'll be seated in the tub. I don't need your help." More bite. It wasn't lost on him that time, given that his hand gently caressing her lower spine stilled.

Looking slightly wounded by her words, he sighed. "If you insist." She eased off his lap, and he strode to the door. With his back to her, he said, "I'll wait here until you've settled in."

It took extreme effort to work loose the five buttons on her shirt, and was even harder to strip out of it.

She peeled the thick gauze bandage from the skin at her side, then slowly worked her jeans down her hips, but quickly realized that getting them past her knees would be a miracle. The excruciating pain wouldn't allow too deep a bend at the waist.

"I don't hear any water splashing," Gavin called out from the threshold.

"I can't do it." *Damn it.*

"Do you want my help?"

"Yes," she conceded weakly.

With eyes averted, he grabbed a bath towel from a folded stack on the shelf and handed it to her. She covered her front as he bent and pulled off her sneakers. He dragged her panties and jeans down her legs, then tried to help maneuver her into the tub amid her attempt to keep a hold on the towel. Frustration bloomed as he expelled a breath and sat back on his shins. "Sienna, this is ridiculous. We're adults. I'm going to help you into the tub whether you want me to or not."

She didn't argue as the towel was tugged from her grasp. He brought both of her legs over the edge and helped ease her down into the heavenly soothing warm water, then grabbed the half-empty bottle of bath gel from the edge of the tub and pumped the citrus smelling soap into his palm. With clinical movements, his hands ran over her body and circled her breasts. Care was given near her wound. Several more pumps of the bath gel finished off her legs, then he got up from his knees.

"Holler when you're ready to get out. Don't attempt to do it on your own." He quickly moved to the door while drying his hands on his jeans, and closed it behind him.

Seriously!

That was mechanical as shit. She didn't consider herself a beauty queen, but goodness, she was completely naked, and he'd hardly batted an eye at her. Not even a slight flare of appreciation was given as he washed her breasts.

Men had hit on her at least once a week at the café where she'd once waitressed in the evenings. She was consistent with her workout and felt her body looked pretty good. Well, now she was sporting a nasty wound that would likely leave an ugly scar on her torso, not forgetting the one above her left eye.

What did she expect, that he'd grope her? *Of course not! Absolutely not!*

Not to mention, she'd kept him at a distance to avoid the headache of dealing with the usual rollercoaster of emotional baggage that relationships often brought. And still, he'd rushed to her hospital bedside and opened his home to her. The man had stolen a way past her steel wall of defense, conquering her not by typical wit and charm, but with patience and a compassionate resolve.

What about the Kavanaghs?

Sienna rested her head back against the tub and closed her eyes to ease the throbbing.

Gavin Crane or Gavin Kavanagh? Are they one in the same?

• • •

Shit.

Braced at the kitchen island with an ice cube pressed to the back of his neck, eyes closed, Gavin tried not to think of the feel of Sienna's soft skin and bare shaven pussy—not one single strand of hair anywhere.

It took herculean effort to remain dispassionate as he stroked the wet curves of her body, over her full breasts and budding nipples . . . *nipples that I'd love to seal my lips around.* He swung open the freezer and grabbed another ice cube, contemplating if he should drop it into his boxer briefs.

Dark eyes, forever long legs, pert breasts, silky smooth skin, damn, she was beautiful . . . and fragile right now. *She's ill, you horny pig, get a grip. And add to it what she now knows about your family, you'll be lucky if she's still here by morning.*

"Gavin?"

He tossed what was left of the ice into the sink and rushed to her. She was attempting to climb out of the tub. "Hey, I told you not to do that." Grabbing a bath towel, he took care in getting her out of the tub, covered her up, and carried her to the bed.

She pointed to the small, multi-colored pouch on the floor by the door. "Could you hand me that? It's my toiletry bag. I need my moisturizer. I'm sure Bailey would've packed it. She knows I can't live without it."

Gavin retrieved the bag. The faint scent of strawberries filled his nostrils as the lotion was squeezed into her palm.

"Will you help? I can't reach my legs. It hurts to bend."

Dear lord.

Squeezing a liberal amount into his hands, he began working it over her legs, while doing his best to avoid watching the movement of her hands beneath the towel as they circled over her breasts and on down to the V of her mound. Yep, he would die with an excruciatingly raging hard-on.

Focusing on his task, he used the opportunity to massage her feet. His fingers worked her arches, her ankles, and slid upward, kneading her calves.

"Wow, that feels amazing." She moaned, writhing with the arch of her body, and closed her eyes briefly, while resting back upon the propped-up pillows. "Mr. Crane, I must admit your hands really do work miracles."

Gavin looked at her, and she smiled, a smile so captivatingly alluring, it stirred up a heavy dose of want within him. "Anything to help you relax," he said as he tried to rein in his need and concentrated on soothing her tension, but her soft purring moans were nearly unbearable.

He slid his hands up her satiny-smooth inner thighs, his thumbs adding just enough pressure, and came within a scant of the apex. Their fingers brushed. He snatched his hand away and hastily stood up. A man could only take so much. "I'll get you a fresh bandage and something to wear." He headed off to the closet. *A muumuu made of burlap would be ideal right now.*

"Just a tank and panties will do," she called out.

Taking several deep breaths, Gavin willed away the erection that threatened to crest as he pulled a pair of pale-blue satin panties and a matching tank top from the drawer.

"It's time to take your meds," he said on his return to her.

After applying an antiseptic to the half-inch wound above her left brow and the other at her side, he affixed the bandages and helped her dress, then retrieved her pills and a glass of water from the kitchen. Holding the medication out to her, he gave a quick look at his watch. "Dr. Burton said every four hours. It's been nearly six."

"I don't like taking pills of any kind. Bad family vibes. My mother suffered . . . suffers from prescription substance abuse."

Gavin nodded, recalling all of what Lucas had told him about Sienna's mother, how the woman hadn't protected her daughter from lecherous scum.

But he let go of the thought; it wasn't his place to cast stones. "You need to take these, sweetness. They'll also help you rest, so you can heal."

Her brown eyes widened in obvious surprise at the endearment. Gavin wasn't sure what had possessed him to say it. He couldn't take it back.

Her gaze stayed fixed on his face as she popped the pills into her mouth and swallowed them down with the water. "Speaking of family, are we going to talk about that ginormous elephant in the room?" she asked as she handed over the glass.

He looked around. "I don't see an elephant." His grin was met with an eye roll. The buzz of his cell phone gave him a small reprieve. He pulled it from his front pocket and read the text from Mike:

Miser got that item you wanted.

No fucking way! Dale had been apprehended. He hadn't expected it would be that fast. His cousin Miser was like a hound chasing a rabbit. It never ended well for the rabbit.

"Is everything okay?"

Gavin looked up from typing out his text. "Pardon?"

Her focus dipped to the phone clutched in his hand and then back up. "You look as though someone kicked your dog."

Dale was about to get a foot in his ass, that much was certain. Relaxing his jaw, he sent off his text, and stuck his phone back into his pocket. "It's nothing."

"I said, we need to talk."

"Yes, I know." He settled the comforter over her, tucking it in at the shoulders. "We will. You need to rest. I'm going to step out to pick us up something to eat. What would you like?"

"Surprise me, but nothing heavy." She reached out her hand, and he eagerly took hold. "Thank you for letting me stay here . . . for everything. I'll try not to be too much of a burden."

"You're not a burden. I care about you, Sienna." *I want you to be mine.*

"Gavin—"

"Try to sleep." Not wishing to hear the many ways she wasn't feeling him the way he was her, he kissed her palm, then gestured to the nightstand. "I brought in your cell just in case you need to reach me. I won't be gone long." He could feel her eyes on him on his way out of the room.

Stepping into the spare bedroom, he slipped out of the light blue button-down and pulled on a black T-shirt. Leaving on the dark-blue jeans, he retrieved his heavy-soled boots from the closet. After making a few calls, he went back to the master bedroom. Sienna lay asleep on her back, her features free of strain, breathing easy. That was good.

The late afternoon sunbeam cut across her cheek, bathing her lovely face in an ethereal glow. *Breathtakingly beautiful.* He could stand there for hours and simply watch her sleep, marvel over her loveliness, but he needed to use the time of her slumber wisely.

Padding quietly to the nightstand, he pressed the remote that lowered the blinds, darkening the room. She didn't make a sound.

As he exited, he made a mental note to pick up food *after* he finished with that fuck-face. That way, his primary reason for going out wouldn't be a complete lie.

Chapter Twelve

The building was dilapidated; chunks of mortar were missing between large sections of faded red brick. The windows were boarded up, and those that weren't, were dusty and broken. The drive in to Baltimore's industrial district had taken him over an hour. It took another half hour to maneuver his way during the crush of downtown gridlock along the southeast end of the harbor where grain factories to textile mills once thrived. Some parts of the area were on a slow trickle back to life. But not here. This vacant parcel of the city had yet to get a facelift.

Gavin exited his car and crossed the gravel parking lot to the steel-plated door. It was the only part of the structure that didn't show its age. He gave the handle a hard pull and stepped inside. Mike's alert gaze met his just inside the door, apparently keeping watch.

"Mr. Crane," Mike greeted.

"Gav."

Gavin's head turned to the call from his right and was surprised to see his younger brother entering from a side door. "Eddie, what are you doing here?"

"That's all I get? It's good to see you, too."

They shook hands and pulled in to a hug.

"Pop wanted me here."

Of course he did. Edwin was acting as the man's eyes and ears. It was a position the young man thrived in and would follow through to the letter.

Gavin turned back to Mike. "Where to?"

"This way."

Dust and granules scraped under their booted feet as they made their way across the abandoned sugar warehouse to a door that took them below ground. Along the hall, wooden doors were spaced wide apart. Some stood open to the interior. The rooms appeared to have once been windowless offices.

"Where did you all find him?" Gavin asked as they trudged down the narrow corridor.

"The guy was caught trying to sneak his way through the back alley to his apartment," Mike said.

"Stupid fuck," Edwin snorted from the rear.

"Miser had stopped by the hospital and managed to get an address from that lady, Faith. . . before the doctor sedated her, that is. Miser tapped into his network on the street and kept a look-out," Mike explained and added, "He ran into some interference, though."

Gavin side-eyed him. "What kind of interference?"

"Two heavies must have been following the dude. They wanted to take a piece out of him also, said the dude owed them money. No worries. Miser took care of it. He—"

"Enough." Gavin raked a hand through his hair. He knew how his cousin, Miser—Nilan was his actual name—tended to *take care* of things. It usually resulted in missing appendages. Damn how he hated all that shit.

They came up to a door at the end of the hall. Gavin braced a hand on Mike's shoulder, stalling his hand on the knob.

"Faith had a friend at the hospital named Diego who looked after her. Where was he when Miser was mastering his interrogation skills?"

"He'd stepped away, I guess."

"And Danny? Where was he?"

"He'd gone to the cafeteria to grab a sandwich before it closed for the night," Mike said low, and started that weight shifting from one foot to the other.

On the one hand, Gavin was pleased that they'd obtained the necessary information about Dale from Faith. On the other, if Miser had so easily gained uninterrupted, direct access to Faith, Dale could have done the same to Sienna. That unnerved him. The reservations he'd had about using his father's men to look after her were now gone.

"Did that dude, Kevin, ever leave my lady's side?"

"Only when the hospital staff came to check on her. Even then, it was less than five minutes or so, and I made sure to be there when he wasn't. I let him know when I needed to take a leak. Trust me, Mr. Crane, your lady was well-protected. There was always one of us there at all times."

Satisfied, Gavin beckoned a hand at the door, and Mike opened it. Seated behind the metal framed desk was the man that started it all, Dale Carter. To his left, Miser stood with a shoulder braced against the paint-chipped wall, his attention centered on his cell phone. The man's casual bearing contradicted just how lethal he could be.

When they were kids, Gavin had nicknamed him Heat-miser because of his flaming red hair, that no matter how he tried to tame, always stuck straight up. Back then, it made him look amusing. Now it personified the man's ruthlessness. To Dale's right was a man that Gavin didn't recognize, who looked just as unfazed. The fact that the man didn't bat an eye said he didn't miss much.

Gavin brought his attention back to Dale. Two empty Five Guys burger wrappers were on the table in front of him as he sucked from the straw of a 7-Eleven Big Gulp. He looked as though he was merely hanging out with his buddies, not realizing that the man to his right would love nothing more than to use him to practice his surgical skills.

Snapping back to the here and now, Gavin stuck his hands in his front pockets to project a relaxed vibe. "Good, they fed you as I instructed." He received an unflappable look up and down.

"Who the hell are you supposed to be, and what do you want with me?" Dale angled a thumb over at Miser. "He said they ain't cops, that someone needed to speak to me about a job that will pay off big. I'm guessing that'll be you. I don't know you, so what the hell you think I can do?"

Feeding the man and seeing to his comfort gave him a false sense of bravery. It was precisely how Gavin wanted him to feel. It put them on an even playing field. He'd also instructed the men not to lay a single finger on the fool.

"Well," Dale said, showing his impatience by checking his watch.

"No, we're not cops." Gavin stepped forward and dragged the desk away that separated them. Miser came out of his relaxed pose and towed it the rest of the way out of the room. The other guy followed. Edwin remained standing behind Gavin, his back against the wall.

Gavin moved in a bit closer. "It was my lady that you beat, shot, and left for dead."

Awareness registered in Dale's bloodshot eyes for a moment, then his stare flattened as he came to his feet. "So that's what this is about? Not some job for me to get paid? Your lady, huh? Which one of those bitches are we talking about?"

Gavin smiled, a tight smile. "Bravado." He nodded. "I like that."

"Am I supposed to be scared of you?" Dale's mocking laughter echoed up through the missing ceiling tiles. "Dude, I dealt with wannabe badasses like you in lock up." He gave Gavin a hard once-over and took a threatening step forward, lips curled upward. "Look at you in your designer get-up and pretty-boy haircut." A rough chuckle. "You got your boys there at your back."

Gavin grinned, not allowing his composed expression to falter. "If you think they're here to help me kick your ass, you'd be sadly mistaken. Their only job was to locate you."

"So it's like that?" He smiled, a wide display of dingy teeth.

"It's precisely like that," Gavin returned. Without warning, Dale came at him with no finesse, attempting a sucker punch. Dodging the bitch-move, taking steps to the left and right, Gavin caught him in the jaw once, twice, a third time, and followed with an upward jab to his chin, knocking him on his ass. His rage unleashed now, he grabbed Dale tightly by the throat, squeezing as he dragged him up until he stood braced against the wall. "You like to beat up on defenseless women." Blood oozed from Dale's nose and the split of his lip, dripping down onto Gavin's wrist. "Motherfucker, I'm going to show you what it felt like for them."

"They gave as good as they got," Dale strained out around his narrowing windpipe. He spat out a mouthful of blood, that Gavin managed to dodge with a quick head tilt, his shoulder catching the brunt of it. "Especially that black bitch." Dale laughed, a foul, grating laugh.

Gavin's surprise knee to the groin and several jabs to the midsection had the man doubling over, gasping for breath. With a sharp gag, Dale upchucked his dinner and Big Gulp.

"Give me a gun." It had been said to no one in particular. In a flash, four revolvers appeared before Gavin. He grabbed Mike's Glock by the barrel and struck Dale in the face twice with the butt of the gun, sending him to his knees. Blood spewed from the gashes above his left eye and across his temple as he lay unconscious in the puddle of his dinner.

"Night that motherfucker, bro."

Gavin's head swung over to Edwin, censuring the boy's tongue with a laser-sharp glare as he handed off the gun to Mike. With clear understanding, Edwin shrunk back and offered up a wad of napkins. As Gavin wiped the blood from his hands and from his shirt, he said, "Drop his punk-ass off a block from the nearest hospital."

"That's not how this works. I got it from here," Miser said without even a hint of interest in his tone, completely disconnected. "Your pop gave me instructions."

"I don't give a shit what he gave you." Gavin now shot his cousin a dagger-sharp look. Miser opened his mouth to argue, then smartly snapped it shut. Though he despised the piece of shit sprawled out at his feet, he wasn't about to have parts of the man incinerated . . . alive or whatever morbid creativity Miser chose to conjure up. "The hospital, Miser, understand? He's wanted by the cops, and likely a number of people would be thrilled to get their hands on his ass. He'll keep his mouth shut about this, believe that."

"Mr. Crane, your father does business with that detective out of Baltimore," Mike put in. "I can contact Mr. Kavanagh for an alternative if you want."

Gavin nodded.

Mike fished out his phone from his back pocket. After a short conversation, he ended the call. "It'll be taken care of. I was told to tell you it'll mean that you now have an additional assignment added."

Gavin flinched, though it shouldn't have been a surprise. Everything with his father came at a price.

Giving a look down at Dale, he spoke directly to Mike, "Get him out of here."

"It'll get done. I got it, Mr. Crane."

"He's a Kavanagh now." Edwin grinned, throwing out right and left air jabs. "Gav, you beat the shit out of that dude. That was epic, bro."

"Shut the fuck up before I perform a repeat on your ass," Gavin snarled and headed for the door.

"Hey, Pop wanted me to find out when to expect you at the house?" Edwin called out.

"When I'm standing in front of him is when he'll see me," Gavin answered on his stroll down the hall.

Chapter Thirteen

Sienna woke in a darkened room, the window shades blocking all light and shadow. If not for the digital clock on the nightstand illuminating, in vibrant red, 5:41 p.m., she'd have been unable to see her hand in front of her.

Lethargy crept into the depths of her fuzzy mind, slowly dragging her back under. She'd slept nearly three hours and felt she could sleep another three. *Damn pills.* She fought against it—too many memories of seeing her mom comatose after taking whatever it was she'd managed to bum off one of her shithead boyfriends.

"Gavin?" When he didn't stroll in, she tried again, and listened for footsteps. Nothing.

With her bladder about to burst, she sat up slowly—achy, groggy—and turned on the table lamp. The wheelchair was parked across the room by the door . . . too far away to be bothered with. Taking a tight inhale of breath, with a hand pressed firmly at her side, she left the bed, and trekked the short distance to the bathroom. As she relieved herself, she wondered if Gavin had returned with the food and left again. Her stomach growled on cue, calling attention to its hollowness.

Hearing her cell phone ringing on the nightstand, she finished up, washed her hands, and then as fast as her body would allow, made her way back to the bed. The ringing stopped. Bailey's name showed on the display. She scooped up the phone and crawled across the bed atop the covers. The effort of it exhausted all her strength. With her right cheek pressed into the cool, soft puff of the comforter, eyelids heavy, she tapped the number. A couple of rings in, the line picked up.

"Hey, Sie. I hope I didn't wake you. I wanted to see how you were getting along."

"You didn't wake me." It came out muffled and raspy. "I'm good."

"You don't sound good. Where are you? Where's Gavin?"

Sienna eased onto her back with much effort. "I'm in bed, well, partially in bed."

"Partially? What do you mean partially in bed? Where's Gavin?"

"He left to get food."

"Left to get food? When did he leave?"

"About three hours ago."

"Three hours!"

"Bails, you sound like an echo. I'm sure he'll be back soon."

"The man lives in Georgetown. There are restaurants and eateries on practically every block. It shouldn't take three hours to pick up a meal. Most of the places deliver anyway. There was no need for him to leave you alone. I shouldn't have encouraged you to stay with him. I see now it was a mistake. Sienna, we're coming to get you. Lucas?" she yelled.

"Bailey, calm down." The girl had leaped to DEFCON 5 in a hot second. "Don't bother Lucas. I'm fine. Gavin has been great, really. I'm going to rest before he gets back."

"Are you sure? Because I can be there in twenty minutes."

"Yes, I'm sure." Silence. "Really, Bails, all is fine here." Why worry her best friend? Besides, Sienna had yet to meet a man that didn't disappoint her eventually. That said, she hadn't expected Gavin would be at her beck and call.

"I'm going to rest. You're pregnant and should try to do the same."

A long sigh. "Fine, but I'll be checking on you."

"All right. Talk to you later." Sienna disconnected. She dropped the phone on the bed, dragged the comforter over her, and closed her eyes.

Thinking of the text message Gavin had received earlier, it seemed to trigger something. His eyes had glazed over in a way she had never seen before, toughening his handsome features into a grim mask.

Kinda scary.

Chapter Fourteen

Gavin entered his apartment and rushed into the kitchen. The damn restaurant had taken forever with his order. Calling ahead evidently didn't make much of a difference.

He set the bag on the counter and washed his hands, then quickly prepared a bed tray with the soup and breadsticks. Pulling a glass from the cupboard, he filled it with ice and poured a can of ginger ale while giving a look at his watch. *Shit.* Sienna should've taken her meds over an hour ago. He shook two pills from the bottle into his palm. With the tray in hand, he headed to the bedroom.

The lamp on, Sienna lay asleep horizontally across the bed, the comforter tangled between her legs. Gavin took in her gorgeous body, long and lean, admiring every tantalizing curve, remembering the feel of her satiny smooth skin, the way her breasts filled his palms as he'd bathed her. Her nipples strained against the scant fabric that exposed her flat belly. Her satin panties draped low on her hips.

He gave himself a mental kick in the ass. Here he was conjuring up the many ways he'd like to explore her body when the woman was in pain and needed his care. *Get a damn grip why don't you.*

Setting the tray on the ottoman over by the fireplace, he moved back to the bed, and ran the tips of his fingers along the arch of her right foot to her pink polished toes, tugging lightly. "Sie-Sie, sweetness?"

Her eyes slowly rolled open, then closed as a measured breath breached her lips. "You're back."

"I had to make a stop. It took longer than I'd expected." No reply. "I see you sleep pretty rough."

Her eyes fluttered open and met his. "I went to the bathroom. When I climbed back in, this was as far as I could manage. I chose not to move."

Gavin's stomach tightened. She'd needed him, and he wasn't here. It wouldn't happen again.

Carefully, he helped situate her beneath the covers, and propped pillows behind her against the headboard, then brought the tray over, settling the short leg stands across her thighs.

"Smells good." She brought a spoonful of soup to her mouth. Her brow lifted, and she smiled. "Yum. It's really good."

"It's minestrone from Filomena's." He pushed the pills on the tray forward. "You need to take these."

Her hand shot out and gripped his right hand, studying his inflamed knuckles, then her eyes flashed to his, locking on like magnets. "Where exactly was this stop you had to make?"

Gavin eased his hand free. "I'm going to take a shower."

"No, you're going to stand there and talk to me." Her inflexible tone left no room for argument. "Where did you go?"

His lips pursed to tell her the truth, that he'd beaten the living shit out of Dale for hurting her, but with the Amazonian warrior air she was sending off, she might get up out of bed and kick *his* ass, despite her injuries. "I met up with my brother, Edwin." Not a complete lie.

"What did he do to deserve a beat-down?"

"He doesn't know when to shut his mouth." That much was absolutely true. Gavin turned to leave.

"We're not done talking."

Turning back, he met her hard, steady stare. If any other woman had spoken to him with that level of sharpness, she would have found herself standing outside of his apartment. But this was Sienna Keller. The throaty rumble of her voice was like an intimate stroke across his senses, easily rousing his pinned-up yearning for her. Add to it his adrenaline that was running on overdrive from the ass-kicking he'd given Dale. He needed to come down from the unexpected rush that it all provoked. Since sex with her was out of the question, a hot shower to cleanse, followed by a cold blast to stabilize, should do the trick.

"I'm going to take a shower, then—" She started to speak, likely to object, no doubt, but he took her hand and pressed her palm to the light scruff on his cheek. "I will return, and we can talk." To his surprise, her fingertips tenderly scratched his jaw, her gaze softening. Slowly, he leaned in, and her eyelids fluttered shut as he came within a whisper of her lips, but he veered off, planting a gentle kiss on her cheek. He drew back from the irresistible temptation, and her eyes flew open. "I won't be long."

"That's what you said earlier."

Ignoring the pucker of those smooth, pouty lips, giving her soup a stir, he took in a spoonful. "This soup's the bomb." Smiling, he left the room.

Gavin wasted no time climbing into the shower. He slumped under the ceiling spout, head down, letting the water douse his frame. The high pressure pounded away the tension in his neck and shoulders.

They were going to talk. The entire drive home, he'd worked out in his mind how he'd explain everything—his family, and where he fit within it. If he told her the truth, would she accept him or would she run? She wouldn't be the first.

He avoided building something solid with a woman. At some point, he'd have to tell her who he really was. Or she'd somehow discover it and end up putting heels to the pavement.

It would be easier to explain that he had leprosy, than to discuss his family. But he wanted long-term with Sienna. Damn, how he wanted that. She'd become his obsession from the moment they'd met. She was beautiful, smart, strong, and knew what she wanted out of life. Most of all, she didn't take his shit, and she spoke her mind. Very few women challenged him the way she did.

He looked at his reddened knuckles. *He's a Kavanagh now.*

As he shampooed his hair and soaped his body, Edwin's words grated his conscience. What he'd done to Dale was in retribution for Sienna, but he'd enjoyed it, every damn minute of it. That bothered him.

The ring of his cell laying atop his jeans on the floor broke into his thoughts. He poked his head out of the spray and saw that it was Lucas. He'd leave a message. The ringing stopped for a long moment, then started up again. Shutting off the water, he grabbed the towel from the hook, then stepped out, and picked up the phone, answering, "What's doing?"

"Where are you?"

Gavin rubbed the towel over his head before wrapping it around his waist, then crossed the hall into his bedroom. "What do you mean, where am I? I was in the shower. And why are you whispering?"

"Then I'll ask, where *were* you?"

Roughness scraped up the guy's tone. "Who are you, my A.A. sponsor?"

"I've spent the past four hours trying to convince my wife that her best friend is in good hands. Bailey called to check on Sienna and was told you were out getting food. You can throw a stone in any direction and hit an eatery. I would've called or texted you, but Bailey was worried and wouldn't leave my side. She kept trying to convince me that we needed to remove Sienna from your care. So, where did you really go?"

Gavin couldn't fault Bailey for being concerned. Of course she would check on her best friend after learning that the man she left to her care came from a family of thugs. It was understandable.

"Gavin?"

"Yeah?"

"Was the man breathing when you left him?"

"Somewhat." He ruffled his fingers through his hair, back and forth, air drying the surface. "I left him with Eddie and Miser."

"Does that mean you're in for the night? Sienna shouldn't be left alone."

"You don't think I know that?" Gavin barked, more out of guilt. "I got this."

"Good."

Momentary silence split between them.

"I better go check on Sienna."

"I would've done the same, made that bastard pay," Lucas said.

Gavin glowered. "You and Sean giving me fucking grief, I know your asses would have."

"We just wanted you to focus. We know how you can get. Call if you need anything."

"Sure." Gavin disconnected. He knew Lucas and Sean, especially Sean, would've made sure Dale paid severely. Sean was into mixed martial arts and was a five . . . or six, who the hell knew, degree black belt in Hapkido. Had it been him, Dale wouldn't have survived his rage, damn certain.

Choosing to go without underwear, he pulled on a pair of light-weight black sweats and a plain white T-shirt, then went to Sienna.

The bed was empty, and the TV was on. Her tray sat at the foot of the bed. She had eaten the soup, but the breadsticks remained.

The bathroom door opened. She stood at the threshold with a hand pressed underneath her left breast over her injury.

"What are you doing out of bed?"

"I needed to brush my teeth." There was a tightness in her voice, as if she was trying not to breathe.

"You couldn't wait ten minutes? I said I'd be back."

A vacant stare for a moment, then she lightly shook her head. "Nah, I'm used to taking care of myself." Her steps were small, slow going.

He went to her, and with extreme care, lifted and carried her to bed, tucking her beneath the covers. "No more getting out of bed without my help, got it?"

She sighed, but it came out choppy. "Gavin, I don't need you babying me."

It was like her to push him away. She was so strong, so beautiful, and so damn stubborn. "Woman, look at you. You can't even breathe without wincing. You have a cracked rib, and you suffered a severe concussion." A flashback to Dale's well-deserved ass-kicking sprung in his head as he pointed at the pills that still lay on the tray. "You need to take your meds."

She shook her head. "I can't—"

"Sie-Sie, look, I get it." He sat down on the edge of the bed and took her hand. "Lucas shared with me the situation about your mother."

Her stare flared and held his for a long, quiet moment. Glistening dark eyes flickered shut briefly, her vulnerability unmasked. Then, she met his gaze again, her features back in leveled control. "Then you understand why I can't take them."

"Sweetness, you won't become addicted; you're stronger than that." He ran a finger over the bandage above her eye. "You're the most self-disciplined woman I know." Retrieving the pills along with the half-full glass of ginger ale, he presented the medication to her in his palm.

"Maybe later," she said.

He wanted to argue, but it would end with him undoubtedly losing the battle.

Placing the pills upon a napkin on the nightstand next to the glass, he picked up the tray and headed out.

"Are you coming back?"

Gavin paused at the door and turned around. There was a look of something in the intensity of her stare he couldn't quite place. "Right back."

As he headed to the kitchen, it struck him. Distrust. That's what he'd seen. It's what he'd seen as she stood hunched in the doorway of the bathroom as well. He'd left her alone to fend for herself. *Shit.*

Lucas had shared with him the story she'd told him about how she had to fight off the men her mother would bring home, getting beaten and nearly raped by them, and how her grandmother, who eventually took her in, died just before she graduated from high school. She'd had to deal with things no one should have to go through. He could see trusting and relying on others didn't come easy to her. He would have to change that.

• • •

The next several days, she slept most of each day away—the medication that he'd insisted she take kept her in a drowsy state. More and more, as the weeks passed, she stayed away from the pills because of it, but continued to appear healthier, stronger.

He had meals ordered in, so he wouldn't have to leave her side. He helped her bathe, which was no easy task, given that she'd relaxed in his presence to the point that she didn't mind fully undressing in front of him. For her, it seemed that she viewed him rubbing lotion over her naked body as a clinical act. For him, it was pure torture. He'd learned to say the alphabet backward in his head whenever he tended to her warm, nude flesh. Too bad that trick didn't work when he'd lie alone in bed as he was now sporting boner number six. Gavin closed his eyes as he shifted his stiff cock in his boxer-briefs. He felt like a goddamn teenager each night when he found himself in need to stroke out his desire. On the upside, it never took long to work himself to completion.

He'd close his eyes and instantly her beautiful face would appear, then her supple body, lush and firm. He groaned through a long, shuddering breath, his fingers locking down tight around his shaft as he spilled his semen upon sweat-soaked sheets.

Damn.

Chapter Fifteen

Sienna paused in her channel surfing at the sight of Gavin entering the room carrying a bundle of bath towels. He dropped the load upon the ottoman and commenced folding. Even in his bare feet, plain white T-shirt, and simple basketball shorts, he made her breath catch. A wealth of blond hair that looked damp and styled by a tousle of fingers, blue eyes vibrant and mischievous, strong, angled jaw, muscular, bold build—it all provoked her desires.

She imagined what it would feel like to have his strong hands stroking her body, not in the way he tended to her, but with the kind of caresses that sent hot shockwaves of sensation throughout every nerve-ending, heating her from her core outward.

Picturing his tongue licking her nipples into excruciatingly hard points, and skating down her fevered flesh to her pulsating clit, she clenched her teeth to suppress the sudden moan that crept into her throat as her gaze sketched out his powerful physique. Just then, his head turned, and he caught her staring at him. Thankfully, her lust-filled gaze had already moved up from admiring his perfectly sculptured butt.

Pushing down her rising desire, she aimed the remote at the TV and flipped through the channels with a casual glance his way. "You do laundry? I would never have guessed."

"I can cook, too." He winked.

"Sure you can." Doubtful, she curled her lips. "Boiling water isn't cooking. Everything we've eaten has been from a restaurant."

"I have a cleaning service, but I've suspended the schedule while you're recuperating . . . didn't want them to disturb you. And by ordering in, I learn what you like and dislike. Now that I have a pretty good idea of your favorites, I'll start cooking for you."

Good gracious, that's so thoughtful, so sweet. She hadn't expected such incredible tenderness from him and had to swallow the lump that started to choke her throat. "I was only teasing. You don't have to cook for me." He gave her a side-eyed reprimand as he perfected a crease in his fold. "Fine, I won't say it anymore." Aiming the remote at the TV again, she asked, "What would you like to watch?"

"It doesn't matter." He carried the neatly folded bundle into the bathroom, then returned and started to drag the bulky chair away from the fireplace, something he tended to do each evening.

"Come lie with me." He stilled, and his head jerked sharply to her, his wide-eyed gape fixed. "Or not." Contemplation showed in his crinkled brow before he rounded to the right of the bed and started to climb on top of the comforter, but she tossed it back and patted the empty, cool space beside her. As he settled in, propping pillows against the headboard, he took care in not unduly disturbing the stillness of the mattress. *My goodness, so frickin' considerate.*

"Have you watched *Chopped*?" she asked.

"Is it a horror movie? I'm down."

She laughed lightly. "No, but the judges can sometimes be pretty brutal. It's a show on the Food Network. Amateur chefs compete and are judged on their dishes." She gave a gesture with the remote at the TV. "See. The concept is similar to the art competition I participated in."

"You're no amateur. Your paintings and sculptures made those wannabe artists' work look like a paint by numbers fun hour."

She laughed, liking his quick wit, and gave him a playful pinch to his thigh. *Wow!* It was rock hard. "That's mean. There were a lot of really good pieces presented."

"No, there weren't." It had been said with finite authority, not expecting a debate. He brought the back of her hand to his lips, offering a gentle kiss—soft and warm against her skin. "Sie-Sie, sweetness, you are an extremely talented artist. Own it."

Calling her sweetness had become a thing with him. She was starting to like it.

The tips of his fingers brushed along her palm and splayed, lacing his with hers. She glanced up from their joined hands and met his warm gaze. This wasn't the controlling, infuriating man she'd bickered endlessly with throughout her art tour and who'd flirted with practically every female patron he set his eyes upon. This man was attentive, thoughtful, and excruciatingly sweet. He was almost perfect. But there was still that Kavanagh issue hanging in the wind between them, that he had yet to confront with her.

"Gavin, we need to talk. I haven't mentioned it these past weeks because I felt so crappy from my injuries. Now that I'm feeling better, I want us to talk about everything, about all of what that agent told me."

He let out a heavy sigh. "Yes, I know. I just don't know where to start."

"Try the beginning."

They settled into watching the TV program. And they finally talked, talked throughout the entire episode. She learned he'd gone to boarding school around the age of six. It had been where he'd met Lucas, Dax, and Sean—his brothers, he'd referred to them. It had led her to think that he didn't have any siblings other than Edwin, but then he told her about Dylan and his sister, Caren.

"So, Dylan's the oldest?"

"Yes, it's Dylan, me, Caren, and Edwin. Oh, and Abbey—Abela is her name. We sort of adopted her after her parents were burned to death in a fire."

Sienna gasped a sharp breath, and he looked at her then brought his focus to their linked hands. Her mind took a tailspin downward to that dark foreboding place where the horse's head resided. She wanted to ask if the fire had been an accident but was afraid of what the answer might be.

"I meant, they died in a fire," he supplemented quietly, apparently reading her silence. "All Dylan cares about is drawing. Even his wife gets fed up with the amount of attention he pours into it."

"Your brother's an artist? I'd love to see his work."

"Not your kind of art. He's into graphic art, you know, like for video games and movies. He's actually pretty good. You know that video game, uh, *Sorcerer's Quest*? It came out last year."

"No, not much into video games."

"Well, Dylan did a lot of the graphics."

"That's pretty awesome. I'll have to look it up."

"Awesome, huh?" he grunted. "He needs to step up, that's what he needs to do. My father wouldn't be hounding me all the time about taking. . ." He didn't continue. Instead, he said, "Now you know all there is to know about me."

"No, I don't. For one thing, you didn't mention your mother. You know about mine; now tell me about yours."

"My mother divorced my father when I was six. She mostly lives in Ireland. I'd been sent away to school as part of the divorce agreement."

When he didn't go on, Sienna cocked her head. "Why? What about your brothers and sister? Did they all get sent away?"

"Just me."

Expressionless again, he didn't elaborate, giving nothing away in his gaze. She needed to know more. "Why just you?" And yet another hesitation. He was being selective, she realized. "Gavin, if you don't want to talk about—"

"My father made my mother choose which of her two sons she would save from him. Edwin was a baby; they shared custody of him until he was thirteen, then he came to live permanently with my father. Edwin wanted it. My mother fought against it at first, but then Edwin became unruly, getting into fights at school and around the neighborhood, so she gave in. Soon after, my sister came over to go to college, then she, too, decided to stay. I think there's some guy she's into. She'll deny it." He shrugged. "My father wanted full custody of Dylan and me. As a compromise, if you want to call it that, he made my mother choose."

"She chose you."

"Yes, because even at six, according to her, I was cunning."

"I can attest to that," she teased, and he grinned while his fingers still entwined with hers delivered a light squeeze.

"My mother felt Dylan was mild-tempered, which is one of the reasons my father doesn't want him to take over the. . ." Once again, he didn't go on. A soft sigh left him. "Okay, these interrogation lights are getting kind of warm. Enough talk about me. Have you tried to contact your mother to let her know what happened?"

"Nope."

"Just nope?"

"Just nope. As long as her debit card reflects a deposit every month, I'm off her radar. So, according to Agent Bryant, your family owns a distillery in Ireland and imports Kavanagh premium whiskey to top restaurants around the world?" Sienna wasn't about to let him skate away from the subject.

"Yes."

"But that's not all they do." It was purposely stated as fact. "Was any of what Agent Bryant told me about your family true? You're Gavin Kavanagh?"

He released her hand and fixed his eyes on the TV. "Crane is my mother's maiden name. It's my name," he said in an almost whisper.

"Those guards at the hospital were your father's men. You ordered them to watch over me. Are you part of your family's business? And I don't mean liquor importing."

"I needed to protect you. I thought that bastard, Dale, might try something."

He didn't admit or deny it, not exactly. "Gavin, I—" a tentative caress of a finger swept across her brow where the bandage covered Dale's mark upon her. Surprisingly, it placated her . . . for a moment. "I've had enough drama to last me a lifetime. I don't need nor want—"

"Sienna, I have no say in the blood that runs through my veins. I didn't get to choose my family any more than you got to choose yours. But that doesn't mean we must live the way they do." He shifted so they faced one another, his stare steady with hers. "I want to be with you. I want to look into your beautiful brown eyes every chance I can," a gentle finger trailed down the angle of her throat and along the dip in her left shoulder, "explore your body, and learn everything there is to know about you." He brought her hand to his lips and placed a kiss at the center of her palm before resting it against his cheek's night scruff. "I suspect you don't want to hear any of that, especially now that you know who my family is, but it's how I feel."

Sienna expelled a shaky breath from both the earnestness she heard in his voice and the hot compelling spark of desire she could see in his eyes.

She felt a strange sense of something she couldn't quite name, but somehow, she knew that she should drop her wall of defense, take a wild gamble, and trust him.

His head lowered until his lips brushed feather-light against hers. "I want you," he whispered before his mouth pressed in, tasting and exploring, altering every thought, every emotion inside her. A hand cradled her nape, and his fingers went into her hair, holding her steady as his tongue snaked deep within with incredible thoroughness.

She settled into his kiss, starved for it, dizzy for it. Her hands took on a will of their own, moving over the corded muscles of his arms and down the hard plane of his chest. A hand went underneath his T-shirt in desperate need to make contact with his chiseled abs, on down, gliding into the waistband of his shorts.

Wow! He wasn't wearing any underwear. Her fingers gripped his long, thick arousal. Velvety smooth steel filled her palm. Her pussy throbbed from the raw power and promise of pleasure it would surely deliver.

Wanting him on top, she twisted, and winced against his mouth from the pulsing ache that lit her side on fire, and he paused in his kisses, going stiff as a board.

"Don't stop." Trying to ignore the pain, she palmed his cheek and tried to draw him back to her, but he resisted.

"We have to stop. You really need to take the pills. It's been nearly a day since you last took them." He brought an arm up and rested it behind her head on the pillows. Gentle fingers played in the fine hairs at her nape. "You'll rest and be pain free."

With her teeth clenched, Sienna eased onto her back, took a breath to settle the discomfort, then turned her head to look at him. "They say sex releases endorphins that relaxes muscles and subdues aches within the body."

His blue eyes brightened; a slow smile creased his mouth. "Is that so?"

"It's what I hear. We can find out." She wiggled her brows and sent him a full grin of mischief. "Let's see if the theory is true."

"I don't want to hurt you."

She took his hand and guided it inside her panties, her hand adding pressure to his. Lightly rocking her hips, her eyes shuddered on a moan as the pleasure of his fingers set her core pulsing, then she opened her eyes and met his awestruck gape. His Adam's apple bobbed rapidly in his throat, his expression shifting from shock, and narrowing to hot carnal desire as she directed his fingers where she needed them most, sliding deep into her wet heat.

Looking at him, she smiled. "I'm feeling better already."

Chapter Sixteen

Holy shit!

Gavin watched her pleasure herself with his hand, her guided strokes over her clit growing bolder, faster. She gave a long downward sweep and pushed the length of his middle finger into her pussy. Wet, warm, and so tight. He lost it. The little restraint he'd had, she'd shattered into a million tiny pieces of need.

He came up on his knees, got in between her thighs, and made quick work of removing her panties. Staring down at her moist folds, he licked his lips, then met her taunting grin. "Woman, you're playing with fire here, know that."

"Am I?" With a hint of a shrug, she parted her legs and drew her knees up, spread wide in wanton invitation. "What are you going to do about it?"

That challenging grin of hers had him wrenching off his T-shirt. He bent and delivered a long, slow sweep of his tongue from pussy to clit, back and forth, ending with a swirl over the engorged button. Her long-awaited taste was like the sweetest ambrosia to his senses.

Her breath hitched when he sealed his mouth on her, sucked her labia, and his tongue drew slow circles over her slick folds before spearing her deep, tasting and lapping greedily.

Her fingers gripped his hair with rough assertion, holding him steady as she rolled her pussy on his mouth. "I want to feel you inside me," she said, through a labored breath.

His head jerked up. "I don't want to hurt you."

"You won't hurt me. I'm pretty sure it'll be quite the opposite."

He came up over her and balanced his weight on his forearms. "I don't think it's a good idea." Damn, he wanted her. The beast inside him demanded it.

She reached into his shorts and took his cock in hand, giving it a light, yet determined stroking. "I want to feel all of you inside me."

His eyes squeezed shut, and he breathed in and exhaled slowly for restraint. "Shit, you're not making this easy."

"Then make love to me."

Gavin's gaze flashed to hers. Dark, hot, and incredibly beautiful. Love . . . that one word summed up how he felt, summed up all that she meant to him. Overwhelmed by the emotional surge it brought, he slipped out of his shorts, lowered, and settled his mouth over hers, their tongues reacquainting as he guided his penis inside her welcoming heat.

His breathing stalled a moment in his chest as a hard shudder rushed through him. This went beyond sex. And he'd had plenty to know the difference. This was the complete uniting of body and soul. The feeling was so intense that all he could do was breathe out her name against her lips as he rode the heady sensation. Then, with careful thrusts, he took his time, moving in long, deep surges, while relishing the way her channel tightened and relaxed in chorus with his rhythm.

Impatient hands slid down his back to his buttocks, squeezing, then back up, her nails raking over his arms, biting into his flesh, digging deep. Her eager need was killing his restraint.

Gavin smothered her mouth with kisses as his cock throbbed and demanded more with each slow glide along the searing friction of her slick inner walls. He'd hungered for this, for her, for so long that he was on fire as waves of sensation rose within him, undermining his meager control. Each thrust became harder than the last until he was pumping in and out of her body with his head buried at the side of her neck, licking and nipping her soft, warm skin, while twisting and grinding, going balls deep into her before he cursed through a long, drenching release.

Damn good.

He couldn't remember the last time he'd come that hard. He'd gone without sex since he'd met her . . . well aside from self-gratification, that is. Even that had been while fantasizing about her. That in and of itself was saying something. Fact was, no one else appealed to him.

Her breath came out shallow, fast, and she moaned. He stiffened and drew back. Her eyes were closed, teeth clenched. "Shit!" Quickly, he lifted off her. "Sie, Sienna?" Looking her over, he raised her tank top to check her wound.

She chuckled softly as she rubbed a hand at the welts her nails left on his arm. "That was worth every bit of pain."

Gavin frowned and bit out a curse. "I shouldn't have done it. This shouldn't have happened. What the hell is wrong with me?"

Delicate fingers brushed back the damp hairs from his temples and at the crease between his brows. "If it's that good in my current condition, I can only imagine how it will be when I'm fully healed and can take you the way I want." Her hand circled his cock and easily pumped life back into it.

The look of her contented grin allowed Gavin to relax a bit. Needing to focus, he removed her skillful hand from his shaft, reached over to the nightstand, and retrieved the pills, along with the glass of water. "Here."

"I don't need it. The theory has been confirmed to be true." She grinned.

"Sienna." A stern look. "Take them."

She resisted for a moment, then sighed. "Fine." As she swallowed down the pills with the water, she watched him, then handed over the glass that he set on the nightstand. "You're upset."

"It was selfish of me. I could've hurt you . . . worsened your injury."

"But you didn't."

"It won't happen again, believe that." He left the bed and put on his shorts. "I'll let you rest."

"You can sleep in here." Her smile was filled with invitation as her hot gaze traveled the length of him.

"No." *I'll want to lick every inch of you while you sleep.* It came out a lot colder than intended. The passion fire in her eyes seemed to dissipate like a pilot light gradually cooling down.

Admiring the long, luscious curves of her body stretched out with one leg slightly bent, the wetness from his seed glistening at the V of her thighs, a reminder of how good she felt and how well they fit together, his cock pulsed, wanting inside her again. So weak he was to her and so damn irresponsible. He hadn't used a condom. "You're not on the pill. That much, I know."

"I get an injection once a year." Her gaze flickered, then she scowled. "I'm selective in the company I keep, and I'm surely not out to trap you with a kid," she bit out.

"That's not…" He clammed up to avoid choking himself further on that foot in his mouth, went into the bathroom, then returned with a wet washcloth.

Before he could tend to her, she took the towel, quickly saw to the task herself, and then handed it back to him without ever looking at him. He brought the comforter over her. "I'm going to catch up on some work."

A coldness crept into her features. She clicked off the TV, then turned her head away from him on the pillow as she brought the blanket up to her chin, shielding herself from his admiring view. "Turn off the lamp . . . please," she said quietly, eyes closed.

Scooping up the glass, he clicked the switch on the lamp and left the room feeling like an ass in more ways than one. He'd turned what was special between them into something ugly. Making love to her had been a gift. He thought about that as he tidied and locked up the place, then headed to his room.

As he slid into the empty bed, still thinking over how he'd fucked up his first time with the one woman that meant everything to him, his cell on the nightstand buzzed. There were two missed calls from Dylan and one from his father. A shudder rushed through him in expectation of what it most likely meant.

Time to pay the Pied Piper.

Chapter Seventeen

The blow from his fist was sudden, sending her to her knees. Son of a bitch! Dazed, she hung on with stubborn fortitude, refusing to fold under, and swung out, clawing him across the face. A large, brutal hand gripped her throat and squeezed, and squeezed, and squeezed. The barrel of his gun appeared between her eyes . . . the resounding clank of its discharge. . .

Sienna's eyes sprung open, her breathing hurried. She clutched the sheet in a strangled hold as her nightmare forced her to relive that horrifying moment over and over.

Dim light washed over the bedroom. Her senses on alert, she frantically looked around and found Gavin seated in the chair over by the fireplace. The ceiling's recessed light angled down upon him, haloing his blond head. Feet propped up on the ottoman and crossed at the ankles, he held an ink pen horizontally between his lips as he flipped through a stack of papers upon his lap. Forehead crinkled, he wore an expression of deep concentration as though studying an unsolvable puzzle. He'd scribble something on the pages and then return the pen between his pursed lips. Watching him, his beautiful presence quieted her racing pulse and pushed away that devastating horror.

Following their sexcapade last week, he'd kept his distance, careful in his touch, and guarded in his side-long gazes when he thought she wasn't looking. It had been wrong of her to tempt him the way she had, but it was so worth the outcome.

Sienna's eyelids drooped, and she exhaled, relieving the pressure that trapped the air in her chest, then looked over at him again, reassuring herself that he was still there. His blue eyes were locked on her.

"Hey, sweetness, hope I didn't wake you," he voiced softly; the deep, smooth cadence was like a calming kiss across her senses. "Need anything?"

"No, thanks."

"I thought I'd catch up on work while you slept. I'll let you rest." He started gathering up his papers.

"No, stay. I like knowing you're here." He stared for a long moment. "Please stay."

"Whatever you want."

My protector. With a smile, she closed her eyes to the soothing tone of his low-spoken words.

Chapter Eighteen

Sienna woke to the sound of mumbled voices. A check of the time on the nightstand, it was coming upon noon. Wow! She'd slept the entire night through and practically the morning. *Damn pills.* With the black-out blinds drawn, it could have been 11:51 p.m. for all she knew.

Carefully, she sat up, brought her legs over the side of the bed, and turned on the lamp. There was a consistent ache at her side, but not nearly as severe as it had been, and her head no longer felt as though she rode a never-ending rollercoaster. Apparently, sleep was just what she'd needed.

With deliberately slow movements, she rose, and trekked in short shuffles to the bathroom. So far, no acute dizziness. That was good.

As she freshened up, she thought about the conversation she'd had with Gavin a couple of weeks or so ago. *We don't have to live the way they do,* he'd said. He was right. Besides, who was she to judge? Her family wouldn't win any awards in the upstanding department either.

Thinking of how she'd pleasured herself with his long, formidable fingers and his cock's caressing strokes along the slick walls of her clenching sex, while his tongue devoured her moans of both pleasure and pain, it had sent her spiraling off the edge in exquisite orgasmic bliss. It damn sure was worth the stab-like shards in her side that she'd endured throughout his deliciously hard rutting.

I want to be with you . . . learn everything there is to know about you. His words had shaken her to her soul and sent what was left of her heart's protective barrier crumbling down. She was in love with him; there was no sense in denying it. The reality of it made her smile.

Stepping out of the bathroom and into the closet, she put on her terrycloth robe, then padded barefoot out of the room.

• • •

"What are you going to do?" Dax whispered and bit off a large chunk of his chili dog. "You could ignore the voicemail message, and say you lost your phone or some shit," he muttered around his chomps.

"That won't fly. It's been three days since my pop left the message, and Dylan keeps leaving messages as well. He said Pop is threatening to send someone to my door if I don't respond. I don't have much of a choice. Dylan's message also said it's a pickup; a pickup of what, he didn't say." Gavin filled his glass with water from the fridge's door dispenser, then rounded the island and took a seat on the barstool. He stuck a wad of seasoned fries in his mouth and chewed, whispering, "All I know is it's tonight, and I have to work it out somehow."

"Are you saying you haven't told Sienna about the arrangement with your father?" Dax whispered.

"No, and I don't intend to. If she knew I was doing these assignments, she'd walk for sure, believe that," he uttered low.

"You don't know that."

"I know her. And she pretty much made it clear to me when we talked about it all."

"I think what you need to do—" Dax paused and looked across the room.

Gavin's head turned. Sienna stood at the start of the hallway. Even in her bathrobe, she caused his breath to hitch. She was a stunning beauty. It was impossible not to want her. Throw in her strength, and her bold, yet genuinely kind temperament, she was perfect . . . and a tempting treat that was out of his reach. After they'd had sex, which clearly put more of a strain on their already tenuous situation, he'd done his best to keep his distance.

He got up and went to her. "Hey, sleepyhead. If you're going to be up, let me get your wheelchair."

"I don't want it."

"You don't want it, huh?" He looked back at Dax, who was stuffing clumps of fries into his mouth. "See what I'm dealing with here." It was said with a smile. Turning back to her, he took her hand and guided her over to a barstool. "This is my buddy, Daxton Pattarozzi."

Dax wiped his hands on a napkin, then shook her hand. "I go by Dax. Nice to finally meet you."

"It's nice to meet you, too, Dax." She eyed the hotdog and fries. "Tell me that's from Ben's Chili Bowl."

"The one and only," Dax said while chewing.

"My fav." She took a fry from Gavin's plate and munched. "Hmm . . . the best ever."

"I have some chili in the drawer warmer for you, thought you might want it later for lunch. I was going to make you breakfast." Gavin went over to the stove to heat up the skillet.

"Breakfast? It's past noontime. I'll have the chili." She ate more of Gavin's fries.

"Bro, she's a woman after my own heart." Dax grinned and stuck the remaining end of his hotdog into his mouth. "I see why you're crazy about her," he uttered around the mouthful.

"Dude." Gavin frowned and gave a sheepish glance at Sienna as he set the bowl and a spoon before her. "Do you need your pills?" Her right brow arched, looking surprised that he'd asked rather than ordered. What would be the point? She would do what she wanted anyway.

"No, babe, I'm good. My side doesn't ache as much, and I don't feel the slightest bit dizzy."

Babe. Gavin blinked, rendered speechless for a moment. She'd never called him that before. He downplayed it, suppressing a grin. "That's great, but don't overdo it. You need to keep resting to heal."

She smiled and took his hand, entwining their fingers. "I will. I heard voices . . . thought I'd take a break from the bed and come say hello."

Gavin and Dax exchanged a look, both wondering just how much she'd heard.

"We were catching up," Gavin said. "What would you like to drink?"

"Do you have any juice?"

"Cranberry."

Her eyes brightened. "That's actually my favorite."

"I'd like to take credit, but Bailey told me."

"It's still sweet of you."

With a glance at Dax, who wore a smirk as he munched away on his fries, Gavin went to the fridge. "Ice?"

"Yes, thanks."

"I stopped by to see how you were getting along," Dax said to her.

"I heard you and Sean Grant flew in from London and came straight to the hospital. Thank you."

Dax nodded with a glimpse over at Gavin, then back at her. "If ever one of us is in any kind of trouble, we come together. That now includes you and Bailey."

She looked at Gavin. Their stares held in a quiet understanding, then she turned back to Dax. "It's appreciated."

They ate and chatted for about an hour. Dax shared stories about Gavin, Lucas, Sean, and himself when they were kids that had her laughing to tears. Several times her breath snatched, and she pressed a hand at her side with a look of discomfort brought on by laughter over something the man said.

"Dax, come on, cool it. I think she's got the picture. You've made it clear; we were four degenerates," Gavin finally said so Sienna would stop laughing and wincing at every other word. He turned to her. "Hey, how would you like it if Bailey came by later? You two could hang out, catch up." He cleared away the dishes, then went back over to her.

"I'd love that!"

"I'll give you ladies the place to yourselves this evening. How's that sound?"

She cradled his face in her hands, pulled him in, delivered a light peck on his lips, and then drew back with eyes exceptionally warm. "That's really sweet. You're wonderful, you know that?"

Damn! That around the clock sleep she'd had must have done something to her brain chemistry. She was being shockingly affectionate. "Of course I know that." He grinned, while again doing his best not to get all lopsided jolly by her behavior. He turned to Dax. "We'll grab a drink later? Maybe hit up Sean and Lucas to see if they'd want to join us."

"I'm in," Dax said with his attention on his water bottle, his expression bland, thankfully giving nothing away.

"I'll go call Bailey." Sienna rose slowly from her seat. "Dax, it was great meeting you."

"The pleasure was all mine. Take care."

Gavin walked her back to her room. She picked up her phone from the nightstand and sat on the edge of the bed. "Is there anything I can get you?" He helped her out of her robe, then settled her beneath the covers.

"No, thanks. You've done more than enough."

"Holler if you need anything." He headed out.

"Gavin?"

At the door, he gave a look over his shoulder.

"You're really sweet. That's all I wanted to say."

Wow! Okay, he let that one wash over him like a warm spring rain. Guilt filled his chest as he thought about how much he didn't deserve her.

He nodded, closed the door behind him, and went back to the kitchen island.

"That's one save," Dax whispered. "Three more to go. What will you do when you get call number two from your father . . . and the rest of them? You won't be able to use the ladies hanging out each time."

"I'll deal with it as it comes."

Dax stood up and stretched his long frame, then moved to the door. With a hand on the knob, he said, "If you need me to join you tonight, I'm there."

"Nah, I got it." Gavin gave a quick look over his shoulder in the direction of the hallway before whispering, "What you can do is meet up at Sean's around five. I intend to make a quick stop there before I head to Dylan. In case Sienna asks about hanging out with you and the guys, I'll be able to say truthfully that I was there."

"Dude, that's called lying by omission."

Gavin frowned. "Weren't you leaving?"

"Just saying."

"Get the fuck out."

With a chuckle, Dax delivered a mocking salute, and exited.

Pain in the ass. Gavin hated to admit that his buddy was right, but what choice did he have? He was taking a gamble by not telling her and just hoped the deck was in his favor.

At the close of the door, he made his way back to the bedroom. Sienna had removed the sheets from the bed. The woman just refused to keep still.

The sound of the shower running drew him to the bathroom. She stood just outside of the glass door with a hand under the water.

"I see you insist on making me worry about you."

"Bailey will be over around three. I wanted to straighten up and take a shower. Will you help me shampoo my hair?"

Gavin helped her out of her tank top and panties. Keeping his attention on the task at hand, he assisted her into the shower.

"You could join me." She beckoned her head in the direction of the warm spray.

Admiring her beautiful, naked, tantalizing form as the water glistened over her smooth skin, he was barely tethered on the edge of his restraint as it was. "It's best for both of us that I don't."

After tending to her hair, with swift hands, he bathed her, then wrapped her in a towel and guided her to the chair by the fireplace. He made quick work of dressing the bed. She came forward and took a seat on the edge. On his knees before her, he squeezed into his palm the strawberry-scented moisturizer and began running his hands over her legs. Soft and smooth as new spun silk.

She removed the towel, exposing her nakedness, and encircled her legs around his back, drawing him in. Her brilliant smile dared him to succumb to the blatant invitation.

Sensual and sexual. *I fucking love that about her.*

Staring at her succulent breasts on down to her bare sex, he licked his lips, remembering the sweet taste of her. "Stop torturing me, woman. You make it damn hard to be good."

"Maybe I don't want you to be good."

With her body spread before him like a decadent smorgasbord, he glided his hands along her legs, over narrow hips, and cupped her breasts. So damn weak to her, he took her right nipple into his mouth, sucking the pebbled flesh into a hard peak, then dragged his tongue up the delicate column of her throat, and finally claimed her offered mouth. His kisses were light, teasing, until she began an aggressive sweep of her tongue over his lips, nipping, licking, and tasting him with a rough and greedy insistence. The act was so provokingly stimulating, his dick pulsed in his jeans as he all but rammed his tongue down her throat. "Sie, I want to lick every inch of you," he breathed huskily, as he slipped a finger between the split of her moist folds and gently circled her clit before pushing the thick digit into her already wet pussy. A shudder was shared between them as her channel clenched and unclenched in time with his deep stroking finger.

The ring of his cell phone jolted Gavin back to his senses. He drew back and pulled the phone from his front pocket. Seeing Abela's name on the display took him by surprise.

Sienna palmed his face, her eyes seeming to glow like hot coals of unquenched passion, and tugged, attempting to force him back to her mouth.

"I need to take this." He stood up and answered the call on his way out of the room, "Hey."

"Hey yourself, stranger. It's been a while."

He stepped into his bedroom and closed the door. The last time they'd spoken had been during Dylan's wedding almost a year ago. They weren't related by blood, but waking up naked in bed with her had been wrong, not to mention downright stupid. He'd reduced his whiskey consumption from that day forward.

"You still there?"

"Yeah." Gavin pulled himself out of his thoughts of the day he'd made the fucked-up mistake of sleeping with her. A lurch curled in his stomach . . . so fucking stupid. "How are things with you?"

"Good, I guess. I asked Eddie how you were, since he's the only one that has gotten the pleasure to see you. I'm sure you're still hot with a great ass."

She was always vocal that way with him. There was a time when his ego ate that shit up. Not anymore. Bypassing the comment, he asked, "So what's doing?"

"I was calling to see if you'll be at the party?"

"What party?"

She chuckled. "Your pop's birthday party, silly. Will you be there? The family would love to see you. I would love to see you. Uh . . . yeah, you got weird after we had se—"

"When is the party?" Gavin cut in, not wishing to be reminded of that night.

"The same time it's always been. The second weekend in September. I was also calling to see if you'd like to grab a drink, you know, to catch up? Like I said, it's been a while."

"My plate's sort of full right now."

A sigh dragged out from her. "Gav, come on, we're talking one drink and a bit of conversation."

Awkward silence filled the space for several seconds as he tried to drum up a reason not to see her without hurting her feelings. None came to mind fast enough. "Uh, yeah, sure, I'd like that. I'll hit you up when I have some time."

"Great. Okay, well . . . it was nice hearing your voice . . . deep, smooth, and sexy." Another soft laugh. "I'm looking forward to that drink."

"Sure thing." Gavin ended the call and raked his fingers through his hair, flooded with a sea of regret. She'd gotten the wrong idea about his feelings for her. To avoid hurting her, he'd put distance between them, hoping she'd get the message. That apparently had been his second mistake with her. They needed to have a talk.

Sienna. He'd left her smack in the middle of foreplay to talk to the other woman. *Damn it.*

The ring of his cell in his hand startled him. *Dylan.* He answered, "What's doing?'

"The meet time is the same, but the location has changed."

"What do you mean it's changed? Changed to where?"

"Not over the phone. I'll tell you when you get here, which will be when exactly? If we want to be on time, we need to be ready."

"How far out are we talking?"

"Dude, not over the phone."

"Fuck, what's the distance!" Gavin barked and looked at the closed door. "How far?" It came out more calmly, but not by much. He could do without all this incognito bullshit.

"Just under two hours . . . one way."

He bit out a curse. "I'll head out in a few."

Chapter Nineteen

Are you kidding me!

Sienna sat slack-jawed, staring at the empty space of the door. Baffled and feeling slighted once again, slowly, she stood up, and made her way to the closet. It took a bit of effort, but she managed to bandage her side and forehead, and then dressed for the day in tan shorts and a pink T-shirt. On her trudge back to the bed, Gavin entered the room and approached her.

"Here, let me help you."

She slapped his hand away. "I'm good." Dismissing the offended look in his eyes, she held her breath and eased down onto the bed.

The sound of the doorbell had them both checking the clock. Without a word, he left the room. Moments later, Bailey bustled in carrying a bright orange floral tote and wearing a smile just as bright. They shrieked excitedly and hugged tight.

"I know I'm early, but I couldn't wait to see you."

"It's fine. Girl, I'm so glad you're here."

Bailey's gaze roamed, studying. "How are you? Have you been resting?"

"She refuses to take her meds," Gavin chimed in from his perch at the threshold with arms crossed and a shoulder resting against the doorframe.

Bailey turned her head to him. "I knew she wouldn't."

"I don't need them. I can manage on my own," Sienna said with a knowing look over at Gavin. Ignoring the dimness in his blue eyes, she brought her attention back to Bailey and smiled. "We're going to have a blast."

"You know it. I brought your favs." Bailey pulled from her tote a box of cheddar and caramel mix popcorn and a bag of mini dark chocolate bites. She looked back at the door. "Gav—" The space where he'd been was empty. She turned back. "I was going to ask if he has Netflix?"

"He does, as well as Amazon, Hulu, all of it." Sienna clicked the remote at the TV on the wall and pulled up the menu.

"Perfect. We're about to series binge." As Bailey kicked off her canvas sneakers and climbed in bed, she said, "I hear the guys are hanging out tonight. Lucas mentioned it before I left."

"Yep." Sienna stared at the empty space of the door. She could hear Gavin's low murmurs but was unable to make out what he was saying. He was speaking on his cell again, that much was obvious, but to who?

"What is it? What's wrong?"

She met Bailey's quizzical stare and smiled as she tore into the box of popcorn, soaking up the cheesy-sweet aroma. "I was craving this, thanks." She received a long look, then her friend relented, picked up the remote, and started flipping through the channels.

About two hours and an empty box of popcorn later, Gavin came into the room carrying a glass of water and her medication. He shook two pills from the bottle and set them next to the glass on the nightstand. "You ladies need anything before I head out?"

The piece of chocolate in Sienna's hand stilled at her lips as she took in his tall presence. Dressed in all black—jeans, a crew-neck shirt beneath a stylish jacket, and heavy soled shit-stumpers— the first word that came to mind was gorgeous. The second was threatening. Her head turned to the nightstand. It was closing in on 5:00 p.m.

"You're getting your party started kind of early." His lips pursed, then there was a pause, a pregnant pause as if he was trying to think carefully before his attention dropped to the floor briefly, then back at her. He'd once claimed that he could read people. Well, she was becoming a scholar in her own right at reading him.

"I'm headed to Sean's place. We'll likely hit up a bar for drinks later." He lowered and came in, aiming to kiss her.

Seriously? Sienna turned away just enough that his lips caught her right cheek. He reared back, head cocked slightly. A questioning look subtly colored his expression before his poker face settled back into place. *Again, seriously? Oh no, buddy, it doesn't work like that with me. One minute you want me and then all it takes is a phone call to change that? Nope, you go do you.* She wasn't stupid. There was no doubt in her mind that the call he'd taken earlier had been from a woman, one who apparently was important enough that he would walk away from having sex with her.

"Tell my husband to behave himself." Bailey grinned, her head bouncing between them, unknowingly breaking into their silent exchange.

"I'm on it," Gavin said to her, yet his eyes remained pinned.

Sienna chose not to move away from the hand that cupped her cheek and resisted turning her lips into his affectionate touch. Damn him for consistently seesawing her emotions.

"You try and rest some. Have fun, ladies." Straightening to his full height, he turned, and left the room.

No words were spoken until the resounding clank of the entry door, then Bailey asked, "What was that about?"

"We had sex."

Bailey gasped. "Sienna, are you nuts? You have a cracked ribbed and a concussion." Her eyes narrowed. "That's it, you're out of her. You're staying at my home. What kind of man would take advantage—"

"I initiated it." Sienna met her friend's tightly furrowed brows. "Yep, all me."

"What were you thinking? You could've worsened your injury. You're here to rest up, not to be . . . be . . ."

"Rocking out," Sienna supplied with a curved lip. "Did you see the man? He's smoking hot with his clothes on, picture him without them. On second thought, don't. Erase him from your mind." Receiving a reprimanding glare, she sobered. "No worries, it won't happen again."

"Good," Bailey huffed. "Why?"

Sienna drew back. "Why? You want me to sleep with him or you don't?"

"Yes . . . No . . ." She shook her head. "I don't know. I picked up some sort of weirdness between you two. What's up?"

"I think he's seeing someone."

"What makes you say that? You're staying in the man's home. If that had been the case, why did he insist on having you here to recuperate? You're supposed to be getting to know him better." Bailey cut a sideways look and shook her head. "I guess that much has been accomplished."

Sienna thought about Gavin's fingers buried deep inside her while his tongue was practically down her throat, yet whoever the woman was on that call enticed him a hell of a lot more.

She munched on her chocolate while saying, "I know the signs. Heck, I've seen Lifetime movies just like this—the text messages and phone calls—rich guy with two mistresses."

Bailey sucked her teeth. "You're being ridiculous."

"Oh really? Well, how do you explain this? We were about to have sex again and—"

"Sienna!"

"Pish." She waved a hand at the objectionable frown. "Yeah, yeah, give me a break, okay. I'd been sex deprived. Anyway, he gets a phone call and bam, I'm all but forgotten." Fiddling with the blanket, she was annoyed that she'd allowed her feelings to cultivate into this all-consuming affection for him. She didn't like feeling vulnerable and unsure, especially where a man was concerned.

"The sex between us had been just that, sex. It didn't mean anything."

"It meant something to you. I can tell." Bailey regarded her with an acumen that came from years of a deeply bonded friendship.

"Nah, I'm good." *Major lie.* Her best friend maintained a concerned frown. "Bails, stopped looking at me that way. Really, I'm okay. Gavin and I are friends." Needing to change the subject, she said, "I met Daxton—Dax Pattarozzi." They stared at one another, then shrieked in unison like high school cheerleaders. "Hottie, right?"

Bailey rapidly nodded. "Oh yes."

"Have you met Sean?" Sienna asked as she tore into another bag of chocolate. "I've seen his pics online of course, but I haven't met him."

"I've met him, and the Internet doesn't do him justice." They shared grins as Bailey aimed the remote at the TV. "So, what will we watch first?"

Chapter Twenty

Gavin made the hour drive to Sean's sprawling suburban estate along the Potomac River.

Before he could press in the code to open the gates, the twelve-foot, glossy black irons parted. Sean must have been alerted on one of his security feeds. The property was outfitted with sensors and cameras that could thwart anyone lurking within twenty feet of the private grounds.

Gavin drove along the black flagstone, flanked by neatly groomed, lofty, aged evergreens, pulled into the circled driveway and parked beside Lucas's silver Ferrari. To his left, over by the side driveway that led to the guest house and to the rear of the property, was a lime green Volkswagen Beetle.

As he exited his car, Dax's car came rolling up. He got out and came forward. They gripped palms and pulled into a hug.

Gavin raised his chin in the direction of the bright green vehicle. "Who else is here? Or, has Sean gone economy friendly?"

"It belongs to a friend of Nate's. I think they're study partners in his master's program. Nate invites her out to play tennis on occasion."

Gavin raised a brow. "Her?" he asked as they made their way up the stone steps and tried the door, expecting that it would be unlocked. "So, Nate has a girlfriend?"

Sean had practically looked after his cousin, Nate, after the guy's parents' plane went down over Nosy Berafia Island when he was ten years old. Their bodies were never found. Nate's father had piloted the plane.

"Yes, to the female friend part, and I'm pretty sure it's a *no* to the second part," Dax answered as they strolled through the expanse of the great room and into the kitchen.

Gavin squinted briefly to allow his vision to adjust. The stark white room was near blinding. Lucas sat at the island nursing a Yuengling, and Sean was standing over by the glass French doors looking out.

"Gav, man, to add to your second question, that's why." Dax directed a comical look over at Sean.

Perplexed, Gavin frowned. "What do you mean?" He stepped over to Lucas, and they greeted one another with their usual handshakes and bro hugs.

"Sean's got a crush," Dax sang out.

Sean came away from the window sporting a scowl. "Dax, shut up. I'm not fucking twelve. I don't have a damn crush."

Gavin and Sean's palms met, and they pulled in. "Dude, you really need to add some color in this place."

Sean looked around his kitchen. "What's wrong with white?" He waved a hand at the stainless-steel appliances and at the ultra-pale gray marble countertops on his way to the fridge. "There's your color." He grabbed three beers, uncapped the bottles, and handed one off to Gavin and the other to Dax. Taking a seat on a metal gray barstool at the island, Sean took a swallow from his bottle. "I was watching Nate's swing. It's too low. She kicks his ass during every match."

"If you say so," Dax muttered, then coughed out, "Crush."

Laughter broke out, and Sean sent his bottle cap rocketing at Dax's head. A quick dodge to the right saved Dax from getting struck by the projectile.

Gavin glanced at his watch. He'd have to leave soon if he wanted to get to Dylan on time. The drive to the bar where they'd chose to meet before heading to the drop location—he still hadn't a clue where that would be—was a good hour and a half at best from Sean's place. "I won't be hanging around here long."

"You could tell your father you're not going to go through with it," Sean said. "You plan to cut ties with him anyway, so—"

Dax sucked his teeth with a side look at Sean. "Dude, come on, you know damn well how the man's father is. Hell, we all know." He turned to Gavin. "Bro, no offense, but that motherfucker's scary as shit. Remember when the three of us would be crazy enough to spend the summer with you? Your father's way of entertaining us would be to see who could break down and reassemble a Glock the fastest, and the one who came in last had to clean them all." Dax chuckled and shook his head as he took a drink of his beer. "Yeah, you better follow through on those assignments if you know what's good for you, my brother."

"How did Sienna take it when you told her about what you're doing?" Lucas asked him.

"He didn't tell her," Dax supplied, and Gavin hurled one of the bottle caps laying on the counter at the guy's head. Again, Dax dodged it, remaining unscathed. "What was that for? You said you weren't planning to tell her."

Chagrined, Gavin glowered. "Like Sean said, shut the fuck up," he groused, primarily out of the guilt he felt. "I'll get the assignments done, and then it'll all be over. Sienna doesn't need to know." He took a gulp from his bottle. The inanity of his words made it hard to swallow.

"Are you serious? You're not planning to tell her what you're doing?" Sean asked. "That's how you intend to play it?"

"I don't think that's wise, my man," Lucas put in. "Look, you know I got your back. I won't say anything to Bailey, but keeping this from Sienna is not a smart move. I wouldn't gamble with this one, bro."

"Yep, that's what I tried to tell him earlier, but you know his ass never listens," Dax casually remarked between sips of his beer.

Gavin's first reaction was to snap off and tell them all to mind their goddamn business, but it wouldn't be fair. They wouldn't listen anyway. Here he was at his buddy's home, using them all as buffers to aid him in his deception. If anything, he should be thanking them for once again having his back. That said, they just didn't understand what he was up against.

Things between Sienna and him were flimsy at best right now. If he told her he was doing jobs for his father as repayment for using his men to watch over her, he could lose her. She may not take kindly to what he'd done to Dale, either, even though it was in retribution for what that bastard did to her. But she was nearly killed. He couldn't sit back and do nothing. Fear quivered in his belly over how easily things could've turned out much worse because of that fuck-nut. That bastard needed to pay.

Gavin's thoughts were disrupted at the sight of Nate and his *girl*friend now standing just outside the glass doors. His head turned to Sean when he went to the fridge, retrieved two bottled waters, and then stepped outside. He handed over the waters to the pair, then chatted with the young woman, whose features resembled Bailey. Her brown skin tone, lean, athletic build, and even her hair that was arranged into a curly ponytail were pretty similar to Lucas's wife.

"Hey, are you all seeing this?" Dax asked as they watched Sean laughing it up with the woman, practically cock-blocking his cousin, Nate. With a light touch on her arm, Sean said something that had her throwing her head back in laughter. She gave him a playful shove on the shoulder.

They all looked at one another. "Damn." Lucas chuckled with a shake of his head. "Our boy got it bad."

"Yep. What did I tell you?" Dax put in.

Just then, she retrieved her phone from the side pocket of her tennis bag, gave a look at it before tapping in a text message, said a few words to Sean while wearing a bright smile, that Sean reciprocated, and then she and Nate went on their merry way. Sean came back into the kitchen, still wearing that floppy, broad grin. Seeing them all staring, he dried his expression and cleared his throat, concentrating on finishing his beer.

"I'm considering throwing Nate a graduation party," Sean said. "I didn't think his ass would make it through a week of undergrad. Soon, he'll have his MBA . . . never could've predicted that."

Gavin noted the guy's father-like proud grin. Nate getting his MBA was a major achievement, considering how much the young man used to party. There was a time when Sean would call Nate at school, but the guy would be MIA for days. Then Sean would show up at his dorm and find him passed out from partying or who knows what. Sean wanted to kick his cousin's ass on a regular basis, especially after the university had placed Nate on probation a second time. Thankfully, the young man got his shit together.

"I guess the maturity bell rings at different times for us all." Dax got up, went to the fridge, and grabbed another beer.

"We're still waiting for yours to ring," Sean teased around sips from his bottle.

Dax threw his head back in an abrupt laugh, then flattened his expression. "You're funny." His tone was just as flat, yet he grinned. "I assume that young woman you're crushing on will be at this little graduation soiree?"

Sean's brow creased. "She has a boyfriend. The guy is a friend of Nate's. The dude texts constantly. It seems he likes to keep tabs on her."

"That's fucked up." Gavin stood up. "I better get going. I have about an hour drive from here, and who the hell knows how far Dylan has us going on from there?" On his way out, he said over his shoulder, "Oh, and Sean, you're definitely crushing on the lady, bro. But as our boy Dax often says, no ring, fair game," Gavin told him on his way out and heard Dax back him up.

"Damn right."

Chapter Twenty-one

Heads bobbed to the pulse of the music. Round bar tables that circled the overcrowded dance floor were packed, and not a booth along the far wall was vacant. Customers sat hemmed in tight at the bar, drinking, and abrupt laughter cut through the fast-paced country beat pounding out of the 1980s wooden block wall speakers.

"I guess this is the local hotspot," Gavin drawled with a look at Dylan beside him. They'd driven out to a rural Virginia town that was so remote, he would bet it wasn't even listed on the map. There hadn't been a car on the road for miles. Looking around the place, likely the entire town's population was in the bar. Not his speed. "I'll wait in the truck."

"No need. I—" Dylan started.

"Well, good evening, stranger."

Their heads turned. A petite, attractive brunette stepped before them balancing an empty tray against her hip. She came up to Dylan, and he leaned in to accept her peck on the cheek. "I didn't think you'd actually show up. When you'd texted to say you'd be in my neck of the woods, I had to double check the number to make sure I hadn't been spammed." Her gaze shifted. "Hello, handsome. Who might you be?"

"He's my brother, Gavin."

"Well, nice to meet you, Gavin, and welcome to Cailin's. I've held a booth for you. This way. I'm Cailin, by the way," she said over her shoulder as she led them through the crowd.

Holding up the rear, Gavin glanced up at the exposed wooden beams and high industrial ceiling fans, and around at the mounted deer heads that lined the knotty oak paneling.

Heads pivoted; hard stares followed them, some in obvious challenge.

They came up to a half-moon shaped booth outfitted in hunter-green leather seating. It aligned with the entrance to the bar, giving Gavin a good view of those coming and going.

He slid into the seat, his spidey senses on full alert. If shit went south, he'd be ready.

Across from him, Cailin and Dylan were having a whispered exchange, heads close, her hand in his. Whatever they were discussing, it brought a pout to her ruby painted lips. She took a step back, and their linked hands severed, a slow separation. Gavin wasn't sure which of them withdrew first.

"I'll send someone over with drinks. The usual for you?" she asked, and Dylan nodded. She turned to Gavin. "And you?"

"Whatever he's having."

Offering up a slight smile that appeared stiff, forced, she went on her way.

Sitting back, Gavin eyed the crowd as he said, "I guess Angie's liberal with your marriage vows." He gave a nod in the direction of Cailin now over at the bar. "You and her?"

"Nah, but she'd like us to start something up again."

Gavin cocked his head. "Again?"

"She was before Angie, you know, first love and all that jazz." He frowned. "It didn't work out. Pop felt she didn't check out. I had to make a choice. Pop wanted to. . ." Dylan broke off. His expression became rigid for a moment, then drawn inward as he looked over at Cailin.

Gavin's brows shot up. "Pop would've had her. . ." Their stares held with clear understanding. "Damn," he voiced low.

"Here you go, boys." The waitress set whiskey-filled glasses before them. "Compliments of the proprietor."

"Then this is for you." Dylan handed over a twenty to the waitress. With a smile, she tucked it between the deep valley of her full breasts that practically spilled out of her leather vest tank top, then moved on.

They both looked at Cailin again over behind the bar. As if sensing them, her head came up from her task of wiping down the weathered mahogany wooden surface and met Gavin's gaze, then slid to Dylan, lingering, before she broke the connection and went back to tidying up.

Dylan continued to stare at her a moment longer, then took a sip from his glass. "It was a long time ago. I have my Angie." His words didn't quite meet his somber blue eyes as he ran a finger around the rim of his glass.

Gavin didn't know what to say to the guy. Having seen Dylan with his wife, there was no question that he loved her, but Cailin undoubtedly had been the man's sacrifice.

He thought of Sienna. Would he be forced to make the same choice as his brother? Could he walk away from her? A sudden foreboding feeling of emptiness swept down on him, that sent a cold streak up his spine. The phantom loss he felt of not having Sienna in his life, the hard surge of emotion had him itchy to get the night over with so that he could get back to her. The mere sight of her would be enough to stifle his anxious heartbeat. He couldn't lose her.

"Two handsome men sitting here all by their lonesome. I saw you two when you arrived, thought I'd come over and say hello. I'm Deidre."

Gavin's head turned to the woman sliding into the booth beside him, catapulting him out of his dismal thoughts. Long, dark hair—glossy. Dark eyes—captivating. Ruby-red lips—full. Milky white complexion—flawless. All a nice combination. Except, she'd been a bit heavy-handed on the perfume; the oddly spicy citrus combination singed the inside of his nose. He looked at Dylan and received a shrug of a shoulder. The woman, Deidre, inched closer. The leather seat anchored the satin fabric of her red mini dress, causing it to severely ride up, revealing shapely thighs.

Her gaze roamed, giving him a thorough once over. "The hair, the clothes," she sniffed and smiled, "you smell really good." She looked between Dylan and him. "You guys stand out in this place like road flares."

Tell me something I don't know. Gavin came to that conclusion the moment they pulled up to the place. Thankfully, it had been merely the patrons' plaid shirts and over-washed jeans that separated them instead of a Quentin Tarantino, *Dusk to Dawn* situation.

"I told you my name. Do I get the pleasure of knowing yours?" she asked while running a slender finger slowly down his arm.

"I'm Dylan, and he's Gavin."

Gavin met his brother's stupid smirk. Dylan was enjoying this.

"Gavin," Deidre smiled, "I like that name. So, Gavin, do you dance?" The side of her right breast skimmed his arm. One hand came to rest on his shoulder, stroking. The other glided over his thigh, skating inward, upward.

Gavin had a thing for bold women. They tended to get straight to the down and dirty. No games, no strings. *Sienna Keller.* Her beautiful face appeared in his head. The way she'd handled him throughout her art tour and continued to do so, whether she realized it or not, no other woman came close to her. Anticipation spiked that he'd get to go home to her. The thought of it made him smile. Beside him, practically melded to his hip, Deidre smiled back in apparent misinterpretation. Her hand trailed along his shoulder, perfectly manicured nails lightly skimming his nape. The other trekked a path up his inner thigh coming within a hair of his cock. He removed the woman's determined hands and slid back, putting much needed space between them. "I do dance . . . with my lady." Did Sienna dance? He'd have to ask her about that.

A hint of a flicker in her dark eyes, and then she narrowed the gap between them once more. Taking his hand in hers, she brought it to her bare thigh and added pressure against his fingers at the inner curve just shy of the apex. "How about I borrow you from your lady for a dance?" Her pinky came up and swayed from side to side. "One little dance won't hurt. We can see where the night takes us from there." Her brilliant white smile delivered all sorts of promises.

Across from him, Dylan's phone rang. Still wearing that stupid grin as he played witness to the woman's flirtations, he took the call, and said a few words as he rose to his feet. "Shit, we have to jet, or we'll be late. I got the time wrong."

Gavin slid over, lightly nudging, forcing Deidre out of the booth, and stood up. "Deidre, it was a pleasure."

"Maybe we could connect some time. Here's my number." She pulled out a pen from her purse and scribbled her number on a napkin, then came in close, coming up on her insteps to whisper in his ear. "If only you knew the many things I'd love to do to you." Her gaze met his, her dark eyes full of that wicked declaration as she took it upon herself to slip the napkin into his front jeans pocket, her fingers lingering longer than necessary.

Filing out behind his brother, Gavin mulled over his interaction with the woman. Had he been tempted?

Not even a fraction.

For him, that said a lot.

Chapter Twenty-two

Hours had been spent TV bingeing and catching up. Dishes of Thai food had been ordered. They ate amid series-hopping a variety of shows, and more chatting.

Sienna gave a look at the clock. It was nearly eleven-thirty. Stretched out beside her, Bailey released a wide yawn, one of many that she'd fought for the past hour or so. "Bails, it's late. You should head home."

"No, I'm fine."

"Girl, you're barely able to keep your eyes open."

Bailey raised her head from the pillow. "I'll wait until Gavin gets back."

Sienna expected she'd say that. "It's not necessary."

Bailey sat up and rested back against the headboard. "Maybe I'll text Lucas. These men are worse than women when it comes to guys' night out. They don't know when to call it a night."

"No, don't bother Lucas. I'm going to take my medication and sleep. I'm sure Gavin will be in soon. You should go." A reluctant stare. "The pills make me sleepy. I'll wait to take them until you call to say you made it home." Sienna shifted and feigned a soft grunt. That got her friend moving.

"Sie, you need to rest." Bailey climbed out of bed and slipped on her sneakers. "Let me get you a fresh glass of water." She grabbed the glass from the nightstand and dashed out of the room. Short moments later, she returned and set its replacement back on the nightstand. "Are you sure you wouldn't want me to stay? I could spend the night. Lucas won't mind."

"You're pregnant and should be resting also. Go home." They came in with tight hugs. "Thank you for spending the day with me."

"It was fun. Like old times. I'll call you tomorrow. She headed for the door but turned back. "About you and Gavin—"

"It's fine." Sienna smiled, doing her best to convey reassurance. "Like I said, he's a good friend." Delivering a weak nod, Bailey left.

Sienna allowed herself to accept those words as she settled beneath the covers. About a half an hour into season three, episode five of *Homeland*, her cell buzzed. She retrieved it from the nightstand and read Bailey's message:

Home. Lucas is in bed. Has Gavin made it in?
No.
Really?
No worries.

To end the conversation, she texted:

I'm taking my meds.
Ok. TTYL. XOXO
XOXO.

Sienna set the phone at her side then picked up the pills. Thinking on it, she dropped them back upon the napkin, and turned off the TV. It took about an hour to shut her mind down before she could fall asleep.

A dull ache in her side woke her. Checking the time—2:44 a.m.—she left the bed and padded down the hall. Easing Gavin's bedroom door open, within the darkness of the room, light filtered in through the partially opened slats of the window blinds. A shadowy silhouette lay upon the bed, low, smooth drags of breath pushing in and out. What time had he come in? She closed the door and wasn't sure what made her go across the hall to his bathroom. Flicking on the light, the clothes he'd worn sat in a heap upon the floor. With careful movements, she bent, picked up the shirt, and sniffed it, not sure what possessed her to do that either. The scent was a mixture of his cologne, stale cigarettes, and a woman's eau-de-stink perfume.

What am I doing? This right here was the reason why she hated relationships—the wondering, the worrying, the whys. They were friends, nothing more. A hard jolt of anguish constricted her chest. Damn him for waking her heart and threading himself into it so seamlessly.

Dropping the shirt, she went back to her bed, popped the pills into her mouth, and washed them down with water. As she lay there staring into the dark, letting lethargy drag her under, she raised her heart's barrier back up, brick by excruciatingly heavy brick. She didn't need the headache, didn't need his affection, his devotion, his drugging kisses, the feel of his strong arms wrapped around her.

Ugh.

Chapter Twenty-three

"Hey, sleepyhead."

Gavin set the breakfast tray on the ottoman and raised the blinds. "Hope you're hungry. I made my five-star French toast."

She squinted at the burst of sunlight that lit up her corneas, turning away from its brilliant flare. Her eyes fluttered open and zeroed in on the bouquet of mixed flowers in the glass vase that he'd set on the nightstand.

He knew he should have let her sleep, but he'd missed her during those hours spent with Dylan.

The way he'd left things with her last evening, he'd hoped the breakfast and the flowers would soften her mood.

"I wasn't sure what flower was your favorite, so I got—"

"A little of everything," she said with a soft smile as she eased upright, and he fluffed up the pillows at her back. "They're beautiful. Thank you."

"Anything in the world for you, know that."

She sent him a peculiar look, unreadable.

Out of a simple need to touch her, he took her hand and pressed a kiss into her palm. "When you taste my French toast, you'll say I belong on that show, *Chopped*."

"That good, huh?"

"You'll see." He brought the tray over and drizzled warm syrup over the fluffy stack. Slicing off a corner, he fed it to her. "Your verdict, madam?"

She chewed, and a smile creased the corners of her mouth. "Very good."

"Believe that." He grinned.

As she cut off a small portion and dipped it into the syrup puddling upon the plate, she asked, "How was last night? You boys have a good time? I guess Lucas couldn't handle the late night." Her head came up from her breakfast, her stare upon him as tight as a trapeze wire.

Gavin winced a little, though the barrage of questions were anticipated. That said, her sun-warm smile had given him false hope.

"It was cool, and what do you mean?"

"Bailey texted to let me know she'd made it home. She said Lucas was in bed. It was around 11:30 p.m."

"Yeah." He wasn't certain what time Lucas left Sean's place, since he himself had only hung around for about thirty minutes. And he did end up at a bar, just not with his boys. Fucking Dylan had gotten the pick-up time wrong. They'd left the bar and had to damn near break the sound barrier to get to the drop that ended up being a good two-hour drive away.

The bar. Deidre surfaced into Gavin's thoughts, and just as easily, he erased her. And he was smart to toss the napkin with her number written on it the minute he'd exited.

A goddamn envelope. Dylan needed back up for that? It had been the only item retrieved. If Gavin didn't know better, he would swear his pop was fucking with him in this whole debt owed bullshit.

"So, you and the guys just hung at a bar all night?" She shook her head with a dismissing wave of her hand. "You know what, forget the question. What you do is not my business. I've been thinking. I should go stay with Bailey. I can get out of your way, let you have your bedroom back, your home . . . your life."

Her eyes were flat, yet acutely unyielding as the chill of those words struck like rough stones.

Maybe it was the bright sunny morning or the sweet fragrance of honeysuckle to her left, though Gavin sensed it, she didn't let her irritation with him show in her tone. That made it worse.

"You're not in my way, and I told you that this room is yours. I don't want you to go. Will you stay?" he rushed out, fear of her leaving welling up tight in his throat. She didn't respond as she concentrated on eating her breakfast. "Sie-Sie, sweetness, I want you to stay. Will you?" No reply. He sighed deeply to relieve the constricting pressure in his chest. "I'll go clean up my mess in the kitchen and then return to help you dress."

"I can take care of it myself. Thanks."

"Sienna. . ." The urge to tell her the truth, come clean about it all rode his conscious hard, but now definitely wasn't the time. "Are you sure?"

"Very sure. Thanks for the breakfast. It's delicious." Her stare was cold, contrary to her warm tone.

As he left the room, he thought maybe this was how it should be between them. Who was he to think he could start something long-term with a woman like her? She was sweet and good, not meant for someone like him.

Last night, as he'd sat with Dylan in the booth of that piece of shit bar, and as they'd driven out in the middle of fucking Nowhere, Virginia to the pick up, he realized that he couldn't drag her down into his family's world, especially after learning about Cailin. He'd seen the ugly ways the Kavanaghs played. He needed to keep Sienna away from that vicious madness.

Seeing her in that hospital after what Dale had done to her, his innate need to fight back ruled his actions. It also created the mess he was now knee deep in with his father. He thought about it all as he loaded the dishwasher, then wiped down the countertop. He'd acted on impulse. Stupid of him.

The rest of the day, they hardly spoke, not for his lack of trying. Her responses were choppy and tepid to just about everything he'd said.

The next day was the same. Even during their visit to the doctor for her check-up, she remained distant with him.

By the end of day three, he'd gotten the message. Though she hadn't packed up and left, she'd removed herself from him in every other way possible. She showered on her own and quickly covered up if he came into the room, prepared her own meals, and did her best not to depend on him. She'd essentially reverted their relationship back to square one. Like now, she sat up in bed with her legs slightly elevated upon pillows beneath her knees, and he reclined in the chair, stretched out with his feet propped upon the ottoman. Distance definitively set, they watched a detective show she said was called *Bones*. He'd had to ask because she hadn't volunteered. No more cuddling and sharing between them.

With arms folded across his chest, trying not to appear as unsettled as he felt, Gavin gave a look over at the bed. Her brows were pinched in concentration as her eyes sat transfixed on the decomposed corpse on the TV screen.

Following her shower earlier—foregoing his help again—she'd gone without the bandage on her face. There was a slight pucker around the wound above her brow, but the swelling at her left temple had diminished.

Watching her chew her bottom lip, his gaze dipped there, recalling the petal softness and the sweet taste of her warm tongue. His attention moved lower. Dressed for bed in a white cotton tank top that was all but see-through, the imprint of her dark areolas and pearled nipples punctuated the fabric. He licked his lips. He could feast on those succulent nipples for hours and never get enough. That got him thinking about her plump, juicy clit that was scarcely gift wrapped in those delicate pale pink panties. His dick pulsed in his sweats. *Fucking madness!* Abruptly, he got up, and she finally looked at him. She'd been avoiding that, too.

"I think I'll call it a night." His eyes shifted to the empty space in the bed beside her, and she met his expectant look before taking a glance at the clock to her left. It was barely eight-thirty.

"Kind of early," she said.

He'd tortured himself long enough. "Yes, I guess. Is there anything I can get you before I turn in? You haven't taken your meds for a couple of days." Again, his gaze drifted briefly to the empty, cool space beside her warm, lithe body.

"I don't need the pills. It doesn't hurt as much anymore when I breathe deeply."

"Glad to hear it." Awkward silence.

Her palm brushed across the vacant area beside her, and his eyes locked in on the movement. "Would you like—" The buzz of his cell in the pocket of his sweats interrupted their first conversation in days. She gave a glance over to the nightstand again, undoubtedly noting the time, then back at him. "Aren't you going to get that?" The gruffness in her tone wasn't lost on him.

"No. What were you about to say?" he asked as the buzzing continued.

"Nothing. Good night." Her eyes cold now, she fixed her attention back on the TV.

Damn it. Gavin closed the door behind him and yanked out the phone from his pocket. *Dylan.* Presuming the reason for the call, it went unanswered.

In bed, scenarios danced in his head of what Sienna may have asked, each resulting in him joining her in bed and them making love in every position he could conjure up. He yearned to wrap himself around her, immerse himself in her scent, her comforting warmth. Restless minutes passed as he lay with images of their joined bodies locked tight in an endless caress.

His cell rang again. *Dylan.* He thought to ignore it but figured the guy would only hit redial.

"Yeah, what?" Gavin answered.

"We need to head out."

Though he'd expected it, he muttered a curse. "How far out this time?"

"From where I am in Woodbridge, it's about an hour. Add an additional hour for you, so get moving. Meet me at my place."

Gavin got out of bed and went to his closet. As he riffled through his shirts, he asked, "Did you confirm the time? Don't have me wasting minutes at some shitty-ass bar."

"It's been confirmed. Pop's really anxious about this one for some reason."

"Is it another envelope?" Gavin dragged on a pair of dark-blue denims. When silence filled the line, he realized why. Damn, how he hated all this cryptic bullshit.

"Are you on your way?"

"Shit, dude, you just called." He balanced the phone between his chin and shoulder to slip on his socks.

"Actually, I called you fifteen minutes ago. Stop fucking dodging my calls."

"Yeah, yeah, if you want me to be on my way, you'll stop yammering and let me get dressed." The line abruptly disconnected. Gavin pulled on a black T-shirt and dragged his lightweight, black leather jacket off the hanger, then grabbed his black Lugged boots. As he sat on the edge of the bed to slip them on and lace up, he tried to think of what to say to Sienna about where he was headed. *You could tell her the truth.* She'd hardly spoken to him for the past several days. The truth right now would surely not work well in his favor. *When will it ever?*

He left the room and went to her. Taking a bracing breath, giving a soft tap on the door, he opened it, and stood within the frame. Still situated upright in bed, she'd gotten beneath the covers. Her stare did a slow slide down his frame, then keen eyes lifted, viper-locking with his, her expression crinkling with bemusement. That look was asking, no, demanding an explanation that he was unable to give.

Swallowing deep did little to work the knot down his throat. "Hey, I'm going to step out for bit." His gaze dipped briefly to the floor. "I can't sleep." Looking at her again, her unblinking stare was focused on him. "Is there anything I can get you before I leave?" No words, just a light shake of her head. "Uh, okay. Try and rest. Good night." A nod. He shut the door, leaned back against it, and closed his eyes. *Shit.* Her suspicious look had been damn hard to stomach. He just had to get through two more assignments, then no more lies. As he headed out, he thought about Dax's words: *lying by omission is still lying.*

Shit.

• • •

The moment Sienna heard the entry door clank shut, she snatched her cell phone and called Bailey. After a few rings, the line connected.

"Hey, I was going to call in the morning to check on you. Is everything okay?"

"Gavin is seeing someone. I'm sure of it now."

"Sie, hold on a minute."

Sienna listened to Bailey say, "Babe, I'm going to take this downstairs. No, don't press pause. You can continue watching. I've already seen this one."

A short moment later, she came back on the line. "Okay, I'm back."

"Hope I didn't interrupt anything."

"No, I'm trying to get Lucas caught up on *House of Cards*. It's like he's been living in a cave. He hasn't seen much of anything. So, what makes you so sure Gavin is seeing someone?"

"He received a call, and just as before, he came in here looking like sex walking, then left the apartment."

Bailey gasped. "Are you kidding me! He left you alone again?"

"Pish, I'm feeling much better. I'm hardly experiencing any discomfort. Did you hear the most important part of what I said? Gavin is seeing someone else."

"You said, *someone else* as if to say you and Gavin are a couple. You told me you two were just friends."

Sienna's eyes closed briefly, then she stared up at the vaulted ceiling; no sense in denying it. "Fine, I like him. I more than like him, okay, are you happy now?" Getting a chortle, she sighed long and slid down, stretching out beneath the covers. "It's not funny. We're not officially a couple, but I thought we were headed there. All it takes is a call from whoever this woman is, and he rushes off to her. Telling me he couldn't sleep, that he needed to step out for a bit. Bullshit. You know how I know it's a lie?"

"How do you know?"

Sienna could hear light chomping in her ear. "What are you eating?"

"Sorry, I'm in the kitchen. I got hungry. It's sweet gherkins and string cheese. Now, how do you know he's seeing someone?"

Pregnancy 101. Sienna would cut her friend some slack in getting the munchies. "I know because he does this thing where he looks down when he's talking . . . when he's about to tell a lie. I'm so doggone pissed with myself for allowing my feelings to latch onto him like some weak little, lovestruck teenager," she ranted in aggravation. "I blame him. I'm telling you, it's like those Lifetime movies—rich guy takes you in, cares for you, gets you to feel safe, makes you breakfast in bed, gives you flowers—"

"He gave you flowers? Aw, that's so sweet."

Sienna rolled her eyes. "Bails, geez, this is a 911 call," she grumbled in growing frustration and blinked rapidly at the sudden, unexpected tears that stung the back of her eyes. "I really need my friend right now. Stay focused. I don't know what to do. That pisses me off the most. I always know what to do."

"Sorry, I'm focused. Have you talked to him about it or have you done what you always do when you think a man has stabbed you in the back—assume the worse, then clam up tight until he can't take the dismissal from you any longer, so he kicks himself to the curb?"

She huffed. "I don't do that."

"Sweetie, you do, and stop it." It was a soft, yet firm chiding. "If you more than like him, which I must say, that's freaking awesome," she shrieked lightly, then quickly grew serious, "come out and ask him if he's seeing someone."

An anxious knot curled tight in Sienna's stomach at the thought, because there was a part of her that had already claimed him as hers. *Damn you, Gavin Crane.* This was the very reason she never let a guy have this deep of a level of control over her feelings. "What if he admits to it?"

"Then you'll do well to put a stiff boot to his butt. I will say that I think you're jumping the gun on this one, though. Lucas said Gavin is really into you, that he's never seen him this crazy about a woman before. I wasn't supposed to tell you that."

Sienna sat up, hopeful. "He did? Did Lucas use the word crazy? Bails, don't sugarcoat it. I need to know."

"Yes, he said the word crazy. Now relax about it all."

She eased back down under the covers. "I'll let you get back to your hubby and movie night. Don't tell Lucas what I said."

Bailey sucked her teeth. "Of course not. As if you needed to tell me that. Call if you need me. Hugs."

"Hugs." Sienna ended the call. She would ask Gavin, put it all out there. Heck yes, she would. If his answer was contrary to what Bailey stated, she'd accept it, and her life would go on . . . *but with a chunk of my heart missing.*

Restless hours passed as she tried to quiet her mind in between quick glances at the clock. Doing her best to wait up for him, sometime around midnight, exhaustion finally prevailed.

Chapter Twenty-four

Gavin stepped into the cool, dark space of his apartment and tugged off his boots just inside the door. Remnants of mud and gravel covered the thick soles. The sudden pelting downpour had done a number on his leather jacket.

Sliding his fingers through his rain-soaked hair, a cool breeze from the kick-start of the air condition feathered across his damp clothes as he crossed the space in his socks and padded down the hall to Sienna's room. He slid the wall switch up a tad in the hall to allow the low recessed light to filter in. She lay sprawled out on her back in the middle of the bed. Damn, how he wanted to stretch out next to her, brush up close against her soft skin, rest contently within her comforting warmth. With a long sigh, doing his best not to disturb her, he closed the door, turned off the light, and went to the bathroom.

After a quick, hot shower, he slipped on a pair of black cotton boxers and climbed in bed. Weariness pulled him under with ease.

When he roused awake not from a nightmare, but from a desperate yearning to hold Sienna, instinctively, he reached out across the bed. Cool sheets filled his palm. Nothing new. It hadn't been the first time.

He glanced at the clock. It was nearing 5:00 a.m. He left the bed and shuffled across the hall to the bathroom. More awake now, on his return, his head pivoted toward the soft light illuminating from the front of the apartment. Stepping down the hall and into the living room, there, over by the window, Sienna sat perched upon a barstool before her easel. He went to her. The slow dawn breaking outside the windows and casting shadows on the buildings across the street had been expertly captured upon her canvas. Rubbing the sleep from his eyes, he stood quietly and watched her work.

"Hope you don't mind, I used a sheet as a drop cloth. It was the one item you forgot to get when you bought out the store," she said without a pause in perfecting the fine delineation of gray mortar on the building depicted at the left corner down the block. Even the condensation on the buildings' windows and the dampened pavement leftover from the heavy rain had been skillfully depicted in her artwork. *Wow.*

"That's really beautiful. Like I said, you're no amateur." He stepped in close behind her and rested tentative hands on her shoulders. When she didn't jerk away from his touch, he caressed and lightly massage the back of her neck with his thumbs. "Couldn't sleep?" he asked softly.

"Something like that. I've been having dreams of that night."

His hands stilled. "The shooting?"

"Um hum."

"Sienna . . . I didn't know."

"I didn't mention it."

"You should've told me."

She shrugged, brushing it off in that brave, warrior woman way that she did. "Painting helps me relax. With the art tour and then everything else that happened, I haven't picked up a brush in weeks. I'm so behind." She looked up over her shoulder. "And yes, I took my meds, but I was too wired from the dream to fall back asleep. Painting makes it all better."

A gorgeous smile was sent his way that he returned ten times over. And she was speaking to him again. It felt good. Damn good.

"Glad to know painting helps, but I'm sorry you're experiencing the dreams." Thinking of the ass-kicking he'd put on Dale, *very well-deserved.* "I wish there was something more I could do to help."

"There is, but. . ."

Had he not been so close and had his hands not been upon her shoulders, he would have missed both her words and her faint shrug.

"There is, but what?" he asked.

"Nothing."

Before he could push the question again, his head turned with hers as she looked out the window, then back at her painting, back and forth. His head pivoted back to the window upon noticing the sketchpad perched upon the low window seal. He picked it up, and hitched a breath. Studying the electric blue of his eyes, which was the only color used in the black chalk drawing of his likeness, it was impressively spot-on. "You drew me."

She gave a look up over her shoulder again, meeting his awestruck gaze, then rose to her feet and faced him. "Had to get my sea legs back . . . or sea hands in this case." A finger skated along the angled line of his chin scruff. "Great bone structure . . . you're perfect."

His skin instantly heated beneath her delicate touch. "I've been called a lot of things, but I can guarantee perfect hasn't been one of them." He returned the sketch pad to the window seal. "Hungry? I can start breakfast."

"It's kind of early for breakfast. I've been up for a couple of hours. I'm going to lie down and try to sleep a bit." She took off the painting apron and hung it on the back of the easel hook. Re-tying her robe, she headed to the kitchen.

Gavin came up behind her as she washed and dried her hands. "Can I join you?" It came out in an almost plea, but he didn't care. He wanted, no, needed her. An unmistakable longing for her overtook him. Palming her hips, he turned her so they faced one another. "These past days with you not speaking to me have been torture. When I woke and didn't feel you near, all I could think about was how much I wanted to hold you, kiss you, and how incredibly miserable I would be if you were not in my life." He leaned in against the contours of her long, luscious frame, allowing the hardness of his arousal to stroke at her belly. "I want to share your bed and feel the warmth of your skin next to mine every night." Her eyes widened with a look of surprise, then hooded in recognition. More reassuring was the way her lithe body relaxed against his.

Slowly, he lowered his head and brushed his scruffy cheek against the softness of hers. "Sie-Sie, sweetness, I'm not perfect, but I want to work damn hard to be perfect for you." His lips brushed along her cheek, feather-light. Satiny soft and warm, damn, how he missed her nearness. It had only been a few days absent of her affection, yet he felt starved for her and could imagine the state he'd be in if she chose to walk away. "I want to be everything you would want," he murmured and met his lips with hers.

Her hands came up to his chest, hard at first in objection, then lightened, allowing him to taste her unhurriedly. His tongue traced her lower lip before tunneling into her mouth, their tongues mating.

He arched his hips, allowing the severe prod of his erection to stroke her middle once more, and she pushed at his shoulders. With reluctance, he drew away from her mouth and stepped back, giving her space.

As she stared back at him, eyes roaming over his face, wary contemplation displayed in the crease between her brows. Then, she took his hand and led him to her bedroom. With her gaze locked with his, carefully, she removed her robe, and he helped her out of her tank top and panties.

He quickly stripped out of his boxers. They got in bed, and with a determined purpose, he settled his shoulders between her thighs, desperate to soak up her familiar scent, devour her.

He gave a sweep of his tongue over her clit, speared her pussy in long, measured strokes, repeating over and over before sealing his lips on her swollen bud, slowly swirling his tongue, taking his time, tasting her for so long, she cried out his name, panting heavily, shuddering, and arched up sharply through two distinct orgasms. Blunt nails pressed into his scalp as she rocked on his mouth, her silky inner thighs agitatedly rubbing against his shoulders.

He would have kept eating her out if his own need hadn't reached a pinnacle of excruciating pain.

He skated his mouth up her body, nipped and kissed over her taut abdomen, and swirled his tongue around her pearled nipples. Glorious minutes were spent enjoying one then the other before he burrowed his face within the valley of her breasts. He slid his tongue along her neck and finally took her mouth, sharing in a delectably wet, open-mouth exploration, heads angling left and right, both nipping, licking, tasting.

Gavin drew back to simply look at her. "I've wanted to lick you all over from the first day I saw you in that tight black dress you wore at the art contest."

"That was . . . was. . ." she blew out a long breath, "incredible."

"Believe that." He grinned and planted feather-light kisses along her shoulder, from one to the other.

Balancing on his left forearm, being careful not to put too much of his weight on her, he guided his cock into her tight, wet heat, and sighed deeply, his breathing shallow and eyes shut for a moment. This was what being connected felt like, completely bonded. Whether she accepted him or not, he would be forever hers.

His thrusts were unhurried as he took her mouth once more in a crushing, hungry rush.

Her hands upon him demanded more, tugging, groping, and scratching across his arms and back. Seizing a tight grip on his ass cheeks, she raked her nails, embedding into his flesh, urging him deeper, harder, showing him the pace she demanded. Her sexual hunger stoked his. He spread his knees, forcing her thighs wide and thrust swiftly, losing himself in the feeling of her as she panted his name through a long quivering breath.

He gripped the sheets as wave upon wave of sensation took over his body until he could do nothing but ride the wild climax that tore through him with a thundering force. Her name came out amid swallowed breaths as he took his release. It was that name that was now forever imprinted on his heart.

Trying not to collapse down on top of her, he moved off to the side and tucked himself in close, relishing in her warmth. Both stared straight up at the ceiling, breathing with a slightly steady rhythm. "Are you okay?" he asked through an exhausted exhale. "I didn't hurt you, did I?"

"I feel weightless," she answered with a soft chuckle, then asked in a rush, "Is there someone else? You know, someone that you just can't turn away from because you two have history. I don't want to start down this road with you if you're involved with someone on the side. It's a complication I can do without. Been there, done that."

The abrupt switch in topic took him by surprise, and he didn't answer right away. She apparently took it to mean he was stalling. With an etched brow, she inched away. Coolness licked his skin where the delicious heat of her body had soothed. He closed the gap, came up on his left forearm, and leaned partially over her. "I'm not seeing anyone. You're all I want. Can I have you, Sienna? All of you?"

Her eyes closed, then, with a soft sigh, her gaze met his again. "Gavin, trust is important to me. I've had to live with disappointment from the lack of it all my life. Can I trust you?"

An unnerving chill washed over Gavin as she stared unblinking at him, expecting an answer. In time, he would tell her about everything—what he'd done to Dale and the assignments he had to do for his father, all of it. He just needed to get things between them on a leveled plane first. "I would never want to hurt you," he finally said. "Sienna, I'm in love with you." He'd been saying that in his head for weeks now. Her breath hitched sharply, eyes wide with a hand pressed at her side over her injury from the apparently sudden jolt his words provoked. "I don't deserve you, I know, but it's how I feel."

Slender hands cradled his face and drew him to her, kissing him with incredible tenderness. Her thumb pulled down lightly on his chin, opening the way for her tongue to snake with his, moist and sweet. "I love you, too," she whispered softly against his lips. "Make love to me again."

Gavin experienced a momentary shock. It was the last thing he'd expected her to say and he wanted to screech like a damn girl from the jubilation of it. If he did, he'd likely start bawling like one, too.

Can I trust you? she'd asked. Reality bloomed, fissures forming deep gashes within his bliss.

As he joined his body with hers once more and had her writhing and moaning well into the breaking light of the morning, he pushed everything else out, and let himself get swept up in their shared moment, fearing he may not get another chance.

Chapter Twenty-five

"You're painting my skin." Sienna laughed. "You're so bad at this."

"Hey, I'm not the artist. You are." Gavin brought up her right foot and blew lightly on her toes to help dry the pink polish. "It looks pretty good to me." He flipped the bottle over. "Pink-ing of You?" He chuckled. "What happened to just calling it pink?"

Sienna took the *OPI* bottle from him and set it on the nightstand, then tugged at his bare shoulders to get him to come forward. "You did good, babe, thank you."

"Anything for you." He kissed his way up her naked body and settled over her. Their tongues met as their sexes came together in a familiar endless embrace.

They'd been fucking like rabbits for days. Sienna couldn't get enough of him. With each day, she felt physically better, and each time their bodies joined as one, their intimacy intensified, surpassing anything she could have imagined.

"Turn over," she said, and without hesitation, he lifted off her and stretched out on his back. Taking his cock in hand, she delivered several swift pumps to the smooth shaft before she drew him in between her lips and grazed her teeth along the length, then pulled back and sucked the bulbous crown.

He hissed sharply and bucked into her mouth repeatedly. "Woman, you're killing me."

"And you love it."

"I do. I love you, don't stop." His breathing was choppy, and his eyes remained transfixed on her efforts of pleasing him.

She toyed with his balls as she took his thick shaft far to the back of her throat. Her jaw muscles locked on, sucking while her hand vigorously pumped and twisted his length at the base. Her tongue swirled along the wet slit, pre-come smearing her lips as she savored him, relishing the sounds of his moans and heavy breaths.

"Sie-Sie . . . baby." A wild guttural groan tore out of him with his back arching sharply, and his eyes rolled back, looking like a man on the verge of exploding.

Grinning in wicked satisfaction that she'd pushed him so close to the edge, she freed his cock from her mouth's assault and climbed on top of him, straddling his hips. She slid her clit up and down the length of his severely hard shaft, her dampness searing fevered flesh, while watching him grind his teeth, fighting his need. "Are you ready for me, baby?"

"Fuck yes! Now."

She lifted and guided that massive part of him inside her. A rush of air escaped him from the heated friction their combined sex provoked. She began moving upon him with unhurried lifts and a slow rocking. He gripped her hips and raised his, encouraging the speed of her movements, but she pressed down to maintain control. "Not yet."

He released a strangled breath. "Stop torturing me. I want to fuck you."

Sienna laughed. "Greedy." Moving up and down on his ridiculously stiff penis in a measured glide, she took her time. The way he felt inside her, stroking along her hot, wet, clenching channel, she wanted to drag out the euphoria for as long as possible. But he grabbed her hips once more and slammed up hard and deep, again and again. Swiftly, he sat up, and circled an arm around her waist. The other held her buttocks tight as he pumped her on his dick.

"Like that?" she panted against his lips, locking her thighs at his waist, rocking her hips swiftly to match his quick hard thrusts.

"Just like that. You've gotten me so worked up with your teasing that I can't hold out. I'm going to come inside you."

He said her name repeatedly, a husky welcoming hymn as their bodies moved in perfect sync to the end of their shared quivering release. Panting with lips pressed together, sucking in shared breaths, they stayed that way through several racing heartbeats.

Sienna reared back and palmed his cheeks. His face was washed with rosy color from their rigorous lovemaking. "You're amazing."

Light fingers brushed at the damp hairs at her temple. Still burrowed deep inside her, his hand pressed at her buttocks to prevent himself from slipping free of her body. "Sie-Sie, sweetness, you're the only one for me."

"Who knew you were such a sweet romantic?" She kissed the side of his damp neck, then drew back. "I'm hungry. We were so busy having sex that we missed breakfast."

"Yeah, you're insatiable, Miss Keller."

Her eyes widened. "I'm insatiable? Your cock gets hard a second after you come."

"Only for you, believe that." He delivered a quick peck on the lips. "What would you like? Name it. I need to make a run to the market. We're out of a few things."

"That soup from Filomena's was really good. Couldn't you just have the groceries delivered? There's PEAPOD."

"Then Filomena's it is." He tapped a finger on the tip of her nose. "And yes, I could, but there's something I want to get you while I'm out."

He would get her flowers, Sienna knew. A fresh bouquet was stationed on the nightstand next to her side of the bed practically every few days or so. Such a sweet, romantic, caring man, and he was hers. All hers.

She rose to get off him and a stream of their combined fluid spilled from her body onto his thighs. He used the bed sheet to clean them both.

"I guess I have laundry to do when I return from the market."

"Let's shower, and then, while you're out, I'll get it started. It's time I begin earning my keep, Mr. Crane," she said with a playful wink.

"Oh, you've more than earned it, sweetheart." Squeezing her butt, he gave it a light, yet resounding whack.

"Ow," she chirped with a slow grin. "You want to get rough, is that it?" She took his semi-flaccid penis in hand and delivered the long length several swift pumps before she guided it back inside her. Feeling him thicken and pulse deep within, an enticing shudder of anticipation rushed through her.

Her short snatches of breath fell in sync with his as she grinded down, filled full to bursting with him once more. "I'll get started on the laundry, but first," her hips rocked with tiny, measured lifts, then she grew swift and aggressive. "I'm going to fuck you senseless, Mr. Crane."

His grin stretched wide. "Oh yes, that'll work."

• • •

As she loaded the washer with the sheets, Sienna thought about how great things had been between Gavin and her over the past few weeks. Never could she have imagined feeling as happy, content, and safe with a man as she did with him.

And the sex . . . wow, he was such a randy man. Earlier in the shower, she'd ended up pinned against the marble as he took her from behind, and then once again in the bed as she'd attempted to dress it with fresh linens. She had to shove him out of the apartment; otherwise, he would've had her braced against the washing machine.

In the beginning, she'd found him disturbingly fixated on her and wondered what his game was. Turned out, patience and determination was his only weapon. During their three weeks on the road for her art tour, he hadn't missed a single showing and saw to her every need. Add to it how he'd been determined to see to her recovery, how he'd catered to her every whim. He was such a wonderful, caring man. How could any woman not fall in love with him?

She didn't let many men get past her fuck-off defense barrier. Her trust was like a tightwire. Many man ended up falling, yet Gavin Crane had managed to scale it without falter.

The man was nearing thirty but had stated he'd never been in a solid relationship. She was essentially his first love. Calling him a virgin in that regard had choked him with laughter.

He'd dated—the term had been used loosely—plenty of women, but he'd never allowed himself to fall in love due to his family's chosen *profession,* he'd said. His family—she wasn't one hundred percent comfortable with that part. Nevertheless, she loved him and was willing to give their relationship a chance.

The sound of the doorbell rang in chorus with the ding of the dryer. Quickly, she started the sheets to wash, retrieved warm, fluffy towels from the dryer, and carried the bundle to the door. She looked through the peephole, but dark Ray Bans prevented her from seeing the man's eyes. If growing up in the Bronx had taught her anything, she knew to be careful who she let into her space.

"Yes?"

"Where's Gavin?" the man asked and jiggled the doorknob.

"He's not in. May I take a message?"

"Take a message?" A gruff tone and more jiggling of the knob. "Who the hell are you?"

"I'll ask the same. Who the hell are *you*?" Her tone was just as combative.

"I'm his brother, Edwin, that's who, and I'm tired of talking through this damn wood. Open the door."

Sienna gave another look through the peephole. The sunglasses were now perched atop his wheat-blond hair. There was some resemblance.

His right eye came in close to the peephole. "You gonna open the door or what?"

Shifting the bundle in her arms to free her hand, she flicked the lock and opened the door.

Giving her a thorough once-over, he stepped inside, then looked around the apartment. "Where's Gavin?"

"He went to the market for groceries."

He gave her another hard scan up and down. "The market? Isn't that what he pays you to do?"

Sienna drew back. "I beg your pardon?"

"You're his maid, aren't you?"

Her lips pursed to curse him out, to school him that domestic help came in all shades, but then she noticed his blue eyes dipped to the towels she held clutched to her chest. Giving him the benefit of the doubt, she calmly said, "No, I'm not the maid. I'm his girlfriend, Sienna." There was a definite flare of surprise in his eyes at that little reveal.

"Girlfriend? So, you're that chick that was shot?"

"Chicks are baby birds," she returned evenly, and a slow grin cut at the right corner of his mouth as he folded his arms across his chest.

He wasn't as tall as Gavin, and though he favored his older brother, his features were less defined. There was noticeable youth in his narrow cheeks and softer build.

"Baby birds," a weak chuckle, "I heard that. You got legs, girl." Catching her scowl, he supplemented, "Balls—bones—you know what I mean." His noticeable attention slid down to her bare legs in her fitted, white short-shorts. "You do have great legs, too, nice and long. I see my brother doesn't discriminate." His smile stretched wide.

Sienna rolled her eyes and stepped over to the couch, dropping the towels on the center oak table. She asked as she began folding, "Edwin, do you always make inappropriate comments to your brothers' girlfriends?"

He came forward and half sat on the arm of the leather sofa, watching her closely. "How's that inappropriate? It was a compliment." His head turned toward the window. "Who painted that? You?" He moved over to the window and leaned in to the canvas, giving it close inspection.

Sienna glanced over her shoulder. "Yep, it's the buildings across the street."

His head swiveled, looking out the window, then at the painting, back and forth several times. "Damn, you got skills." With hands in the front pockets of his low-slung denim jeans, he moved about aimlessly.

"Anyway, like I said, it was a compliment. The last chick . . . woman Gav hooked up with didn't have nice legs . . . all knocked-kneed and whatnot. Glad he dumped her. She didn't even do a good job cleaning his place."

Sienna's head jerked up from her task. She'd been half-listening to the young man, but those last words penetrated. "Gavin's last girlfriend was his maid?"

Edwin cut a cheeky grin. "I wouldn't use the term girlfriend. I'll just say she was hired to clean but didn't do much cleaning when she was here, if you know what I mean. I don't know how he does it. My bro's got skills with the ladies."

That pinched a nerve, and it had Sienna questioning her choices with Gavin as she listened to the immense pride that tinted Edwin's voice. She could see that the young man admired his older brother's roguish lifestyle. She resumed in folding the towels and asked, "So your brother isn't much into monogamous relationships?"

A colorful chuckle was his reply before meeting her stare, his eyes flaring slightly. "But he likes you."

"I don't know, Edwin. Your words are contradictory." It was said with a forced grin.

"No, really, he does. Why do you think he bloodied and broke that dude's face that shot you? Gav went Mayweather on his ass." He laughed.

Sienna jerked her head to him, and his boxing air jabs stalled. "What did you say?" She dropped the towel mid-fold and took a step toward him. He stepped back, forehead pinched tight, finally getting a clue that he'd flapped his gums far too much.

Edwin looked at his watch. "I got somewhere to be." Quick steps put him at the door. "Tell Gav I'll holler at him later. Good meeting you." He exited without another word.

Sienna stared at the closed door as Edwin's words trickled like icy tendrils down her spine. A chilling dread caused a gnawing ache where her assailant left his mark. Her mind flashed back to that day she'd noticed Gavin's bruised knuckles. Images of the bloody horse's head followed. Her stomach lurched so violently she almost didn't make it to the bathroom.

Chapter Twenty-six

Gavin entered the apartment and brought the groceries to the kitchen island. He pulled out the bouquet of daylilies from the bag and carried them to the bedroom. The sound of drawers being aggressively opened and closed drew him to the closet. Entering, he picked up a bra at his feet. Looking around, some of the hangers were bare where Sienna's clothes had been. She stood over by the shelves, taking down her shoes.

"I see you didn't like the way I arranged things." She swung around. The warm glow in her eyes that he'd grown accustomed to when she looked at him was completely gone. She came forward, snatched the delicate lace from his fingers and shoved it into her pink duffel bag stationed on the dressing island, then went back to yanking items out of the drawers. A sudden anxiousness twisted a knot in the pit of Gavin's stomach. "Sie-Sie, what's going on?" He set the flowers next to the duffel bag and went to her. "Sweetness, what's wrong? Talk to me." An attempt to soothe whatever was bothering her with a stroke at her back was rejected with a vehement jerk away from his touch. "Sienna, please talk to me. Tell me what has you so upset."

She swung back around, facing him. Her hands came down solidly on her hips. "Talk to you? Okay. You're out of fabric softener, you like fucking your maids and then dumping them, oh, and of course, you killed Dale."

Gavin's eyes widened in surprise, and then leveled in denial of her charges. Fear of her walking away, and anger directed at whatever source had caused this five-alarm blaze to roil, lit him hot. He compelled himself to focus. "Who told you that?"

"Your brother, Edwin, stopped by. Aside from him *complimenting* my legs," hard air quotes, "we had a pretty interesting chat. Do you deny any of it?" When he didn't answer, she turned and shoved more of her things into the duffel bag.

"You're going to leave me just like that? After everything we've shared?"

"Yup, that's right, Mr. Kavanagh."

A strangled breath of alarm left him. "You can't. I won't let you." He reached for her, and she repelled him with an aggressive jerk of a shoulder. "I didn't kill anyone."

Her fiery gaze locked tight on him. "Did you hurt Dale in any way?"

"That motherfucker shot you and left you and your friend for dead. He's lucky all I did was kick his ass," he growled in defense.

"How did you find him?"

Gavin didn't reply. He didn't have to. Her eyes narrowed in revelation.

"You had those men that were at the hospital find him, your father's men, your men."

"You're not leaving me." He started pulling out her things from the duffel bag with a frantic urgency and shoved them back into drawers. "You're not leaving. You said you loved me. We can talk about this."

She yanked her clothes from his grip. "I asked you what happened to your hand, and you lied to me."

Again, he knew his guilty silence was displayed like Vegas lights.

The doorbell rang.

"That's probably Bailey." Sienna zipped the bag and slung the strap on her shoulder. "I'll get the rest of my things when I can." She shoved past him out of the closet.

With his heart jackhammering in his chest, Gavin grabbed the jewelry box she'd left on the counter and rushed after her. "Sienna, wait."

She pulled open the entry door, and Bailey stood in the frame. Green eyes narrowed tight on him.

"Hey, Bailey." If looks could kill, Gavin was certain he'd have a knife at his throat.

"Don't you hey me," she snarled. "You and that husband of mine had better stay out of my way. Lucas knew about what you'd intended to do to Dale, and still, he let me convince my best friend to stay with you. His butt will be sleeping on the couch indefinitely. He can thank you for that."

Gavin winced. He'd gotten his boy banished to the couch. *One problem at a time.* He turned to Sienna. "Everything I did was to protect you."

"Gavin, you had Dale hunted down, and you brutally beat him. Who does something like that?" Her lips curled with a look of disgust. "If that's not bad enough, you lied to me about it."

"What do you want me to say?" he yelled. "I'm not fucking sorry that I kicked that bastard's ass for hurting you."

"I guess if someone cuts me in line at the supermarket, you're going to seek revenge and take them out, is that it?"

Gavin exhaled and rolled his eyes. "Come on, of course not. You know this situation was different. That asshole needed to pay for what he'd done to you."

"You just don't get it." She shook her head and stepped out of the apartment.

The sudden well of tears glistening in her eyes threw his mind into a wild state of distress. Her warrior woman, kick-ass attitude he could handle, but this, to be the cause of her tears. . . He grabbed her wrist, holding firm to his lifeline. "Sie-Sie, sweetness, I love you. Please don't leave." He noted Bailey's gaze soften at those words, allowing her anger and discontent for him to slip a small fraction. "This is for you. It was your birthday gift." He offered her the jewelry box.

Her eyes widened with a look of surprise, and a tear slipped down her cheek. Lips trembling, she broke free from his hold. "Bye, Gavin."

Bailey took the box from him, and the door closed behind her with a quiet clank.

"Fuck!" Pacing the floor, while raking all ten fingers through his hair, squeezing tight, Gavin inhaled and let go a slow release to calm his sputtering pulse that boxed against his ribs, then yanked out his cell phone from his front pocket. He pulled up his contacts and delivered a hard stab of a finger on Edwin's name. A couple rings in, the line connected.

"Sup?" Edwin said on the other end.

"It's been a while since I kicked your ass," Gavin gritted. "Know this, I'm going to choke you out when I see you."

"Bro, all I said was your lady had nice legs. What's wrong with that?"

"You said a shitload more than that!" Gavin's chest heaved a frantic beat from both anguish and anger.

"What is she? Black and Chinese . . . Japanese or something? Where'd you find her? She's hot."

"Are you fucking mental?" he boomed, utter rage pounding in the center of his skull. "You're like twelve in a twenty-one-year-old's body. You wonder why Pop is slow in pulling you into his operation. Because you have diarrhea of the mouth, that's why! You need to learn when to keep your damn mouth shut!"

"Whoa, relax, bro, damn. I didn't tell her about Pop's business or the jobs you're doing for him. That says I do know when to shut up. Hey, I stopped by to see if you could ask Sean to hook a brother up, to let me use his private suite at the Capital One Arena tomorrow night. It's the Caps' pre-season opener."

Incredulous, Gavin clenched his teeth, jaw locked tight. "Like I said, wait until I see you, Eddie," he growled and thumped a finger on the *End* button.

Chapter Twenty-seven

"Thanks, but I'm not hungry." Sienna waved away the offering of her favorite popcorn that Bailey held out to her. Seated on the couch, she snuggled beneath the cashmere throw while aimlessly clicking the remote at the widescreen on the wall before her.

"You have to eat something." Bailey placed the bowl on the side table, sat down next to her, and dragged some of the blanket across her legs. "You picked at your breakfast, and you didn't eat lunch. All you've done these past two weeks is paint and sleep." She looked at the TV. "And watch Iyanla Vanzant, *Fix My Life*."

"It's a good show. She's got great advice. And I have orders to fill from my tour. I'm almost caught up on my painting."

"Yes, but you need to eat at some point." A comforting hand stroked her arm. "Sie, that was a really beautiful necklace Gavin gave you for your birthday. A man doesn't spend that kind of money on a woman unless she's important to him."

"How did he know I'd had a birthday? I hadn't told him." Looking at one another, "Lucas," they said in unison. Sienna swallowed hard to keep from choking up. "It is beautiful. He's thoughtful that way." She was unable to stifle the slight quiver in her voice.

"Sweetie, if being without Gavin makes you this miserable, you should talk to him."

She shook her head. "He sought Dale out, and from what I understand, beat him to a bloody mess, then lied to me about it. Who knows what else he's lied about. Maybe he wasn't honest about not seeing someone else."

"A relationship that's built on the foundation of lies is never stable," Bailey said.

Sienna looked at her friend. She had to hand it to her, the girl could find an idiom to suit any circumstance.

"The person that did what he did, I don't know him. That level of retaliation has mob written all over it."

"He was a man scared to death of losing you who wanted Dale to pay for hurting you."

Sienna lifted her head from the plump cushioned throw pillow and shot Bailey an astounded stare. "How can you condone that type of behavior?"

"I didn't say I condoned it. I don't, not at all. I just understand where his head had been with what he'd done. Sie, when Kevin told us that you'd been shot, the thought of losing you was a pain I never want to feel again. Gavin felt that same pain. I read it on his face when he saw you lying in that hospital bed. Should he have done what he did? No, absolutely not. But I have to say, now that I have had time to calm down and look beyond the falsehoods that Gavin, as well as Lucas, Sean, and Dax, who all played a part, told, I can understand Gavin's position. I wanted to stab Dale in the throat myself for what he'd done to you."

Sienna couldn't argue that part. "If I'd had a knife within arm's reach, I would've used it on that asshole, too. He made me break my favorite sculpture on his ass."

"The ballerina you made of Misty Copeland with the gold slippers?"

Sienna nodded.

"I loved that one. That bastard." They both scowled, then Bailey said, "He deserved the beating he got from Gavin. He got off easy if you ask me. Lucas said they cut him loose afterward. The police are still looking for him. No telling where he is now." A gentle hand clasped Sienna's, lightly squeezing. "Anyway, I'm only saying consider talking with Gavin. It's been over two weeks. I'll bet if I looked at your cell phone, as of today, there are likely new messages to add to the ten or so messages from him that you refuse to listen to."

Sienna looked at her and swallowed the welling tears back. "I'm not ready."

"I understand. But really you should eat. I made clam chowder while you were napping. It's Lucas's favorite."

"I suppose I should eat something. Oh, also, this Friday I'm scheduled for my checkup. Gavin usually goes with me." A tear rolled down her cheek, that she hastily swept away with the back of her hand. "Will you come with me?"

"Yes, of course. Hey, how about we go to the spa on Saturday? Ever since you gave me that spa package, I've become addicted to clay wraps. You and I could lie back and get pampered, then go shopping. My treat. Come on, Sie, it'll be fun."

Sienna wasn't in the mood for doing anything, except finding a deep, dark hole to crawl into, but she understood her best friend was trying to cheer her up. "I guess. Sure, why not." She gave Bailey a tentative look. "I'd like to visit Faith. I tried calling, and I texted her several times, but she hasn't responded."

Bailey met her stare. "Funny you should say that. I've been thinking about her lately, wondering if she was okay. I was beyond done with Faith after what she tried to do with Lucas, but when I learned how she'd helped you, saved you during Dale's attack, I couldn't hold onto my anger anymore."

Bailey and Faith's relationship had been rocky at best on a good day. But Sienna longed to have their trio-sisterhood bond again. "Does that mean you'll come with me to see her?"

"You're right; we should check up on her. Yes, I'll come."

"Great."

Chapter Twenty-eight

"Guys, help me out here. What should I do?"

Gavin looked around at his friends. He, Dax, and Lucas lounged on the plush leather furnishings in Sean's corporate office. Across the room, Sean practiced his golf swing on the indoor, narrow putting green stretched out along the floor. "She's not speaking to me because of what I did to Dale. She'll see the assignments that I've been doing for my father as another betrayal."

"I say tell her." Shoulders angled inward, knees loose, arms stretched with a slight bend at the elbows, Sean gave the golf ball a light tap with his nine iron and watched it drop into the shallow hole. He glanced up. "At this point, what could you lose?"

"I agree, just come clean," Dax said as he got up, strode to the sideboard, and refreshed his glass with a quarter of Chivas Regal, then returned to his place on the couch.

"What they said," Lucas added. "I'm deep in the shit with my wife because of all of this."

"How's that couch treating you?" Sean wore a broad grin. He slung his tie over his shoulder and bent to retrieve the ball from the hole. "Is it comfy?"

"Yes, Lucas, does she at least let you see her naked before you have to retreat from the room?" Dax wickedly teased.

"Fuck you both," came Lucas's friendly rejoinder around a sip from his glass.

"I'm afraid we can't help you there," Sean taunted, and they laughed at their buddy's misfortune.

"There are eight bedrooms in that house. I'm not benched on a goddamn couch," Lucas groused. His head swiveled to Gavin seated beside him. "For fuck's sake, man, talk to the woman, tell her everything. Bailey will champion Sienna's cause until her best friend is happy, and I'll pay the price until that happens. I'd like to get back to sleeping in my own bed and making love to my wife on a regular basis if you don't mind."

"Well, Sienna isn't speaking to me; there's not much I can do about that. My calls and text messages to her go unanswered. When I come by your place, she won't leave her room. There's not much more I can do." Gavin finished off his scotch, set the empty glass on the table in front of him, and stood up. "I've danced with you ladies long enough. I better get going. Got a two-hour ride tonight."

Sean came forward, and Lucas and Dax rose to their feet. Gavin delivered a handshake with a bro-slap on the back to each of them.

"You said it's just envelopes that you've been transporting back and forth?" Sean asked. "That's it?"

"That's it." Gavin sighed in annoyance. "Damn ridiculous. The envelopes are sealed. Dylan and I don't have a clue what's in them. All I know is whatever it is, my pop treats it like the nuclear codes or some shit."

Sean's desk phone buzzed. He crossed the room and press the intercom. "Yes, Carol?"

"Sir, Keira Blair is here to see you. She's down in the lobby. I don't have anyone by that name on your calendar for today. Should I send her away?"

"No," Sean rushed out. "Send her up."

"Yes, sir."

He closed the line, then looked at them all, flashing a grin. "Get out."

"Who's Keira Blair?" Gavin asked as he observed Sean quickly adjust his tie and combed his fingers repeatedly through his hair.

"She's Nate's friend, the one that was over playing tennis that day when we hung out," Dax answered and turned to Sean. "What is she doing here?"

Sean grabbed the empty glasses on the table and carried them over to the sideboard, tidying up as he said, "I'd told her to stop by if ever she wanted me to help her put together a business model. She's trying to start an event planning business. I didn't think she'd actually take me up on it."

"So, you're just providing your professional expertise?" Lucas smirked with arms folded at his chest.

"Yes, that's right."

Gavin, Dax, and Lucas looked at one another as they watched Sean stride over to his bookshelves and started straightening knick-knacks, then he hastily moved to his desk and neatly arranged and stacked papers.

"Dude, really, look at you." Dax laughed, and Sean looked up. Before he could respond there was a soft knock upon the door. His assistant, Carol, entered. The woman, Keira, stepped inside, then Carol closed the door behind her.

With a large, black handbag hanging at the crook of her arm, she cradled a leather portfolio at her chest. The other hand held a cup-holder with two grande-size Starbucks cups. Her conservative, pale blue blouse was tucked neatly into a fitted gray skirt, that hit high enough above the knee to expose well-toned legs. The severe arch of her pumps gave emphasis to the shapeliness of her calves. Dark curls framed her attractive, warm-brown features and bounced about her shoulders as her whiskey-brown gaze moved between them, then settled on Sean. "I hope I didn't interrupt anything. I probably should've called. My last appointment canceled at work, and my evening class was also canceled. I had some time and thought I'd take you up on your offer to help me with my business proposal."

No one spoke for an awkward moment, then Sean walked forward. "No, you're not interrupting. They were just leaving." He took the coffee carrier from her and set it on the table. "I'd be happy to help. Have a seat while I see them out."

As she sat down on the couch and opened her portfolio, displaying its colored tab pages, then pulled from her handbag a MacBook Air, propping it open, Gavin could see she was all about business. That said, Sean on the other hand, looked eager to simply have her share the same space with him. Gavin understood that consuming level of adoration for a woman who was driven, who knew what she wanted, who had her shit together.

Sean walked them to the door and pulled it open. He brought a hand down on Gavin's shoulder. "Hang in there, bro. I'm here if you need anything."

"You play it smart, my man," Lucas whispered to Sean with a look over at the lady, whose full focus was centered on her notes.

"No worries. I want to help her, that's all."

Thinking of Sienna, Gavin found those word's awfully familiar. "You keep telling yourself that," he drawled low, glumly.

They headed for the elevator.

"Dude, only one assignment left after this one, then you're free," Dax remarked.

"Yeah." But was he really free? Gavin felt as though he was a walking, highly incurable, contagious disease. Aside from his friends who were apparently immune, he never allowed anyone to get too close, to get caught in the web of his family shit. With Sienna, he'd found the antidote, the one woman to set him free.

You just going to leave me?

That's right, Mr. Kavanagh.

She'd called him Kavanagh. That's how she saw him now, what she saw in him. A contagion. He thought about that as he headed out to do his next pickup.

• • •

"Dylan, stop fidgeting, damn. Just looking at you makes me agitated."

Seated in the passenger seat of the man's Suburban SUV, Gavin cut a look at him. "And put that cancer stick out. I don't need the stink of that shit in my clothes again."

"Afraid your lady will yell at you?" A stupid grin showed severely straight teeth, courtesy of six and a half years of braces following a lacrosse stick incident.

"I said get rid of it."

Dylan put his window down and flicked the cigarette. "How's your lady coming along? Has she recovered from her injuries?" When no reply came, his head turned, and he stared for a long moment. "Eddie told me she's black."

Gavin shot him a challenging hard look. "Yeah, and?"

He shrugged. "And nothing. I already knew. Mike mentioned it."

"What about Pop? Does he know?" Gavin now stared at him with slight unease.

"Nah, everyone knows when to and when not to bother Pop. Anyway, I thought your ass might be gay."

Gavin sat up sharply. "Where have you been? All the women I've been with. That nicotine must've wiped out the few observation brain cells you had."

Dylan threw his head back in a laughing outburst. "I'm just fucking with you, bro." With a sobering grin, he opened his middle console and pulled out a small bag of Sour Patch Kids. "It's good you met someone. I'd like to meet her. I hear she's an artist." He tore into the bag and offered up the candy.

Gavin waved him off as despair stalled his breath in his chest; he had to give himself a moment for it to settle. "She left me," he voiced low. His brother's eyes stretched wide. "Eddie mouthed off to her about what I'd done to that motherfucker that shot her."

"You hadn't told her?"

Gavin shook his head.

"Mistake number one. What about this? Does she know you make these runs with me?"

"Four assignments, then I'd be done. She would've never had to know. I couldn't risk how'd she'd react."

"Mistake number two. Bro, I tell Angie everything. It's against Pop's rules, I know, but I don't care. I realized long ago, if I was ever lucky enough to find a woman that was willing to take on this life, despite everything, I would hold nothing back from her. Look, neither of us want this life. If you want that woman long-term, I'm not talking your customary one-month attachment, I'm talking wife, kids, dog, the whole nine, bro. If that's what you want with this one, you can't hold anything back from her. Fuck Pop's rules."

Gavin sat quietly, digesting the man's surprisingly wise words. Though Dylan was the oldest, he'd been pegged as the runt of the litter. Pop was categorically wrong. He'd mistaken lack of strength with quiet defiance.

His brother hadn't been given refuge and security at a private boarding school to shield him. He'd lived in the murky reality his entire life and fought against it. No, he wasn't weak, far from it.

Their heads turned at the sound of tires crunching the gravel; both squinted against the intense headlights advancing toward them.

Gavin checked his watch. It was a couple minutes shy of 1:00 a.m. "It's about time."

Stepping out of the vehicle, Dylan tucked the revolver in the back waistband of his jeans beneath his navy-blue sport coat before stepping back to grab the aluminum attaché case from the backseat floor of the vehicle. "You're coming to Pop's birthday bash, right?" he asked casually.

Standing within the frame of the passenger door, Gavin didn't answer as he secured his Glock at his back beneath his leather jacket.

"Dude, you had better show your face."

"I'll think about it." Gavin rounded the truck, and with hands clasped behind him, he took his place a step behind his brother's right.

Eyes set straight ahead on the two men exiting the blacked-out Yukon, Dylan cocked his head and whispered out of the corner of his mouth, "Grovel at her feet to get her back and bring her by to meet the fam." In a blink, he was in complete control as he addressed those before him, "Gentlemen."

Watching his brother, his calm, calculating finesse, Gavin knew that yes, their pop was grossly mistaken.

Chapter Twenty-nine

Sienna had been pampered at the spa the entire morning. The masseuse masterfully worked out the tension in her neck and shoulders. Afterward, she and Bailey spent the entire afternoon at CityCenterDC, shopping at the many couture boutiques. If her BFF had had reservations before about spending her husband's money, the girl didn't show it today. And Bailey had been very generous with her card swipes. They wouldn't need to shop for fall wear the entire season.

Sienna released a sigh of calm. Devoting the day to herself helped to clear her head of the many issues crowding her brain.

Turning to Bailey in the driver's seat, she took her hand that rested on the center console, and gave it a light squeeze. "This was fun. Thank you. I didn't realize how much I needed to get out, to just breathe, you know?"

"I know, right? I'm glad it helped." Bailey glanced over a couple of times as she drove. "I like the burgundy tips in your hair. Nice touch. The cut and style reminds me of Halle Berry in *Swordfish*. You're rocking the look, girlfriend."

Sienna ran her fingers through her soft, willowy locks. "I thought I'd try something different." Grinning, she rubbed her inner thighs together. "Girl, that platinum spa package is where it's at. I don't think they missed one single hair follicle anywhere." She reached over and stroked Bailey's thigh. "You're smooth as a baby's butt." She winked. "Does that mean Lucas will be returning to the marriage bed tonight?"

"I guess he has suffered long enough. He tried to shower with me this morning, but I'd finished and dressed to leave for our spa appointment. Poor baby. He's so horny right now." She giggled, sounding only slightly contrite.

"Bails, come on, put the big guy out of his misery; give the man some lovin'."

"Oh, I intend to." She looked over, fashioning a subtle grin. "He isn't the only one suffering."

Pulling up to the security gates of her home, she hit the remote. The heavy wrought iron gates parted, and the Bentley rolled along the gray cobblestone.

Sienna sucked in an anxious breath at the sight of the black Lamborghini parked in the circular driveway. Beside it was a metallic-black, Cabriolet Porsche convertible and a dark gray Maserati Gran Turismo. Backdropped against the stately white brick mansion and balanced by the centered, three-tiered fountain, the vehicles were displayed like priceless jewels. The only thing missing was a rotating platform to display the cars from all angles.

"Sie," Bailey looked over, concern blanketing her face, "we could take a drive. Go see a movie. Something. Anything you want."

"Who do the other cars belong to?"

"Dax's the Porsche and Sean's the other one. I didn't know Lucas was having them over."

"It's cool." It wasn't, not really. Sienna wasn't quite ready to face Gavin, but life seemed to enjoy throwing her curveballs that tended to smack her dead center between the eyes.

"You're sure?"

"Pish." She waved a dismissing hand, deciding she'd tug up her big girl panties. "Yes, I'm good."

Bailey pulled the car into the garage, and they got out.

Entering the kitchen, the men all stood around the center island counter stuffing their faces with a smorgasbord of buffalo chicken wings, mini burger sliders, loaded potato skins, and a variety of chips, dips, and a host of other eats.

"Wow, babe, look at this spread," Bailey said as she and Lucas embraced, greeting one another with pecks on the lips. "Had I known the guys were coming over, I would've prepared something before I left this morning."

"No need. I called a caterer."

"I see that." Bailey turned to the men and smiled. "It's good to see you all." They each returned the greeting.

Across the wide slab of Egyptian marble, blue eyes, deep and intense, were pinned on Sienna. Needing to get out of the direct line of Gavin's stare, she said hello to Dax, then crossed over to Sean with an extended hand. "We haven't met. I'm Sienna Keller."

"It's a pleasure to finally meet you, Sienna. I'm—"

"Sean Grant. I know who you are. You're Paris Hilton on steroids—hotel heir, but without the sex tape . . . I hope," she joked to try to lessen her anxiety at having Gavin's focus laser-locked on her every movement. It didn't help one bit. "Thanks for the plush accommodations during my art tour. The Grant Royal suites are amazing."

"It was my pleasure."

Her gaze traveled the length of him—about six-four easy—broad shouldered—thick, wavy dark hair—sea-green eyes. She then turned to Lucas. "I suppose you have to be tall and gorgeous to join your club, is that it, big guy?" An appraising scan was delivered to all the men, with her assessing gaze lingering on Gavin the longest, then she turned back to Sean. "Do you all have a friend who isn't hot? If you do, poor guy must have a hell of a time with you four as his wingmen." Sean blinked, and a slight grin split the man's exceptionally pretty mouth, looking unsure how to respond.

Dax delivered Sean a slap on the back. "Come on, man, you know you're a pretty girl. Own it."

Light chuckles filled the room briefly, then Lucas said, "We're headed downstairs. The Nats might actually make it to the playoffs." His attention narrowed in on his wife's shopping bags. "How many pairs of shoes did you get this time?"

Bailey smirked sheepishly with a raised chin. "Maybe I didn't buy any."

"She bought three," Sienna supplied.

"Of course she did." Holding his wife affectionately around the waist, Lucas said to the guys, "You all should see our closet. Shoe boxes are stacked to the ceiling. I might have to find her a support group."

Bailey gasped and playfully slapped his chest. "I'm not addicted."

"You are," Sienna and Lucas said in concert, and again, chuckles broke out.

Gavin rounded the island and came up to her. "Hey, sweetness," he voiced softly. "How have you been?"

Though her heart pounded against her ribs, and her stomach unexpectedly tightened from his mere closeness, she managed to work her tone into an intentionally cold reply. "As good as can be expected."

Gentle fingers brushed behind her left ear, toying with wisps of hair at her nape as he studied her features, then met her gaze. "I like your hair. You look lovely. Uh, you think we could sit and talk a bit?"

An awkward, deafening silence now held everyone.

She simply wasn't ready to talk. Thankfully, sensing her distress, Bailey lifted her shopping bags at nearly eye level, drawing everyone's attention. "Well, we're off to go play dress-up." She linked their arms and whisked her out of the kitchen.

Sienna's pulse didn't calm until they'd made their way to the room she'd been occupying. She sat down at the foot of the bed and toed off her flats. Burying her face in both hands, she released a long, anguished breath. "I've missed him so much. I love that man, Bails." She looked up, and her friend's warm gaze stared back at her from across the room. "I just can't accept what he did. And then the lying, how can I trust him?"

Bailey took a seat in the pale blue suede armchair stationed over by the bay window and brought her feet up on the ottoman. "I understand your position, but did you see how his face lit up when you walked in? I can see he misses and loves you, too. And he calls you sweetness. That's so cute."

Sienna swiped away the tear that slid down her cheek. "Yes, it is. But I need more than that. I deserve more."

• • •

"The look on her face said it all." Glum, Gavin dropped down in the black leather recliner. "She's done with me."

"Yeah, she didn't seem happy to see you, bro." Munching from a bag of jalapeño flavored tortilla chips, Dax reclined his chair and stretched out his frame. "Looked pretty bad."

"I have to agree, it didn't look good for you, my man." Sean uncapped two bottles of Dogfish 90 Minute IPAs and handed one over. "But not all is lost."

"His ass had better fix it," Lucas grumbled from his seat on Sean's right while aiming the remote at the theater screen to set the surround sound. "I need my wife back ASAP."

"How can I fix anything if she's not speaking to me? You all seem to forget that part," Gavin groused.

Sean sat forward and angled toward him. "Here's what you do. Don't go to her today. We all could see she wasn't that pleased to see you. The ice has been broken, nonetheless. Show up tomorrow bright and early with flowers and candy. Shit, use my gulfstream to take her to Paris if you think it would help you. In other words, brother, beg."

Seated at the far end in the line of theater seats, Dax leaned forward. "Sean, are you speaking from firsthand experience?"

Lucas threw peanut shells at Dax's head, then turned back to Gavin. "Listen to Sean. Tell Sienna about what you've been doing for your father, and how you had little choice after you fucked up by calling the man in to handle Dale, but that you got Kavanagh involved because you feared for her safety. Then, as Sean said, kiss her feet."

"It's for a good cause," Sean added.

"In all seriousness, they're right." Dax came out of his reclined pose. "Worth a shot. Plus, your ass won't find a woman that damn hot any time soon, so you had better hold on to her like a fucking parachute."

Heads fell back in hearty laughter and mumbled agreement.

Gavin sat forward to look past Lucas and Sean. "Dax, women discover that toy chest you keep and are smart to put heels to the pavement." It was partly a joke. The guy was into some kinky shit. "None of the previous women I've been with come close to my Sie, that I'll agree, but what about Veronica?"

"Are you referring to that life-like blow up doll you keep tucked away in your closet?" Dax puffed his cheeks and blew. Beer sprayed from Sean's mouth. Lucas was close to choking with laughter. "I'm just fucking with you, bro," Dax added, yet they all continued to buckle over in boisterous amusement.

Unable to suppress a chuckle, Gavin sat back and sent them all a solid salute of his middle finger as he took deep swallows from his bottle.

They were right about one thing. What did he have to lose?

Chapter Thirty

The car pulled up to the palatial estate just off the coast in Osterville, Massachusetts. The driver assisted Sienna and Bailey out of the car, then retrieved their luggage from the trunk. He insisted on seeing the two small carry-ons to the door. She and Bailey thanked him, and with a polite incline of his head, he went on his way.

It was a private car service, one that Lucas had been adamant she and Bailey use for the drive to Faith's parents' home from the private airstrip where his jet had landed.

If someone had told Sienna when she was a young girl eating week-old take-out or savoring stale crackers from the barren cupboard, while her mother lay passed out beneath whoever had been her chosen companion from the night before, that she would be cruising in a CEO's private jet, riding around in Gavin's kickass Lamborghini, and even getting to rub elbows with people such as Sean Grant, the hotel mogul, she would have suggested they seek professional help. Talk about life's curveballs. Sienna thought about how much her life had changed as she and Bailey took the wide steps up to the stately ornate front door, and Sienna rang the bell. Moments later, the door opened. Faith's stepmother, the regal Mrs. Sullivan, stood before her and Bailey wearing a smile as bright as her yellow floral, perfectly fitted dress and sunny yellow pumps. A matching floral hairband neatly held back rich red, wavy tresses from her attractive, narrow-angled face.

"Good afternoon, ladies. It is such a delight to see you both, please come in."

Entering the opulent foyer, they set their bags just inside the door.

"Mary?" Mrs. Sullivan called out softly, and in a flash, the woman appeared, as if she'd been prepped to be summoned.

Sienna pulled her attention away from the maid, Mary, scurrying up the stairs with her and Bailey's carry-ons. "Thank you for letting us come out to visit. We wanted to spend a little time with Faith."

"Yes, thank you, Mrs. Sullivan. I hope it's not a problem for us to stay," Bailey said. "We can go to a hotel."

"I wouldn't hear of it. It's no trouble at all. Your rooms have already been prepared. I was glad you called. Faith hasn't been the same since that day." Her gray eyes lowered, and her warm smile waned in a quiet instant as she shook her head. "She has struggled so. The incident with her poor mother was such a tragedy. This recent matter, I fear, has regressed the progress she had achieved with her therapist." With a sigh, kind eyes met theirs again while projecting a hint of a smile. "I'm happy you all are here. It's sure to lift her spirits. Come, Faith is looking forward to your visit." She preceded them through the house and out onto the terrace. "Mr. Sullivan is away on business. He's sorry he couldn't be here to greet you." The terrace looked out over the infinity pool and onward, beyond the manicured shrubbery to the breathtaking view of Nantucket Sound.

Faith lay stretched out on a lounger, cocooned up to her chin beneath a blanket. She stared out at the water, it seemed, in a comatose state.

"Faith, honey, your friends have arrived." Mrs. Sullivan shooed them forward, then retreated into the house.

Faith's head turned slowly toward them. Her long, lustrous blonde hair was now cropped into a short, boyish style. Blue eyes widened and instantly watered. "You came." Her stare settled on Bailey and tears spilled over. "I didn't think you would, but you came."

Bailey sat down on the edge of the lounger and drew Faith into a hug, then took her hand in hers. "Of course we came."

Sienna rounded the lounger, took a seat, and hugged her next. "We missed you. How's your shoulder?"

"Stiff, but okay." Her red, weary eyes shifted between them before she burst into a sea of tears, sobbing into her palms. "I'm so sorry."

They hurriedly embraced her once more. "Shh," Sienna soothed, while looking around for a tissue. A box sat on the small, round glass table to her left. Scattered at her feet were wads of balled-up tissues that she hadn't noticed, evidence of Faith's abysmal state.

She pulled several tissues from the box and gently dried her friend's face. "Don't cry. Here, your nose is running."

"I want to thank you for saving my life. If you hadn't done what you did that day, I don't believe I would be sitting here right now. But what happened is in the past. It was Dale who—"

"He threatened to hurt you and Bailey," Faith interjected as she reached over to the side-table and grabbed another tissue to wipe her eyes.

Sienna and Bailey exchanged gaping looks, then Sienna removed her crossed-body purse and angled her frame, bringing her right leg under her to sit more comfortably. "Hurt us how? Dale wanted you to seduce Lucas into sleeping with him, so you could bribe him for money. That much we know."

Faith blew her nose as more tears rained down. With red eyes fixed on Bailey, her expression filled with grief. "I'm sorry for what I did to you."

Bailey took her hand again. "Are you saying Dale had planned to hurt us if you didn't go to Lucas for money?"

She nodded. "He took me to this apartment in Southeast D.C., near the Anacostia River."

Sienna tapped Bailey's arm. "See, I told you I'd overheard him planning something bad." She turned back to Faith. "Go on."

"He owed money to these guys. Dale initially told me it had been gambling losses that he owed. I tried to help him, but my father found out. He got angry that I was involved with Dale again and kicked me out." She dropped her gaze, her voice an almost whisper. "I felt I owed Dale for what happened years ago. It was my fault he'd gone to jail. He'd wanted to expand his operation, so I'd put him in contact with a friend I knew from high school, a guy that used to supply all the kids with stuff at parties here on the Cape.

"Dale didn't name me in what took place during that drug bust at the apartment, but I—"

"What happened when you went to Anacostia?" Sienna cut in, wanting to stay on topic and not looking to be reminded of yet another tornado that once swirled around the three of them.

Facing them again, Faith drew her knees up, hugging her legs close to her chest. "There were these two really big, scary looking guys. The one named Turk was angry with Dale because a package that Dale was supposed to pick up had gotten seized by the police. That's how I learned that it was drugs. He'd told me he wasn't dealing anymore, but he'd lied to me."

"Go figure," Bailey muttered with an eye roll, not bothering to mask her discontent.

"Dale owed Turk the money that he didn't receive from the pickup that had been seized. To make up for it, Turk told Dale right there in front of me that if he didn't bring him the money, he would expect Dale to turn me over as payment. I-I would've had to be with Turk for several hours," she said, lips trembling, tears flooding, rushing down her cheeks. "He took a liking to me."

Sienna frowned. "You're saying you would've had to sleep with that guy as payment?" Getting a nod, she frowned harder, her anger closing her throat. "That bastard would've had you do something disgusting like that to get his ass out of the mess he brought on himself," she gritted. "Sick prick."

Faith rested her forehead atop up-drawn knees. "Dale said it was either Lucas or Turk," she said through broken breaths.

Sienna looked at Bailey when she reached out, and a gentle hand stroked Faith's arm. She'd expected to see anger in her friend's eyes over Faith's attempt to sleep with Lucas but met green eyes clouded in sorrow for their friend.

"I never liked that bastard. I always told you that he'd been using you. Why didn't you come to us?"

"You said he threatened to hurt Sienna and me," Bailey interjected this time, her expression now harsh, yet her hand upon Faith's arm kept up a tender caress.

"Yes, after those guys threatened to do him in, Dale got so crazy. I mean, it was as if he'd snapped. He'd been given two weeks to come up with the money he owed. If I didn't do what he wanted, he said he'd send the drug dealers after you both. He also said he'd have them go after my family if I said anything to anyone. What took place years ago—" Faith started.

With a heavy sigh, Sienna shook her head. "Look, I really don't want to rehash—" she paused from the light touch upon her hand.

"Please, let me explain. I should've been honest with you both back then. For that, I'm sorry, and I'm so very sorry for what you both went through in that police raid because of me." Tears welled in her eyes once more. "Your friendship is important to me. You two are all I have. That's why I want you to know everything."

Sienna and Bailey looked at one another for a long moment, then Sienna nodded, figuring maybe it was best to air all the dirty crap that happened, then perhaps they could wipe the slate clean and move on.

"Dale had taken the full rap for that drug bust years ago because my father had convinced him to leave my name out of it. In return, my father had promised him that he'd ensure Dale served no more than three months. But Dale had been given the full twenty-eight. He called me when he was released and asked to meet. He'd said he wasn't dealing anymore, that he'd changed, but that he'd lost a load of money gambling with some guys. He'd been trying to win money to get himself back on his feet. At least that had been the lie he'd told me."

"So you felt you owed him because he didn't implicate you in the bust and because of your father's betrayal," Sienna said.

"Yes. Dale threatened to have my father killed. I didn't know what to do. As you said, he was using me. I realized that he hadn't changed, that he only wanted revenge against me for everything that happen to him years ago. There was no doubt in my mind that he would have hurt you. . ." Her eyes dipped briefly to the hand Sienna subconsciously held pressed below her left breast at the area of Dale's mark. A pulsing, dull ache seemed to occur whenever the man's name was spoken.

"I found out that those men he'd been dealing with also ran a prostitution ring. They were the ones behind that news report about all those teen girls that had gone missing in D.C."

As Sienna listened to Faith detail all of what she'd gone through and what Dale had intended to do, more and more, she was beginning to understand the strong stem of Gavin's anger, feeling he'd been justified in what he'd done to that sick asshole. As Bailey had said, Gavin let him off easy. Dale should have been cemented under the jail cell.

Taking a breath, Sienna compelled herself to push it all away. Having lost enough sleep over it all, she didn't need to add to her nightmares.

She took Faith's hand in hers. "Dale, and everything that happened between the three of us, all of it is history now. Let's focus on friendship. I want us to get back to the way we were freshman year. Can we do that?" She and Faith turned hopeful stares on Bailey.

Staring back at them, Bailey took Sienna's hand in her left and Faith's in her right. "I'd like that."

"Bailey's pregnant," Sienna blurted and placed a hand on her friend's slight baby bump.

A soft smile brimmed Faith's lips. "I'm going to be an aunt?" She jumped up to her knees, blue eyes bright, excitement returning color to her cheeks. Looking between them, her features grew hesitant. "Right?"

Smiling, Bailey nodded.

"I'm going to be an aunt!" Faith screeched and pulled them into a crushing hug. "Sisters forever, right?"

Sienna smiled. "You know it." The ring of her cell phone broke into their sisterhood moment. She pulled it from her purse. Seeing a New York number that she didn't recognize was no surprise. Her mom often changed her number to go M.I.A. at the close of a relationship. That way, the man in question could no longer reach her.

Damn it. With all that she'd been through, the monthly deposit had been forgotten. She answered the call, prepared to reassure her mom the money was on its way, but before she could speak, an unfamiliar voice spoke in a mechanical calm, laying out details like a skilled doctor setting a bone break with one quick snap into place to minimize the shock.

"Thank you for letting me know." Sienna disconnected and sat stock-still. The quiver started in her belly, small at first, but swiftly intensified until she was hugging her middle. The frigid shiver crawled up to her chest, and her shoulders began to tremble as the tears broke free.

"Sie, what's wrong?" Bailey asked, concern tightly creasing her brow.

Faith gaped. "Who was that on the phone?"

"A friend of my mom's," Sienna managed through strangled sobs. "She called to tell me my mom is dead."

Both of her friends gasped, then, as one, embraced her as she wept, wept hard for her mom's warm hug that she'd longed for and held out hope for, but now would never get. For those many times she'd yearned for a smidgen of affection of any kind. For the many times she'd strangled back her tears to stay strong during those moments she had to swab cold compresses to her mom's face and neck to help bring her back from the hell she'd slipped into. For the vomit she'd mopped up from a freshly washed floor. And for the days and nights of sheer terror when she'd hide in the dark recesses of her closet to escape the cruel and brutal groping hands of those lecherous unwanted touches.

When her sobs had waned to short sniffles, she pulled out of her friends' supportive grasp.

Faith quickly snatched up several tissues and handed them over, while offering a gentle stroke on the shoulder. "What happened?" she asked softly.

Sienna dried her eyes. "An overdose. She regularly took a prescribed medication for a leg injury she'd suffered from dancing years ago. She often combined other pills . . . I didn't know what they were half the time. This time she'd added something to help her sleep. The combined dosage stopped her heart." A tear rolled down her cheek.

Faith handed her another tissue. "We're here for you."

Bailey took her hand, squeezing lightly. "Yes, tell us what you need."

Sienna dried her eyes once more and looked between them. Her throat ached with the excruciatingly heavy strain of her emotions. "You both are here . . . together with me. That's all I need for now." Staring back into sorrowful blue eyes and anguished-filled green ones, Sienna's tears rained down, her grief overtaking her in racking spasms. They drew her back into their joint embrace, and she held on tight. The years of loneliness in her life had been great. Without the two of them, she'd be completely alone in the world.

Her thoughts drifted to Gavin once more.

Chapter Thirty-one

At the gravesite in New York, a small group gathered and listened to final respects offered by the pastor to Lydia Keller. When Gavin had learned of Sienna's mother's death, he'd reached out to her immediately, but she wouldn't take his calls and wouldn't see him.

During the service, he'd sat quietly in the back of the church watching her as people offered their respects, and now he stood in the rear listening to the pastor speak of loss, and watching Sienna, with Bailey and Faith at her side, as she lay her mother to rest. Lucas stood behind his wife, his hand supportively upon her shoulder. Gavin wished he could do the same for Sienna. He'd lost that privilege. They were over.

An intense yearning gripped his chest, tight and fast, that he found himself cutting through the small group to stand beside her. He heard a slight intake of breath when her gaze turned away from the casket to look at him. Her eyes were shielded behind dark shades, but he sensed by her lifted brows that she was surprised to see him. No other reaction from her followed, and she turned away.

Then, suddenly, warm, slender fingers entwined with his hand. She didn't look at him or speak, just held on, and angled her frame with a tilt of her head to rest upon his shoulder. He wanted to draw her in close to carry the weight of her grief within his embrace but thought better of it. He'd let her lead and give her however much she wanted to take.

About twenty minutes later, the service ended. He couldn't tear himself away from her.

"Thank you," she voiced low. Her fingers squeezed his before their hands separated, and without another word, she walked away with Bailey and Faith at her side.

He watched her until she got into the limo. It took immense strength to stay planted and not follow her.

Lucas approached and palmed his right shoulder. "Give her time."

Gavin swallowed the aching lump choking his throat. "Yeah."

Chapter Thirty-two

The chime of the security alarm jolted Gavin upright out of a sound sleep. Several beeps followed; someone entered the code to disarm. Resting back upon his pillow, he expected one of the guys, all of whom had the code and a key to his place, to come strolling into his room. It had to be that knucklehead, Dax.

Gavin gave a look at the clock illuminating on the nightstand—5:07 a.m. Eyelids heavy, he tunneled his head beneath the pillow in preparation to block out the impending disturbance. Sleep called to him, and he easily drifted off.

What seemed like short moments later, the fragrant aroma of fresh coffee woke him like a lover's morning kiss. He got up and turned on the table lamp, then stalked out of the room, intent on revoking Dax's damn key access privilege.

Crossing the living room into the kitchen, his lips pursed to curse at the guy, he froze. Sienna stood before the stove. A small glass mixing bowl was nestled in the crook of her arm as she beat the eggs within. She was here. Was he dreaming? It had been about two weeks since the funeral, and there hadn't been a day that he hadn't checked on her through Lucas. Rubbing his eyes, he padded forward. Her head came up from her whisking. Her focus moved to his bare chest, on down to his black boxer briefs, then back up, connecting with his. A ghost of a smile touched her lips.

"Lucas let me borrow his spare key." She turned away and reduced the fire beneath the skillet that sizzled with strips of bacon, then started another skillet to heat. "Hope you don't mind?" Her attention came back to him as she resumed whisking her eggs, then a slight pause. "Maybe you do mind."

Gavin blinked. He was so surprised to see her, he hadn't realized that it had been posed as a question. "Why would I mind? This is your home, too." With the mixing bowl secured in her arm, she filled a cup with coffee and held it out to him.

He accepted it as he sat down on the barstool. "It's five in the morning."

She poured the smooth eggs into the heated skillet, scrambling. "I couldn't sleep. Do you like Canadian bacon?"

"I like bacon. Period." In minutes, a plate of fluffy eggs and bacon was set before him. Staring at him with a quiet intensity, she rested back against the counter while sipping a glass of water with lemons floating in it. "You're not going to eat?" he asked as he took a sip from the cup.

She raised the glass in her hand. "I'm not hungry."

"I would guess not; it's hardly morning. How are you?"

"It's been difficult, but I'm okay. Thank you for coming to the funeral."

"You don't need to thank me. I called Lucas to see if you needed anything. I wanted to be there for you, but I figured you wouldn't want—"

"I needed space," she said softly.

Space from him, he surmised. "Your visit with Faith seemed to turn out okay," he said after a long silence. "Lucas said she stayed over for a few days."

"Yes. It was nice to have her and Bailey there with me. It gave me a lot to think about. That's one of the reasons why I'm here."

Gavin stood up and rounded the island, coming up to her. "I'm glad you came. I want us to talk, talk about everything."

"I want that, too."

Taking her hand, he guided her over to the couch and took a seat next to her. "Before you say anything, I ask that you hear me out. Can you do that for me?" A slow nod was her reply. Gavin rubbed his hands on his thighs to settle the trepidation quivering low in his gut, bracing for her expected reaction. "I've been working for my father."

"What!" She bolted to her feet, eyes hard, brows low. "Damn it, you lied to me . . . again!"

Gavin stood up. "I know by not telling you, it's a form of lying. But you said you'd listen." He took her hand and met resistance. "Let me explain. Please, baby, just sit down, and let me explain everything. You came here to talk, so let's do that."

She made an aggravated snort, expression dark, cutting, but returned to her seat.

Exhaling a deep, quiet breath, he sat down, and got right to it. "I owed my father a debt for the use of his men that protected you. It was a stupid move to call on him for help. I was just so damn scared when I found out that you had been shot, I wasn't thinking straight. All that mattered was protecting you. I didn't know what that shithead, Dale, might try to do, so I had my father's men guard you until I arrived from California. For that, I've been given assignments to complete."

"Assignments?" Her features shifted from infuriation to quizzical. "What type of assignments? Like being a hitman or something?"

"No. I had . . . have to act as my brother's second when he goes out on jobs that my father orders."

Her stare at him sharpened. "These jobs," she air quoted, "are what exactly? And you said *have*. Does that mean you're still doing work for him?"

"It's been primarily package exchanges. I have no idea what's in the envelopes, and I couldn't tell you who the individuals are that we meet. Frankly, I don't want to know. It's not social. We get in and out. I agreed to three assignments. My father tacked on a fourth when I had his men find Dale. After I met with the guy, I—"

"After you beat him up, you mean."

There was a strange impassive reserve about her regarding that part of his confession as she got up, went to the counter, and took a sip of her water. "I have one assignment left," he finally said when she returned to her seat with her glass.

"When is it?"

"Don't know. Whenever I get the call from Dylan."

"All the phone calls and text messages. . . So you weren't out with another woman when you didn't come home until who knows when?" He observed her expression slide from quizzical back to prickly displeasure.

Gavin frowned that time. "Hell no! I love you. Even if you choose to walk out that door after learning everything I've just told you, I won't stop loving you. You're all I want, believe that." His mood was anxious as he watched her sip her lemon water. Seconds that felt like hours passed with no words spoken, and then, she stood up.

"Is there anything else you need to tell me? Quite honestly, I've heard enough. I told you I don't want drama in my life. I've had enough of the shit to last two lifetimes."

"That's everything. There's nothing else." Gavin rose to his feet. He'd laid everything out, and now, she would leave him. It had been a pipe dream to think he could have someone as wonderful as her. "I want you to know that I'm sorry for keeping this from you. I was afraid you'd . . . you'd. . ." Scrubbing his fingers across his forehead, there was nothing else he could say. "Anyway, I'm sorry." He stepped out of the path of the entry door.

Taking his hand, she led him down the hall to the master bedroom, took off her canvas sneakers, stripped out of her T-shirt and shorts, and slid beneath the rumpled bed sheets. "Are you just going to stand there?" She aimed a cool stare at him when he didn't move.

The relationship thread between them was warily thin; Gavin hadn't wanted to assume. He took off his underwear and climbed in next to her. He wanted to make love to her, but right then, he needed the feel of her in his arms more. Pulling her in close, her back against his front, they lay there silently, their leveled heartbeats catching a steady rhythm.

"I'm sorry for keeping those things from you. I'll be upfront with you about everything from now on," he said softly as he listened to the even pitch of her breathing, not certain if she'd fallen asleep.

"I know you will," was her low, yet firm reply after short minutes had gone by.

She rolled over, and he stared down at her face, taking in her lovely features. He'd missed simply looking at her. He kissed the well of her collarbone on down to the split of her breasts, drawing in the familiar scent of her skin. His tongue swirled over her stiff nipples, from one to the other, gave a long lick down the center of her body, and settled between her soft thighs. No time was wasted devouring her pussy. Starved for her taste, he sucked her clit, his teeth worrying the rapidly swelling bud before sucking more. He licked the smooth lips of her sex, separated her labia with his thumbs and speared her with his tongue in deep, long strokes. He kept it up, feasting as she bucked and rolled her hips wildly through long breathy pants. He continued to eat her out long after she'd climaxed, lapping greedily the sweet taste of her, then came up, and settled back between her smooth thighs.

She laced her fingers in his hair and brought him down to the crush of her mouth, nipping his lips, stabbing her tongue deep within, kissing him with a rough hunger, then finally reared back wearing a floppy grin. "Oh, how I've missed that skillful tongue of yours," she breathed.

"And I've missed tasting you, touching you." Keeping most of his weight on his left forearm, he studied the mark at her side. "What did the doctor say about your rib during your last visit?

Has it healed as it should?" He lightly brushed a finger across the fading scar above her brow. "And this?"

"All good. I'm fully healed." Her nails ran back and forth over his buttocks, adding pressure, which brought his cock snug within the shelter of her slick folds.

Gavin brushed his lips over hers, sharing more of her sweet taste as he sheathed himself deep inside her in one smooth thrust. They both let out deep exhales from the overwhelming rush of sensation.

With a bow to his back, he captured and nipped her right nipple before clamping down on her breast, savoring. Coming back to her mouth, his hips rocked with a non-stop thrusting. He slid a hand between their moist bodies and fingered her clit, circling in swift determined strokes, as she gasped out her pleasure, eyes closed, her head pressed into the pillow, back arching.

"Oh yes," she panted and raised her hips to meet his powerful thrusts. Her face pressed into the side of his neck, and he felt her nuzzle, nip, and lick his fevered skin.

Gavin drew back to look at her. She was hot, carnal pleasure incarnate, complete and utterly wonderful in every way. "I love you, Sie."

She palmed his face in her hands. "I love you, too, and I so love this penis of yours right now." She grinned. "Turn over."

He withdrew from her welcoming heat and rolled onto his back. She straddled his hips, the hot dampness of her pussy lips scorching his dick as she came down over him, her erect nipples grazing his chest, teasing the fine hairs while offering up gentle kisses along his neck and shoulders.

He reached down to align himself with her opening, desperate to be wrapped inside her tight comforting heat once more, but she raised up slightly, preventing their joining.

"What are you doing? Sweetness, if you only knew how bad I want you right now, you wouldn't tease me. I need to be inside you like an addict needs a fix."

She laughed. With her eyes never leaving his, a hand balanced on his hip as she guided his cock back inside her, excruciatingly slow. Offering small lifts, her eyes shut, and she moaned. "I can feel every single inch of you, so full, so hard, so deep." Her hand then reached back and gripped his thigh as she rocked leisurely back and forth.

The slow, wet glide caused a rush of blood to flood the head of his cock. Gavin had to grab hold of her hips to still her movement, otherwise he'd come too soon. She pushed his hands away and began to ride him with a fierce purpose.

He watched her, mentally recording each new expression as she took her pleasure. When her hand went between her legs and stroked her clit while the other pinched and rolled her nipple, from one to the other, he hissed a shaky breath. "Yes, play with yourself. Keep that up, don't stop."

"Fuck me, Gavin, baby."

In a flash, he sat up. His arms circled her waist, and he came up with her on his shins. Holding her buttocks tight, he began power driving his cock in and out of her. Her face buried in the side of his neck as moans and pants of warm breath licked his skin.

"Don't stop. I'm going to come," she panted in short bursts.

Gavin pumped his hips even faster, deeper, grinding her pussy with determined force. His teeth grazed and nipped her shoulder. Her breath hitched sharply, and she cried out his name as her body began shuddering, her core contracting around his dick in quick ripples. He squeezed her buttocks in both hands as jets of come pulsed from him, filling and overflowing. Her cheek rested on his shoulder; warm exhales fluttered across his chin. When they could take in an even breath, she climbed off him, and they stretched out beneath the cool bed sheets.

Snuggling close, her leg draped over his hip and his arm slipped across her narrow waist. Neither moved nor spoke for long minutes, simply bathing in the afterglow of their lovemaking.

Her head came up from the crook of his arm, her features languid, yet displaying a satiated grin. "That was . . . oh my god, baby, you know how to work it."

She scraped her blunt-cut nails lightly across his moist chest, provoking his sexually charged flesh to shiver from the sensation, easily stirring his cock back to life. "Me? Woman, you put it on me. I see someone was horny," he teased, and she playfully nipped his chin. Her expression suddenly grew serious. He tensed. "What is it?"

"Though I don't approve of what you did to Dale, I understand why you did it. Faith explained he'd threatened to send the drug dealers after Bailey and me if she didn't do what he wanted. There were other heinous things he'd intended to do to Faith had she not cooperated."

"That bastard would've done something like that?" Gavin clenched his teeth to tamp down the swift surge of anger. She palmed his cheek, her fingers stroking the tight angle of his jaw.

"Like I said, I get why you did what you did. He deserved the beating you gave him."

"Damn right."

"As for you working for your father, you said you have one job left to do?"

"Yes."

"After it's completed, your debt will be paid." She paused. "Gavin, I don't want any part of that world. If that's the direction you see yourself going—

"It's not." He fingered the soft spray of fine hairs at her temple. "My father would like me to come into his organization, but I have no desire to be part of that life. When I finish my final assignment, I'm out."

Soft, slender fingers threaded in his hair at the nape. "That's great to hear."

"Sie-Sie, you're important to me. I've never wanted any woman as much as I want you. You're so goddamn wonderful." He came up on his left elbow to look down at her face. "Sienna, will you marry me?" She gasped sharply and flinched against him. "I know I don't come from what you might call good stock, but—"

"Yes."

Gavin blinked. "Yes?" She nodded, her smile wide. "Hell yes!" he shouted and bounced her up and down on the bed. "She said yes!"

Sienna laughed. "You're too much."

His mouth settled over hers, enjoying the familiarity of her soft lips and warm tongue, angling his head to take all that he could. Finishing with several light pecks, he drew back. "Let's go look at rings today."

"Today?"

Grabbing the remote from the nightstand, he put up the blinds. "The sun's almost up. It's supposed to be a nice day. What better way than to spend a beautiful Saturday with my fiancée looking at wedding rings." There was an eagerness he felt to get a ring on her finger, he realized, needing the small security of her commitment. "Well, sweetness, what do you say?"

"Okay. Sure, let's do it."

Gavin gave her a quick kiss on the lips, unable to remember a time when he'd been as happy as he was in that moment. "Lucas has a great jeweler. You've seen that rock Bailey's sporting. I'll shoot him a text to get the number and see if we can get an appointment today." He reached to the nightstand for his cell, but it started ringing. Seeing Dylan's name on the display, he released a cursed breath.

"Who is it?"

"Dylan."

"Does that mean you'll have to do a job?"

"Yeah, likely," Gavin muttered, the fucking assignment ruining his happy moment. He'd become engaged to the woman of his dreams. They were going to look at rings to make it official, but now this damn assignment he'd have to do would prevent it.

"Gavin?"

Pulled from his thoughts, he looked at her. "Hmm?"

"It stopped ringing." They both looked at the phone. "There's a voicemail message. Are you going to listen to it?"

"No."

She stared at him, her brown eyes probing. "Why?"

"Because I know what it's about."

"All the more reason to answer it. Get this last job over with."

She was right. Complete the final assignment, and then put all of it in his rearview mirror. Without listening to the message, he called Dylan back. A few rings in, the line picked up.

"Gav, hey," Dylan answered.

"Yeah, what?" Gavin growled. Receiving a kiss at the center of his chest, he leveled his tone. "What time and where?" he asked as Sienna crawled on top of him. Gentle kisses skated across his stomach. Her lips laved along the hard angle of his hips, and she moved downward, giving his dick a long swipe with her tongue before she took him into her warm mouth. "Shhhhit," he hissed.

"No, it's not that. I was calling to see if you're coming to Pop's party this afternoon. Gav, are you there?"

Gavin bit the inside of his cheeks to focus. "Yeah, I'm here. I-I," he looked down, and dark eyes stared back at him as she masterfully suckled the head of his cock. "Fuck yes, just like that," he whispered. "Right there. Keep that up."

"Dude, what the . . . are you . . . damn, man, you could've just said you were busy."

Gavin swallowed deep. "Uh, yeah, I'm . . . I'm busy right now." Dropping the phone on the bed, he tugged Sienna by the shoulders to get her to release him and had her lie on her stomach.

With a light tug of her hips, he got behind her and spread her legs with his knees. He trailed a path of nips and licks over her smooth buttocks and along her spine, drawing out soft purrs from her.

"I have great hearing, bro," came from the open phone line, followed by a light chuckle. "Gav, it's his birthday. You know the fam's flying in from Dublin and Cork. Conal McCrae, the southeast head, is leaving his sick bed to be here. He and Pop go way back, as you know. Come pay your respects. After, if you want to jet, then jet."

"You can hear what I'm doing, yet you keep yammering. I'll think about it. Gotta go." Gavin ended the call.

Easing into her sex from behind, he brought his legs on the outside of hers, adding pressure, forcing her thighs to close tightly around his length. His movements were slow and controlled, enjoying her. She took his hand and brought it between her legs, guiding his fingers to stroke her clit, unabashed to show him what she needed. He worked the pebbled flesh as he nibbled her earlobe, and her inner muscles clenched down on his shaft with each slow thrust. Her breathy sighs were long and deep as he took her body with loving tenderness.

Entwining their fingers, his paced quickened, thrusting with gratifying fury, until their release struck with fierce spiraling force, and both collapsed to the mattress.

Exhausted, sweat slicked their heated skin. He placed a kiss at the warm pulse of her neck as he worked to catch his breath. A sudden buzz from his cell reverberated beneath them. She fished the phone out and held it up. He opened the text message from Dylan, and they both read:

If I must suffer through this day, so should you.

"Will you go?" Sienna muffled partly into the pillow.

The annual birthday bash was pretty much the only time Gavin showed his face at the house, and even then, it was a very short stay.

She looked over her shoulder. "Well?"

Gavin shifted his weight off her, came in close, and rested his head on the pillow to face her. "We planned to look at engagement rings."

"You should go. It's your father's birthday. We can look at rings later this week."

"I'll go only if you come with me." There was a hesitation. He played on it. "Picking out rings would be more fun. Do you have a particular style you like?"

"I'll go."

Shit, she'd read his game. "Sienna." He stared at the filtering sunbeam cutting across the far wall, trying to think of something to say that would sway her.

"We're engaged. I'll have to meet your family at some point."

Gavin drew her close, her back to his chest, still unable to believe she'd said yes. "You'd rather go to a birthday party than shop for an engagement ring?"

"No, but your brother sounded like he really wants you there. Babe, it's one day."

One day from hell. "So, that's it, huh?" A nod. "Then I guess we're going."

"For now," she yawned, her eyelids low, "we're going to sleep." She turned in his arms. Her caressingly warm, nude body nestled against his, and she draped her thigh across his hip.

Letting out a resigned sigh, Gavin sheltered her within his frame as a foreboding knot coiled in the pit of his gut.

Then again, may as well get it over with. Better to let her meet the clan at a joyful family gathering, instead of during an *All Hands on Deck* family crisis. For the most part, according to Dylan, things had been quiet on the home front. But was it the calm before all hell broke loose?

Chapter Thirty-three

"My goodness, babe, this is where you grew up?"

Sienna gaped out the window shield of the Lamborghini at the massive, gray stone mansion of her fiancé's childhood home. The Kavanaghs' compound was situated a little over two hours south of D.C., in Richmond, Virginia. The monstrous estate seemed so contrary to its rural surroundings.

If she had blinked, she would have missed the obscure turn-off onto the private, narrow, winding gravel that led from the main road and was hidden among overgrown bushes and aged willows.

"It's one of the family homes. Except for major holidays and long breaks, I was away at school," he said as they were waved through the gates by security.

Sienna recognized one of the men manning the grounds. He'd stood at attention outside her hospital room. The man acknowledged her with a subtle incline of his head.

Her sole purpose for coming had been so she could see firsthand what she was getting into with marrying Gavin. Eyes opened, no surprises, no regrets.

All of the men were armed to the teeth. *Quite an eye-opener, so far.* "Guards? Really? You guys keep this level of heavy for a birthday party? And Virginia? I would've expected . . . I don't know, some place like—"

"It's a conceal and carry state within the northeast territory." He cut a look over, his stare drilling into her. "You were the one that wanted to come. We could be doing the whole champagne and diamonds hour right now, but nooo, you wanted to come here. And know that this isn't your everyday backyard barbeque."

"I guess I didn't realize. . ." She left the rest unsaid as she stared back at him in understanding. *Life at the Kavanaghs,* she presumed.

He parked close to the grand slated front steps of the entrance. There, a man sat perched on the top step of the landing smoking a cigarette. Watching them, he came to his feet and leaned back against the white stone pillar.

Sienna turned back to Gavin. "We're already several hours late." Looking around, there were only two other vehicles parked on the front driveway. "Everyone has already left."

"Oh, they're here, believe that. They're parked over on the side field of the property. We can still leave."

She picked up the small, wrapped box from her lap. "We bought a gift. We can't leave."

"The hell we can't." He plucked the box from her and chucked it into the glove compartment.

"Babe, come on." She pulled it back out, then brushed her thumb along the tense, chiseled angle of his right cheek. "We're here now, and that man over there has called your name twice."

"That's just Dylan."

"Your brother? Then introduce me." She took his hand in hers and pressed a kiss on the back of it. "Let's hang out for an hour or so, and then we'll leave, okay?"

With clear reluctance, he stepped out, rounded the car, and held the passenger door open for her to exit. They came up to Dylan.

"I see Pop's got you out here nursing your impending emphysema."

Dylan pivoted his head to release the billow of smoke. "He stinks up the place with those Cuban cigars, but I can't have a smoke anywhere inside the house."

"Good." Gavin snatched the cigarette from between his brother's fingers and flicked it onto the pavement.

Dylan frowned. "Damn, come on, dude, not you, too."

"I don't want that shit anywhere near me or my lady, got it?" Gavin turned his head to her beside him. "This is my fiancée, Sienna Keller."

Dylan's eyes widened. "Fiancée? No shit? Really?" A broad smile broke across the man's mouth. "Congrats." The brothers shook hands and pulled in with slaps on the back, then Dylan stepped over and kissed her cheek. "Welcome to the family. You're as beautiful as I pictured you'd be. Not sure why you're with this lump." He playfully gave a one-two punch to Gavin's chest.

Sienna smiled. "It's great to meet you, Dylan." The eldest brother was about the same height as Gavin, but slimmer. His burnt-blond hair and light freckles sprinkled across the bridge of his nose gave him a boyish charm.

"I want to keep the engagement quiet for now," Gavin said to his brother.

Sienna cut a puzzled look at him, and he took her hand in his, offering a light squeeze, but no other explanation was given. Before she could ask why the heck for, the entrance door opened, and out walked Edwin.

"Gav, I didn't know you were in the housssse," Edwin sang out. "Dyl, Pop's looking for you." His attention shifted. "Sienna, right?"

Sienna nodded, noting how the young man's gaze flickered down to her legs in her coral cotton sundress and back up, back and forth. He then looked at Dylan.

"See, I told you she has great legs."

Gavin shot him a murderous scowl. "And I'm not opposed to kicking your ass in front of the entire family. You're due one, that's for damn certain."

"Dude, can't you see it's a compliment, damn."

"Vanish, Eddie." Gavin glowered, and the young man quickly retreated.

"Maybe one day he'll grow up," Dylan remarked on a chuckle. "Let's head in."

Holding Gavin's hand, Sienna walked with him into a grand entryway. They crossed the space and pushed through another set of gilded glass French doors that opened into an enormous great room with a thirty-foot or so, skylight-cathedral ceiling,·oversize couches, heavy oak tables, and several double wide chairs. A lively tune, mostly of string instruments, poured in through the three sets of French doors that lay open wide. It gave her a good view of the festive crowd dancing out on the lawn.

Inside, people congregated, chatting, dancing, and munching on party food served by circling waiters. There had to be at least fifty people inside and what looked to be double that outside. Many donned party hats and even wore costumes. Sienna felt she'd walked into a circus. The only thing missing was a man swallowing fire.

"I'll go see what Pop wants." Dylan crossed the room and stepped outside.

"Are all these people your relatives?" Sienna was astounded by the mass of bodies dancing, drinking, and singing.

"Not all. My pop likes to do it up old school, like back in Ireland when he was young," Gavin said as they strolled forward.

It hadn't been voiced very loud, but there was pitch added to hear over the music and mingled chatter, yet seated on one of the couches, three ladies' heads turned—two twenty-somethings and one elder woman. The ladies stared back at Sienna with a scrutinizing eye. As if on cue, their gazes slid from her to Gavin. The attractive blonde yanked off her party hat, jumped up from her seat, rushed to him, and practically leaped into his arms. His sister, Caren, Sienna presumed. The young lady and she exchanged an acknowledging smile.

The dark-haired young lady came forward next. A subtle smirk that could only be described as a play on sensual, curved the lady's mouth as she slipped both arms around Gavin's waist, rose on the insteps of her spiky-heeled sandals, and kissed him smack dab on the mouth. Sienna's eyes fluttered. *What the hell. . .*

"So you decided to come," the young lady said, her attention solely on Gavin.

As if remembering her standing beside him, with his cheeks flushed full of color, he gave a look over, and Sienna returned a questioning stare. He was smart to take her hand.

"Uh, Abela, Caren, this is my lady, Sienna Keller."

Caren's ocean-blue eyes brightened. "Wow, Gav, you have a girlfriend? And you're actually allowing us to meet her?" She smiled warmly. "It's nice to meet you."

"I'm starting to think I'm an anomaly," Sienna said jokingly as she shook Caren's hand. "It's nice to meet you, too."

"You *are* an anomaly in a way. My brother is very private, that's all."

"Gavin, you didn't mention a girlfriend when we made plans to meet," Abela cut in.

Meet? Sienna jerked a look at Gavin. To say he looked uncomfortable in his skin would be putting it mildly.

Receiving an assessing once-over from Abela, Sienna also realized that the girl still hadn't acknowledged her. Abela's behavior was like that of a jealous ex. *Have she and Gavin . . . no, that would be frickin' creepy.* Gavin saw her as his adopted sister.

"Where are your manners, boy?"

Their attention flew to the elder woman who spoke from her seat on the couch. With Gavin's hand on her lower spine, Sienna was led before the woman.

"Nana Rue, it's great to see you." He bent and kissed her cheek. "Did you have a comfortable flight?"

"God-awful. I hate flying," she groused in a thick Irish accent.

"Rowena Kavanagh is my grandmother," he said and looked back at the woman. "Nana Rue, this is my lady, Sienna Keller."

"Ma'am, it's a pleasure to meet you." Sienna stuck out her hand and received a weak shake and rapid release.

An index finger righted the black, hard-rimmed glasses up the bridge of the woman's narrow nose as she delivered a scrutinizing scan up and down. "Where are you from?"

Sienna blinked. "I beg your pardon?"

"What are you? Your family?"

"Nana, that's not important," Gavin lightly chided.

Dylan came back inside, and Edwin was close on his heels. Behind them, a man pushing another man in a wheelchair entered. The big, strapping man was bent near the frail man's ear, whispering as he guided the chair forward.

"Happy birthday, Pop," Gavin called out, and both men looked up. The man behind the wheelchair straightened to his full height.

Wow!

With the gift in hand, Gavin led her over to meet Murtagh Kavanagh. Sienna had pictured the mobster king to resemble the guys from the movies. She wasn't too far off. Gavin was about six-four and even he had to look up to meet his father's gaze. He was a hulking bear of a man. Yet, in contradiction, his reddish hair with sprinkles of gray was parted on the right and neatly combed back, reminding her of the 1940s, polished look. His pale blue button-down fitted over broad shoulders, a taut abdomen, and tucked within neat, gray slacks. Raw power—confident without the cocky.

"Pop, this is my lady, Sienna Keller," Gavin said.

There was a slight flare of surprise in his eyes before he extended his large, strong hand. "So, you're the lady my son would move heaven and earth to protect."

"I wouldn't say heaven *and* earth." Sienna grinned. The man's stoic, green gaze pinned down on her, and the medley of voices in the entire room seemed to dull. What was she thinking? This man could have her clipped with a mere wink of an eye. Bailey had often said Sienna was her own audience at times. Perhaps this was the time to take heed of that.

Loud laughter suddenly broke from the man, startling her. The rock you on your heels, wind tunnel resonance kind of surprised sound. It shook her up mainly because he'd look ready to munch on her insides just a moment before. The entire room quieted, appearing to have gotten struck by the force of it.

Beefy hands came down on the narrow shoulders of the fragile, bald man in the wheelchair. "I think I like this lass."

Did he actually say lass? His Irish accent hadn't been as pronounced until just then.

Murtagh tapped the wheelchair-bound man's right shoulder once more. "Conal, you remember Gavin, my middle boy?"

"Of course. Look at you. You've grown into a fine man. I remember when you were no taller than my knee." Conal's spindly fingers patted Murtagh's hand that palmed his right shoulder. "You got yourself three fine boys. Blessed you have been, my old friend."

"Mr. McCrae, it's a pleasure to see you again." Gavin shook his hand. "Sorry to hear about your health."

"The cruel bastard may win this battle, but I won't make it easy."

A hoarse chuckle brought about a rustling cough. He used the handkerchief on his lap to wipe away the light spittle as Sienna once again was given a blatant look over. *What is with these people?* "Aren't you a pretty lass," he said in an almost strangled voice.

Lass again. She smiled politely. "Thank you."

"Gavin, you got yourself a beauty there," Conal said.

Gavin looked at her, his love for her openly expressed in his gaze. "I know."

He handed over the gift box. "Here you go, Pop. It's a gold cigar clip."

"Thank you. It's just what I needed. I can't seem to find my favorite one. It has grown legs," Murtagh said in an elevated tone, and everyone's attention seemed to swing to him on cue.

Queasiness threatened to churn in Sienna's stomach from the whiff of grilled fish carried on the warm breeze. She turned her head away to escape the pungent herb aroma. Her eyes widened at the sight of a man running a large knife down the belly of a dead pig, its entrails spilling into a bucket. *Ew, gross.* To his left another fresh full pig rotated over a fired spit. She swallowed repeatedly, trying her best not to vomit. Giving a look at Gavin, she was glad to see the look of concern in his eyes, having picked up on her distress.

"Hey," he called to a waiter carrying a tray of empty glasses, "can we get a glass of water with lemon?" The guy nodded and hurried off.

Feeling a bead of sweat starting to break out above her top lip, Sienna ran a subtle hand across her mouth and took slow, quiet breaths, doing her best to mask the rising tide.

"Pop, you said you wanted to have a meeting." Dylan broke the sudden silence.

"Pop, can I join?" Edwin asked, his blue eyes wide, hopeful.

"No, Eddie," Murtagh answered. "But, Gavin, I do want you in on this."

Gavin shook his head. "Nah, my lady's not feeling well. We're going to head out."

Sienna looked at Murtagh. His hard stare said the word no was unacceptable.

Taking Gavin's hand, offering a reassuring squeeze, she smiled. "I'm fine, really." In truth, she needed to sit before she fell on her face. "I'll wait over there on the couch."

"You're sure?" Gavin asked, his gaze holding hers in an almost plea.

"Yes, I'm sure." Sienna wasn't about to come between him and the big guy. They'd have their meeting, and then she and Gavin would get the hell out of there. She'd seen all she needed to see.

She walked away to show all was fine. Before she could sit, Nana Rue's hand flew out and gripped her wrist. Sienna stared puzzled at the woman as she was tugged to stand directly before her. Weathered hands came down on her hips, adding a light pressure, then both hands moved to her stomach.

"Are you pregnant?"

Sienna gasped. "No! No, I'm not pregnant." Her tone whipped up slightly.

"Then what else could it be about you that he sees?"

Insulted, she withdrew her arm from the woman's hold not too gently. "We're engaged." The words just flew out.

The woman's gray eyes stretched wide as saucers, and she pushed back hard against the couch with a hand clutching her bright floral smock over her heart.

Sienna and Gavin's, heads turned to his father whose stare narrowed, lips thinned. Within that tense moment, the waiter returned and handed Gavin the glass of water. He came forward and gave it to her. Taking small sips, she sat down in the armchair, and tried to ignore the many eyes upon her.

"Wow, Gavin, are you two really engaged?" Caren gaped. "Now that's what I call a birthday surprise." She laughed.

The entire room played witness. *So much for keeping things quiet.* Sienna sent Gavin an apologetic look and met an expression like none she'd ever seen before. To say he looked pissed would be putting it mild. *Damn it.* She chanced another look at Murtagh. He stared back at her, projecting a shitload of menace. *Ugh.*

"Do you have any Irish roots in you at all?"

Nana Rue's question drew her attention. "I don't believe so."

"You don't look just black, so what else are you?"

"She's black, damn, Nana, stop with the goddamn questions!" Gavin thundered, and Sienna jumped. Shit, the entire room felt the rumble. The old woman's gray eyes glazed over in shock, chest heaving out quick breaths.

Sienna had never witnessed Gavin at this Richter scale of pissed off. And it was her fault. She should never have insisted he come here. It was clear now why he was so adamant in not wanting to introduce her to his family—the mobster Addams family.

"Let us have that meeting, boys," Murtagh finally said, his inflectionless tone belied by his hard-drawn features as he wheeled Conal across the room to a set of closed double oak doors. Dylan followed.

"Pop, can I come?" Edwin called again in eagerness to join the men's meeting, but was ignored.

Gavin leaned in, and Sienna pursed her lips, ready to receive his parting kiss. Instead, he whispered at her ear, "You wanted to come. Hope you're satisfied." He reared back. Eyes hard, a tick worked in his clenched jaw. Without another word, he straightened and walked away. She didn't look away from him until the office door closed behind him.

Her insides tightened. He was off the charts angry . . . at her. She wanted to offer an apology for putting him in this crazy situation and wondered what was being discussed behind those closed doors? Likely, nothing she would want Gavin to get mixed up in. Him being pulled into whatever Murtagh was meeting about was also her fault. Her mind ran through many chilling scenarios of what it could be. Cutting off her active imagination, she turned her head away from the office doors and was met by Abela's glare. The girl sat with arms folded at her chest and legs tightly crossed. She'd remained quiet throughout all of it. Sienna didn't need to be a Rhodes scholar to read her—anger, filled with jealousy, and covered in a thick coat of *bitch, you're not welcome here*. No doubt, Abela had a thing for Gavin. A massive knot of possessiveness over Gavin swelled in Sienna's chest.

Frickin' great, I have an adversary. Jim frickin' dandy.

Looking around, apparently, she'd become the party's main attraction. Many pairs of eyes and low whispers were still focused on her. *I so don't need this shit.*

She'd been tempted to march over to those double doors and drag Gavin out so they could get the hell out of there. The man that stood at attention outside the door in his fitted black suit, hands clasped in front of him, bright red hair standing straight up on top of his head, and eyes alert, quickly curtailed that idea.

Seated upwind to the open doors, another good whiff of the grilled fish and roasting pig aroma combo filled her nostrils. *Ugh.* She placed the glass of lemon water on the side table and rose to her feet.

"Can you tell me where the bathroom would be?" The question was directed at Caren. Abela . . . and likely Nana Rue would have her pee on herself.

Caren's head came up, pulled away from whoever she'd been texting while grinning profusely and bounced up out of her relaxed pose. "I'll show you." As they made their way out of the room and down a long hallway, Caren looked at her. "I can't believe my brother is getting married. Dylan and Angie were married a little over a year ago. Since that time, they've been trying to get pregnant."

"Is she here?"

"She's out back catching what's left of the sun. If I'm out there five minutes, I look like someone set me on fire. I try not to stay out very long."

"Abela isn't very talkative." Sienna gave a look over to read Caren more than hear her.

"She'd been looking forward to seeing Gavin all day. You on his arm was a bit of a surprise."

"I got the impression she and Gavin are pretty tight."

"You can say that." Caren's lips curved at one corner as if holding in a really juicy secret.

They came to the bathroom door. "Thanks. This place is enormous. I would've found it eventually, but it may have been too late."

"It's not a problem." Caren turned to leave but pivoted back. "Hey, don't pay any attention to Nana Rue. She's old country. The Irish bloodline is important to her." She hugged Sienna, then stepped back and smiled. "Welcome to the family."

"Thank you." As Caren strolled off, Sienna thought about that as she entered the bathroom.

Welcome to the family. It was some kind of family she was about to marry into, that's for damn sure, like one she'd never imagined.

Chapter Thirty-four

"Engaged! What the hell were you thinking, son?"

"I was thinking my relationship is none of your business." Gavin glared back at his father's objectionable scowl.

"Watch your tone with me, boy. I'm still your father."

The man's Irish brogue thickened with each word. This was Murtagh Kavanagh, the boss, the top dog of the Irish Republic Army, northeast territory speaking now, not his father.

To avoid telling him to go to hell, Gavin pushed down the mounting aggression. "What do you want? Why am I in here?" He took note of the pulsing vein in the vexing man's hard-set square jaw.

"Murtagh, this may be a good thing," Conal chimed in from his wheelchair parked just inside the door.

"Good thing? I don't see it. We know nothing about her. No good sense. He gets wooed by a pretty face, breasts, and ass—"

"You watch your mouth!" Gavin lunged, restraint gone, but was shoved back by Dylan.

"Pop, Sienna's a lovely woman. You don't have to worry," Dylan rushed out.

Gavin shot Dylan a venomous look but let it go as fast as it came. His brother was trying to step in as peacekeeper as he'd often done over the years when Gavin and their father went at each other. "Dylan, not I, nor my lady, need you defending her to him," he gritted.

"Engaged. Your grandmother was right to ask the woman if she was carrying. What other reason would you have other than plain stupidity? Engaged or not, she will be checked out, you understand," Murtagh made clear. "Let us hope I'm satisfied with what I find."

"You'll stay out of my business." Gavin's challenging tone contradicted the rapid punching his heart was putting against his ribs. Remembering the story told to him about the day his father stabbed his uncle in the chest with an ice pick and watched him bleed out as he took his last breath only because he received intel that Uncle Teb had spoken to the Feds, Kavanagh's definition of *checking out* could be a life or death call for the person in question.

Gavin also wondered if Dylan experienced the same suffocating tightness in his chest when he'd had to walk away from his first love, Cailin. Could he give Sienna up so easily at his father's command? *Fuck that.*

He set a steady stare on the man, pitching his voice low and threatening, "I'm going to marry Sienna no matter what you find out about her or her family, and you'll stay away from her, got it?"

Murtagh's brows dipped, but only a fraction. With a glint in his eyes, he rounded his desk and took a seat. "You do have my spirit, that is to be sure. Your mam knew the minute you entered the world that you were a solid one. It's why she wagered to keep you in the divorce, and why I wouldn't hear of it. She thought if you went to that boarding school, it would keep you away from me, away from your family."

Gavin sighed and asked again, "Pop, why am I here?" He wasn't about to trash his mother with the man. No doubt, there were still bitter feelings that she'd had the good sense to walk away. No one turned their back on Murtagh Kavanagh. No one. But his mother had . . . and it came at a price. Gavin had been the cost—her sacrifice.

Murtagh looked at Conal. "Now how do you see this situation as a good thing?"

Conal angled his chair toward Gavin. "Your father and I have agreed to merge our two families." Receiving surprised as well as puzzled looks, he went on, "I don't have much time left on this blessed earth, and I'm leaving behind no sons to replace me."

"Those package exchanges you and Dylan transported were agreement negotiations between Conal and me," Murtagh put in.

"There are many who don't want to see this merger happen. We had to be discreet, keep it close to the vest," Conal continued.

"What does that have to do with me?" Gavin's head bounced between the two men.

"We want you to sit over the southeast," Murtagh answered.

Gavin shot Dylan an accusatory glower. "You knew about this. It was all a setup. That's why you insisted I come today."

"I didn't have much of a choice," Dylan muttered with a glimpse over at their father.

"There shouldn't have been a need to hoodwink you, son. You should be here on your own merit. But you stand there scowling." Murtagh sighed and reclined back in his chair. "Be that as it may, this merger will make me the largest head in the country. The entire eastern seaboard would be under my name. As Conal mentioned, many don't want to see that happen. I need someone I can trust at my side, someone strong enough to handle situations, should they arise."

"Once you are married and she births you a son, you can start building a legacy," Conal added, his expression soaked with pride, as though he'd just handed over the monarchy.

Knots of unease coiled tightly in Gavin's stomach. He felt his knees giving way beneath him, but fought against it, letting none of his anxiety show. "I don't want it." Clear and precise.

"Son, this is an honor Conal is offering you, that I'm offering you," Murtagh said.

Gavin shook his head. "I don't accept it." He turned to Conal. "Thanks, but no thanks." His attention, as did Dylan's, flew to the resounding pound of their father's club-like fist slamming down on solid oak.

"This is how you react to such a gift, like a petulant whelp!"

Gavin did his best to maintain calm. "It's not for me, Pop. Groom Eddie. He wants to be brought in. Teach him, mentor him."

Murtagh's head cocked sharply. "It's not for you? Who do you think you are? Legally changing your name to Crane, you think that changes the blood that runs through you?" His tone cemented with fury. "Who do you think has kept you protected? It's my name that has been your protection, not your mam's."

"I'll do it," Dylan spoke up.

"Dylan?" Resolute, unshakable sternness stared back at Gavin. Dylan was trying to shield him, he understood. "Dyl, you don't want this, either. Tell him."

"I said I'll do it." Dylan looked between the two leaders. "I can handle it."

"No offense, my boy, you are the eldest, yes, but your skin's not thick enough, that I well know. Your brother, Edwin, is too quick-tempered. He has a lot of growing to do before I can set him loose. Gavin, you've always been the strong one, lethal when a situation calls for it, yet levelheaded. Take that bloke you went after for harming your lady. The way you sought out your enemy and handled the situation is exactly what I would have done, which is why I'd hoped you would stand beside me and take your place as my successor when the time comes."

Like hell I would. Those were shoes Gavin had no intention of wearing. There was no way he would drag his future wife into this hell. And going after Dale had been a stupid impulse of anger that he regretted. It was what got him tangled in this shit in the first place. Never again would he be so reckless.

"Give the territory to Cousin Emmett . . . or Cousin Miser. Even he should be able to keep his psychosis in check if he knows what's at stake."

Murtagh scowled. "What the hell do you think this is? You think you can just—"

"I'm not dead yet," Conal cut in and wheeled his chair forward, pivoting it before them. "Gavin, give it some thought. I'm sure you'll see the importance and significance to your father—your family—of you succeeding me. To that end, there is one more pickup we need you two to make."

Murtagh slid across the desk the familiar brown envelope. "Conal's man will be there in an hour."

Gavin's eyes flickered between the men. "Now? I can't do this now. I have to get Sienna home." He shook his head in weary frustration. "This will have to wait."

Murtagh crossed his arms at his chest, his brows low. "Need I remind you of our agreement, son?"

"As if you'd let me forget," Gavin groused.

"The drop is not far from here. You'll be back before your lady notices you're gone. We'll look after her. You needn't worry," Murtagh said.

"I can handle this, Gav; you don't have to come." Dylan grabbed the envelope.

"He's going," Murtagh ordered. "It's his final assignment, and he will see it through."

Gavin didn't want to leave his brother unprotected. He closed his eyes and pinched at the ache between his brows that started to form, sighing deep. Just one more assignment, and then he would be out, set free, the shackle unlocked and removed from his neck forever. Picturing his freedom, he said, "Dyl, I got you."

"Now, that's what I like to hear." Murtagh grinned and tapped an index finger at his temple. "Like I said, levelheaded." Rearing back in his chair, he stroked his chin, and stared stone-faced at Gavin. "So, you wish to marry that pretty lass?"

"Don't." Gavin glared back in stark warning, and the man brought up his hand, palm out.

"I have a proposition for you. I won't have your fiancée or her family looked into if—"

"Like you did with Cailin," Gavin ground out with a glance at Dylan.

Murtagh looked at Dylan, his expression bland. "It had to be done. She could have been a plant, a mole filtering information to her uncle." Not a hint of contrition was conveyed in the irksome man's green gaze.

Dylan scowled. "You were wrong about Cailin. I meant more to her, we meant more to each other, than that," he voiced in an even monotone that stumbled only slightly when he'd said her name.

Gavin heard the hurt from the loss, undercut by contempt rumbling just below the surface of his brother's calm.

Murtagh rose to his feet, large hands splayed atop the desk. "Well, that's far behind us now. You have Angie. She turned out to be a good fit for you and our family. Though I still wait for her to give me a grandson," he grumbled and returned his attention to Gavin. "As I was saying, I won't have your lady checked out, in exchange that you agree to consider Conal's and my offer. You can use the time to think on it while my good mate still graces this earth," he said with a look of sincere fondness at Conal.

"That seems fair enough, I say." Conal nodded.

Gavin's mind scrambled in a multitude of directions. He could keep his father's hired claws away from Sienna, protect her, but he'd have to step in as head of the southeast territory to do that. Losing her was not an option, and protecting her was priority one, so where did that leave him in this situation?

"What is discussed here stays here," Murtagh said, drawing Gavin out of his thoughts. "You're not to disclose any of this to that new fiancée of yours. Dylan understands not to say anything about the business to Angie, and so shall you with your Sienna."

"Are we done?" Gavin asked, yet he'd already taken wide strides to the door. Getting a nod, on his way out, he exchanged a look with Dylan that said, *fuck your rules.*

The great room was swollen with even more guests having a good time. Gavin looked around for Sienna. The chair where he'd left her was now occupied by his grandmother. From as far back as he could remember, crotchetiness had always been her M.O. Cutting his way through the festive throng, he approached her. "Nana Rue, have you seen Sienna?" Her head came up from her Words with Friends app on her iPad. At eighty-six, the woman's mental faculties were acutely sharp.

"Why don't you find yourself a nice Irish girl? That's what you need. Or do what your brother, Dylan, did. You can hardly tell that Angie has Mexican in her."

Out of the barest respect to her age, Gavin bit the inside of his cheek to refrain from calling her a goddamn racist. And Angie was part Latina. He wasn't in the mood to give her an Ethnicity 101 lecture on the difference.

He crouched down to meet her eye to eye, so she wouldn't miss a single word. "Nana, Sienna will soon become my wife." She jerked her chin up, lips puckered in distaste. "She has accepted me," he waved out at the parade of overly liquored up people around them, "despite all of this crazy." Receiving an indignant huff and a harsh look away with arms folded at her chest, Gavin stood up. "Whether you choose to accept that or not is up to you. It won't change those facts."

Spotting Caren entering from the hall, he went to her. "Where's Sienna?"

"I showed her to the bathroom earlier. We took a walk in the greenhouse. On our way back, we spotted Uncle Niall disposing innards over by the shed. She headed back to the bathroom. I'll give her a few minutes."

"No, I'll go. Look, I have to make a run for Pop. I need you to keep an eye on Sienna for me."

"Pop already put me on entertainment duty before you got here. He figured if you showed, you'd likely have one of your friends, maybe Dax with you, so you would have an excuse to leave. He wanted you to stick around for that meeting."

Gavin's eyes narrowed. "Of course he did." It was like their pop, always calculating his opponent's next move. Even his sister was in on the ruse. They'd all played him.

"We just didn't expect you'd bring your girlfriend. You've never let us meet any of the others before."

Looking around at the wild bunch, *that's why.* "Caren, you know how this party can get. Watch out for Sienna, got it?"

"Don't worry, I'll keep her company. She's so sweet, Gav. I can't believe you're engaged." She gave him a tight hug.

"Thanks." It was still shiny brand new to him as well. If only he could take a moment to enjoy the feeling.

Gavin strode off down the hall. Hearing his name called, he turned. Abela was making her way toward him. "Abby, hey."

"You haven't called me that in a long time." She came up and draped her arms around his neck, her hips pressing in.

"Abby . . . Abela. . ." Her body coaxed him back against the wall.

"Gav, what we did wasn't wrong." Delicate fingers snaked in his hair at the nape. "We have history, a good, long history. What you think you have with her doesn't come close to what we have together." A seductive grin creased her lips as her hand slid down his chest, skating onward along his stomach to his cock.

Gavin tried to jerk his hips back to escape her determined fingers, but the wall at his back impeded the action. "Abela, stop this." He reached down and gripped her hand, and the other went up to dislodge her arm secured around his neck.

A few steps down the hall, the bathroom door opened and out stepped Sienna. Her eyelids fluttered for only a moment before setting them fixed as she aimed her footsteps directly in their path.

Gavin quickly came out of Abela's hold. "Hey, sweetness, I was looking for you."

"Not very hard, I see." Her stark gaze shifted to his right. "Abela, will you excuse us." Her tone was deceptively soft contrary to her dark, laser-lock, no nonsense stare. He knew that look all too well and what it meant. He or Abela, or more likely the both of them, were about to get an ass-kicking.

Abela delivered Sienna a hard study from head to feet, then turned back to him. "Gav, we'll continue our conversation later." She delivered an eye roll at Sienna, turned, and strutted off with an exaggerated sway in her red shorts that scarcely covered the rim of her pale ass cheeks.

They remained silent until the hall emptied out.

"You fucked her, didn't you? And I can see that barely-there tank top and those ass-grabbing shorts she chose to wear today were for you, too."

She shot him an accusatory look of disgust. When he didn't answer, a hard shove to his chest with both hands let him know her full irritation.

"Ew, she's like your sister. That's just gross. This place is wild. And I thought my family was messed up." She shook her head, her eyes rolling upward then landing rigidly back on him. "This is next level bat-shit crazy."

Gavin couldn't defend himself or his fucked-up family. He only said, "I'd had too much to drink when it happened with Abela. It was only once . . . over a year ago . . . after Dylan's wedding."

"Double ew, and she evidently wants to hook up with you again."

Her look of repulse added to his shame. "It won't ever happen again, believe that."

She fisted his polo shirt and jerked him close, pinning narrow eyes upon him. "It fucking better not if you want to keep that exceptional appendage of yours swinging between your legs, got it?"

He could see she meant every word, yet a smile broke across his mouth, unable to help it. He was bordering on masochistic because he found her Amazonian, kick-ass attitude so fucking hot. "You're vicious, woman."

"Believe that," she mocked, her glower finally waning.

Palming her cheeks, he kissed her slowly, then with a sudden eager need to devour her sweet mouth, his tongue snaked within, deepening the kiss. For long minutes, he enjoyed her, while ignoring the occasional intrusion of people traipsing up and down the hall, then drew away from her deliciously soft lips with much effort.

"I swear you get sweeter with each kiss."

A light brush of her thumb stroked across his moist lips. "You're pretty yummy yourself."

"I want to apologize for how I acted earlier. I shouldn't have gotten upset with you. Being around my family tends to make me agitated."

"They are a wild bunch, that's for sure. It's fine."

Circling an arm at her waist, holding her close, he wanted to whisk her away from all of this madness. "How's my fiancée feeling?"

Her lips curved into a dimpling grin. "Your fiancée . . . you like saying that, don't you?"

"Damn right." Returning a grin, his joy was near bursting, but then he got serious. "How are you feeling? I heard you encountered Uncle Niall. Can I get you anything?"

"I'm good. Seeing that whole pig out back being gutted, those little beady eyes bucking out, then watching that man pick through the soupy blood and guts, it almost did me in, but I'm better now."

"Good. There's something I need to tell you." Gavin looked from side to side.

"What?" She did the same.

"Not here." Taking her hand, he led her out of the hall and upstairs.

"Where are we going?"

"To my old bedroom." They strode down the long corridor, entered the room, closed the door, and he backed her up against it. Dropping to his knees, he slipped his hands beneath her dress and circled to her buttocks, stroking, kneading. Eyes closed, he buried his nose in the V of her mound, inhaling deep, his need spiking in a feral, intoxicating rush. "Damn, I love your scent." His fingers snaked around the delicate lace of her thong and dragged her panties off her hips and down her long, lean legs.

Her hands gripped his shoulders, prodding him back. "Didn't you have something you wanted to tell me?"

"Yes." He peeled her panties off over her sandals, then slid his tongue between the split of her silken-shaven pussy lips, in search of her juicy clit. Her right leg came to rest on his shoulder, spread wide in invitation, aggressive fingers tightly clutching his hair. His tongue laved the sensitive pearl before clamping his mouth on her, sucking hard. Rocking her hips, she tossed her head back, her breath sawing out in quick bursts as she gripped his head, rough and insistent, to keep his mouth pressed against her sex.

Licking, swirling his tongue, and sucking, he kept it up until her body quivered and she panted heavily through her release. Coming to his feet, he kissed her on their way to the bed. Within mere seconds, they were both naked. He tossed the heavy gray comforter aside, and they settled atop the navy-blue gingham sheets. He got in between the curve of her soft thighs and guided his cock inside her wet heat as his tongue rimmed her right ear and nipped at her lobe. "You're so beautiful. I love you," he whispered.

"I love you, too," she breathed raggedly. "What was it you wanted to tell me?"

Gavin licked a path along the column of her throat and bowed his back to suck on a pebbled nipple, indulging himself upon her succulent bud, from one to the other.

Her knees came up; fingernails embedded in his ass cheeks. "You started this, now move, baby, fuck me."

"Oh most definitely." He brought both her legs up at the bend of his arms and pounded her pussy, thrusting hard and deep, twisting his hips, grinding into her, pelvis to pelvis. Her pants of warm breath at his ear had him surging with such force, completely lost in his need, her body shimmied up the mattress, nearly banging her head on the headboard.

Her nails raked down his back to his buttocks and held tight as she arched up sharply through a long shuddering orgasm, then her rough pants became soft, satiated purrs. He kept thrusting until his entire body locked down tight, and he emptied deep inside her.

Delightfully drained, he collapsed upon her long, exquisite form, aware that she carried his dead weight. He was just too gloriously spent to move but forced himself up on his forearms to bear the bulk.

"That was the best one yet," he uttered around the silky glide of tongue on tongue.

She reared back. "You've been rating our lovemaking?"

"Come on, you don't think that was damn good?" He grinned, his breathing somewhat labored.

She smiled back. "Okay, that *was* pretty amazing."

A knock came at the door before it opened. "Gav—"

"What the fuck, Dylan!" Gavin grabbed the blanket to shield her.

"Oh, sorry." Dylan promptly closed the door. "I've been looking all over for you. We need to get going."

"Going where?" Sienna looked at him. "What is he talking about?"

"That's what I wanted to tell you, but you distracted me with these pretty, brown tits." Chuckling, he flicked a finger over an engorged nipple, and she playfully slapped his hand away.

"Dude, come on. We're already late," Dylan called from outside the door.

"Give me ten minutes, damn," Gavin yelled back. His cock slipped free of her warm sheath, and he got up. "I have to do my last assignment."

"Now?" She followed him into the bathroom en suite. As they washed up, she asked, "Where exactly are you going? Is it safe?"

"I don't know yet, and you don't have to worry." Gavin searched the cabinets and found a basket of unopened toiletries beneath the sink. He took from it a packaged toothbrush and a tube of toothpaste. In between brushing his teeth and rinsing his mouth, he explained what took place in the meeting.

"You said no, right? You're not ruling over no southeast."

"I said no," he replied to her reflection in the mirror. "But my father doesn't take too kindly to the word no. He expects me to reconsider, or more like insists on it. No is not an option."

"Trust me, I got that impression about him." She sighed long. "I know this is your family, and I would never tell you to stay away from them, but," she shook her head, "I can't deal—"

Gavin stepped to her and waved a thumb between them before taking a gentle hold of her shoulders. "You are my family first and foremost, understand?" Getting a weak nod, he brought her chin up with his index finger to hold her gaze. "Sie-Sie, you mean the world to me. I have to protect you by doing whatever that takes."

Her brows furrowed. "Whatever that takes? What is that supposed to mean?"

"We'll talk about everything when I get back."

"When will that be? I can take the car home."

"No, stay put. There are no lights on that road we turned onto to get here. That's on purpose." Getting a feeble nod again, he kissed her forehead and left the bathroom. "I'll only be gone about two to three hours at most. You can hang out in here if you want. The TV remote is on the desk there." The sun had almost set, tinging the room with a dusky light. He turned on the desk lamp. "There's also a study downstairs with lots of books. Caren can show you where it is." He quickly slipped on his clothes, then turned to her standing at the threshold of the bathroom. His breath caught. Arms loosely folded beneath her perky breasts with a shoulder braced against the doorjamb, she stood leisurely in all her naked splendor. Perfectly sculptured curves and soft angles—beautiful. She was everything he'd imagined he'd never have.

Her brow crinkled. "What?"

Gavin blinked. "What?"

She swirled an index finger in the direction of his face. "You're looking at me all weird."

"I'm imagining eating you out again later."

Smiling, she came forward and wrapped her arms around his neck. "Are you ever not horny, Mr. Crane?"

"Eh." A shrug. "Since I met you, I pretty much stay erect." He stroked the curve of her left ass cheek before delivering a hearty slap. She yelped, then a grin slid across those pouty lips. "Get dressed so I can concentrate." Scooping her clothes up off the floor, he handed them over. "I'll have one of the staff bring you up something to eat."

"No. I'm not helpless. I'll find something on my own. The last thing I need is for your father to think I expect to be served."

"He wouldn't think that."

She gave him a sideways look, lips pursed. "Umm hmm, right. I didn't miss the split-second scowl on his face when I stupidly broadcast to the entire room that we are engaged, before he flashed back into Mr. Big, Bad Grizzly."

"I'm glad you announced it. I shouldn't have tried to hide it." Staring at her now dressed in her bra and panties, could she look any hotter? Unable to resist, he came up to her, pushed the lace aside, and suckled on a puckering right nipple.

"Your brother's waiting." Slender fingers threaded in his hair and held firm.

"Let him."

"There has to be a kitchen in this monstrous place somewhere."

"There are two," he said as he flicked his tongue back and forth over her stippling bud.

"Two kitchens?"

"The regular one and another smaller one on the basement level."

"Wow, I guess organized crime has served you all well."

Gavin's head came up from her breasts. That's what it took to get him flaccid. He drew away and took a seat on the edge of the bed to put on his shoes.

The way his family earned their wealth had always curled knots in his stomach, mainly because he benefited from many who suffered at the hands of his father. Pushing his guilt back down that mental dark abyss, he stood up. "When you enter the great room, turn left, and go through the double doors. That'll be the kitchen."

"Babe, I'm sorry. It was supposed to be a joke. Bailey often says my jokes are for my own amusement." She brought the fitted dress over her head and shimmied it down her slim hips, then came in close and wrapped comforting arms around his waist. "I'm sorry."

Gavin released a weary long breath. "What you see here, all of this, it's not my life. I'd rather have nothing than the burden this shit carries. I want you far away from all of this. But I may not have—"

A pounding blow came against the door. "Gavin, man, let's go!"

"We'll talk about this later." Giving her a quick peck on the lips, he exited.

Chapter Thirty-five

Sienna made her way back downstairs and was nearly run over by a woman that zipped past her, shrieking in laughter as she attempted to escape a man that chased after her with a red feather boa. Evidently the party hadn't waned. There seemed to be even more people present. The drinking, dancing, swearing, singing . . . yep, a three-ring circus, that's what it looked like.

She was startled by an abrupt grab of her right wrist and swirled around into strong arms.

"Aren't you lovely. I arrive late and find a rare jewel. May I have this dance, my lady?"

"Maybe another time." Sienna tried to peel out of the embrace of the handsome, drunk, and apparently high young man. His bloodshot blue gaze lulled and roamed over her face before settling on her mouth.

"I could eat you up." His head lowered; warm liquored breath feathered against the side of her neck.

"Dude." She shoved hard at the solid wall of his chest. His head lifted and puckered lips came in, aiming for her mouth. She reared back as far as his strangled hold would allow. "I'm pretty sure Gavin would take issue with this." Pushing at his chest once more to get free only made him tighten his purchase.

A drunk and high as a kite admirer, geez.

She'd offer him one last chance to let her go before seeing no other alternative but to introduce the young man's nuts to her knee. "Look, you need to back off."

"Shane, let her go!" Caren rushed forward and pried the man off, unknowingly saving him from an otherwise crippling blow to the balls. "Do you want Gavin to take your stupid head off? Go away before I tell him what you tried to do to his girlfriend . . . fiancée, and then I'll watch as he kicks your ass. Shoo, damn you." She shoved him, and he stumbled away. "Sorry about that. Cousin Shane's really a good guy. He just tends to party a little too hard, is all."

Sienna straightened her dress and took a breath. "I can see that. Thanks for the rescue."

"No problem."

"I was on my way to the kitchen to see if there was anything light I could munch on. I don't think I'll be able to eat that poor piggy after seeing his insides spill out of him." She gulped back the bile at the thought.

"I'm sure we can find you something." Caren led the way.

They stepped into a massive kitchen filled with servers bustling about.

Caren pulled open the industrial-size fridge. "Hmm, what about fruit?"

Sienna shook her head. "No, thanks."

"Can I help you ladies?"

Their heads turned to the right. Before Sienna could respond to the bald man who must have been the head chef, given that he was the only staff dressed in a white uniform, while the others were in full black, Caren said, "Tom, she's looking for something light to eat."

"Ah, of course. Would a bowl of vegetables in chicken broth suit you?"

"It would . . . and crackers if you have any. Thank you." Sienna smiled appreciatively.

"And a glass of water with lemon, if you wouldn't mind," Caren added with a smile that Sienna found genuinely warm directed at the man.

"Coming right up."

They took a seat at a small table near the back of the kitchen to keep out of everyone's way. Within minutes, a steaming bowl of goodness was set before her. Sienna inhaled and let the savory aroma soothe her hunger before digging in.

"Have you and Gavin set a date, and will you try to get pregnant right away?"

Swallowing down the mouthful, Sienna brought up the cloth napkin from her lap and wiped her mouth. The girl was direct, she had to give her that. "No, not yet, and Gavin and I haven't discussed when or if we'll have kids."

"If you do, my father would want his first grandchild to be a boy."

Had Sienna not looked up again, she would have missed the very brief scowl that creased Caren's forehead. There was an undercurrent of something felt in her words . . . not sure what. "I don't think your father wants me in particular to become his daughter in-law, let alone give him a grandchild, boy or girl."

Caren's eyes widened, and she shook her head. "Not so. He's been out back telling anyone who'd listen that Gavin's engaged and that you two will give him a grandson. He's super excited." She made a hand motion resembling a drink at her mouth. "He's a bit tipsy, I'll admit. Pop likes his whiskey, but I know he's thrilled. He's not one to get jolly about much. You seemed to make him laugh. That's saying a lot." She nodded. "Yes, he wants you and Gavin to marry, and for you to give him a grandson. If he could, he would demand it."

Sienna didn't know if she should be pleased or worried about that. The latter most likely.

"What about you? Are you seeing anyone?"

Caren looked around then leaned in, whispering, "Don't tell anyone. There's this guy I've been talking to at my gym."

"Why so secretive?"

"If my father finds out, he'll want to have him checked out."

Sienna leaned in, mirroring her pose, and whispered, "Checked out? How?"

"You know, have him and his family checked. If he isn't satisfied with the report. . ." Brows puckered, she sat back and let the rest of her thought hang in momentary suspense silence. "How's the soup?"

"Very good, thanks." Sienna wanted to know more about this *checked out* business. That all too familiar spine chill started a slow roll down her back over what the answer might be. The topic was placed on her mental list of things to discuss with Gavin later.

A sudden yawn escaped her. The weight of the entire day was starting to catch up with her. She finished up the soup and then brought the bowl and glass to the sink. One of the staff kindly took over the chore of rinsing and placed the dishes in the dishwasher. The kitchen ran like a well-oiled machine.

"I think I'll go lie down in Gavin's room if that's okay."

"Sure, of course. Let's exchange cell numbers. You can text me if there's anything you need." They quickly did so and then left the kitchen.

"You'll likely not get much rest. There will be fireworks later. Eddie's out back now setting everything up. He does this really cool light show. He goes all out. The presentation seems to get bigger and bigger each year."

"Caren?"

They both turned around. Abela stood a few yards away, keeping her distance as if Sienna carried a contagion. "I see you're being summoned." She stared back at Abela's venomous scowl. *Really? You want to take it there with me? Bring it.* A slight flare of understanding appeared in the woman's cold, brown eyes. Abela was smart to look away. Turning back to Caren, Sienna smiled. "Maybe I'll come down once the light show starts."

"Sounds good." Getting another call out from Abela, Caren trotted off.

Sienna took note of Abela's side-eye before the pair ambled away. *Like I got time for that nonsense.* Dismissing the woman, she made her way back to Gavin's room. Leaving the desk lamp on, she took off her sandals but remained dressed and climbed into the large bed, settling atop the comforter.

It took effort to quiet her thoughts about many aspects of the day before she drifted off to sleep.

Hours later, a cool hand stroked over her hip and in between her thighs, waking her from a rather sound sleep.

"Hey, sweetness."

Smooth lips and light kisses grazed her neck. She rolled over into strong, cradling arms. That Shane guy could learn a thing or two from his cousin. "You made it back." Fully dressed, his clothes carried a hint of nicotine.

"Yep. Did you get something to eat?"

"Um hum." Resting her head in the crook of his shoulder, nuzzling close, she draped an arm across his waist and a leg over his hip, stroking the heel of her foot up and down his jean-clad leg in complete contentment.

Loud bangs, followed by whistling sounds rang out before the room was bathed in streaks of Technicolor light.

"How can you sleep through all of that noise? Eddie's got an entire arsenal of fireworks. He'll be at it for who knows how long."

"I was really tired. Your family knows how to bang out a party, that's for sure."

"True that. When it comes to celebrating, they go at it pretty hard." His hand slipped inside her panties, and a middle finger leisurely massaged her clit.

"So, that was your last assignment?" A soft pant. Sienna rocked her hips against his skillful touch. "You're done, right?" More loud pops and crackling broke into their intimate space. She reared back to look at him. "Gavin, I asked, are you done?"

"Sie-Sie, I'm going to do whatever it takes to keep you safe, know that."

She frowned. "What does that have to do with what I asked you? Are you planning to continue to work for your father, become leader of the southeast as he wants or not?"

"That's not quite what it's called."

She shoved his hand from between her legs and came out of his embrace, contentment instantly evaporated. "Leader, ruler, dictator, who gives a damn what it's called. Are you planning to take the job, that's all I want to know?" Again, no reply. He merely rolled to his back and stared up at the intermittent rainbow of color casted across the vaulted ceiling. Hurt, undercut by betrayal, she released a deep exhale for calm, sat up, and brought her legs over the side of the bed, slipping on her sandals. "I guess that's my answer."

A caressing hand stroked along her spine. "My pop wants to strike a deal with me. He'll let us be, if I agree to look after his southeast territory," he muttered. "I didn't say I'd do it."

She looked back at him. "But you're thinking on it. I can tell. You keep saying how I'm your family first and how you want to keep me away from all of this. Now you're about to take over as mob boss for that old guy in the wheelchair." Anger and frustration mounting, she waved a dismissing hand. "You know what, forget it. You do you. I'm not going to—" Thundering booms rang out in quick succession. In a speed that stunned her, he leaped from the bed, and grabbed her with both hands on his tumble to the floor, rolling her beneath him. His hand cradled her head and pushed her face into the crook of his neck.

"Gavin, what the hell!" She tried to rise, but his full weight pinned her solidly against the cool hardwood floor.

"That's gunfire. Stay down."

Sienna went stock-still as loud screams were heard. She'd thought it was more fireworks.

When the popping stopped, he drew back just slightly and ran a hand all over her. "You're okay?"

She nodded, feeling her heartbeat in her feet. "What happened?"

"I don't know." He got up, yet stayed low on his way to the window. "Stay down." With his back shielded against the wall, he widened the wooden slats of the blinds, leaned to the side, and peeked out.

"What is it?" The room was situated at the rear of the house with a good view of the backyard party. "Gavin?"

"Security is fully armed. Everyone must have fled inside. Tables are overturned. What the . . . there's a body. . ." He raced to the closet.

"A what!" Sienna watched him search the top shelf, reached far in back, and pulled out what looked like a men's shaving bag. "Gavin, what's going on?" Her breath hitched at the sight of the gun he pulled from it. The chamber was quickly clipped opened and checked. Fully loaded. "You keep a loaded gun in this room?"

"Every room in this house has a loaded gun in it." The matter-of-fact tone in his voice was scarier than the look of that black steel in his hand.

"Is there a gun at your apartment?" His direct stare was answer enough. She rapidly shook her head. "All of this . . . this place . . . I have to get the hell out of here."

"You stay put and stay down." He stalked to the door.

Ignoring his clipped command, she rushed to him. "No, I'm coming with you."

"Sienna, I need to see what's going on. You'll be safe in here."

"I'll be safe with you. I can't sit in here. Wh-what if something happens to you?" Her voice bubbled over in a stuttering panic, eyes instantly watering.

He drew her close and kissed her lips before his forehead came to rest lightly against hers. "I'll be fine."

She drew back, but her hands remained clutched on his arms. "You don't know that. You didn't pull out that loaded gun for shits and giggles."

"I just want to be prepared if shit goes even more sideways." Seeing her ready to object, he finally conceded. "Stay close to me."

"Okay." Heck yes, she would. As if she needed to be told twice.

He eased open the door and peeked out, then they slowly made their way downstairs with him checking corners and corridors along the way.

The great room was packed in chaos. Mothers were cradling their crying children; men were yelling and rushing around in a confused disarray. Through it all, Eddie, along with several other men, was trying to get everyone to settle down.

Sienna found Dylan, who was consoling his wife, Angie, she presumed. Among them were Caren, Abela, and Nana Rue. "Gavin, there's your family over there." She searched the crowd. "Where's your father?" With his towering height, the man should be easy to locate, but he wasn't there.

"Everybody shut up!" Gavin roared in a resonance that abruptly brought the entire room to heel. He tucked the gun in the front waistband of his jeans, took her hand, and then they moved to the center of the room. "Emmett, get the women and children downstairs now. Who's on the security gates?"

Dylan came forward. "Not sure. It happened so fast. Everyone was watching the fireworks at the time it all went down."

Gavin scowled. "Fireworks! Are you fucking kidding me?" A stiff index finger pointed at several men in black suits. "You, you, and you, see that the gates are secure."

As Emmett ushered the women and children out, he looked back. "What about her?"

Sienna met the man's direct stare, then turned to Gavin, lightly squeezing his hand. "I'm not leaving you."

"She stays with me."

"You sure about that? You don't need her hanging on you with all of this shit going down. She'll just get in the way."

Gavin's brows dipped low. "Are you sure you want to stand there and argue with me?" The man evidently thought better of it and walked on.

As Gavin barked out orders with no objection, strutting around with that gun openly displayed at his middle, Sienna was getting kind of turned on seeing him in this light. She frowned. *What the hell! Ugh, that's sick and twisted. This place is rubbing off on me.* She shuddered at the ugly thought.

With the room now free of frightened, wailing women and children, she felt she could breathe and think a little better. It lasted mere seconds as her breath lodged right back up in her throat at the sight of the blood-soaked, overturned, *empty* wheelchair.

"Dear god!" Her head jerked to Gavin, who stared at the crimson puddle staining the oak hardwood floor.

"Where's Pop and Mr. McCrae?" Gavin asked with an anxious look at Eddie. "No one was doing their fucking job, that's how this happened! Watching fireworks," he growled.

"They're in the office with Mr. McCrae," Edwin said. "Pop was hit in the shoulder. McCrae took two in the chest. He was the target, sure enough. Dylan and I were told to stay out here to get everyone under control. We should be in there with him. What if Pop dies?" He looked at his older brothers with heightened fear in his eyes.

Sienna's attention drew to a staff person on his knees now sopping up the blood from the floor. She looked out through the open French doors. Several more staff in their shadowy black uniforms were righting tables and chairs and cleaning up debris, all working with a mechanical calm as though this was a normal day in the life when one works for a mafia kingpin.

Still holding a firm grip on her hand, Gavin crossed the room to the office. His brothers followed.

Chapter Thirty-six

A straight up gangster.

Seated shirtless in the armchair in front of his desk, bristles of red hair with sprinkles of gray split his lumberjack wide chest. Legs spread and braced steady, Murtagh clutched a bottle of Kavanagh brand whiskey as another man worked a sharp tool into his shoulder, digging it in deep. He hardly winced as he brought the bottle to his mouth, swallowing down a hefty gulp.

If there ever had been an image of what Sienna pictured a mob boss to look like, the man before her was a clear-cut depiction.

Blood oozed from the open womb. He used a towel already stained in blood to wipe his chest. She turned away to stop herself from vomiting on the mafia king's buffed black shoes, only to see a figure stretched out on the floor, covered . . . no, he was skillfully shrouded in a blue and green checkered wool blanket like sausage within casing. *Mr. McCrae.* Her hand flew to her throat; a shiver rushed through her as she stared at the motionless man. *This is madness!*

Gavin's arm slipped around her waist, stroking her side. "Sweetness, you shouldn't be around any of this. Go downstairs. We'll leave as soon as I'm done."

"I'm fine." Not wanting to leave his side, Sienna swallowed down the bile.

"Pop, are you okay? That looks pretty bad." Dylan handed him a clean towel from the desk, that was used to wipe away more blood streaming down the man's chest.

"I'll live if Bran here can pull the bloody beast from my shoulder."

"What the hell was this about?" Gavin asked.

"I told you, son, there are those who don't want to see me have McCrae's territory. Conal suspected he had a traitor in his camp, someone that wanted him dead, sooner than later, so they could take his seat."

"Pop, this was an execution," Eddie barked. "I'll bet that fucker's wishing he was dead now that Miser's got a hold of him."

Gavin turned to Eddie. "What are you talking about?"

"Miser capped one of the dudes who shot Pop. The other one who shot Mr. McCrae was caught before he could get away. Miser has him out back in the tool house." Eddie's grin was sickly malicious. "He'll get him to talk."

Dear god! I'm about to marry into this freak show. What exactly was Miser doing to the guy? Sienna's imagination went into a rapid tailspin of possibilities. She felt the added pressure of Gavin's hand at her side, easily reading her unmasked scowl of fear and disgust.

"They were both sacrificial lambs," Murtagh said around swallows from his bottle. "They snuck in to do a job with no expectation of leaving alive, that much is certain. What they don't know is Conal and I had already worked out the logistics. Those papers you and Dylan shuttled back and forth were legal ease to get the matter settled. The docs have already been sent up to the top head in Ireland. We—" Murtagh's green eyes locked on Sienna as though he'd just noticed her standing there. He scowled. "Gavin, your fiancée should go downstairs with the women and children. This is a private business matter."

Gavin turned to her. "Go. It shouldn't take long. Like I said, we'll leave as soon as I'm done here."

"No, you won't be leaving," Murtagh chimed in. "There are things we need to iron out in your new role." He looked over at the man beneath the blanket; his eyes filled with grief. "We were mates from infancy. He was my brother. Those bastards took him before he was ready."

"I got it, sir." Bran, the makeshift medic in a dark suit held within a narrow tweezer a mangled blood-soaked bullet. He dropped it into the silver ashtray on the desk, and then began cleaning and dressing his handiwork.

"It's about bloody time." Murtagh chugged from the bottle of whiskey once more. When he looked at her again, he cut a small smile. "Sienna, darling, you go relax. It would seem this engagement has become quite timely. Let's hope you birth me a grandson soon after the two of you wed. I have big plans for him."

Listening to the man's thick accented voice that he attempted to lace with warmth, sweat trickled down Sienna's spine. She turned to Gavin. "What does that mean?" Her head turned back to Murtagh. "What plans?"

His small smile was now a wide grin. "I will see that my grandson is properly groomed. Legacy, lass. We Kavanaghs have been around a long time. I intend to make certain that we continue for many years to come."

The rapid beat of her pulse was felt in every nerve-ending throughout her body as fear and anger filled her full to bursting. She sent him a hard warning glare. "If you think you're getting your hands on any child of mine, you must be nine kinds of crazy."

"Sie-Sie, I got this." Gavin lightly squeezed her hand.

Murtagh threw his head back in that roaring, blow-your-cheeks-back, wind-tunnel laughter, eyes crinkled tight. "Oh, lass, I do like you. Gavin, you did well with this one. Now if you birth me a grandson, you will win my favor, all the more. And we will have the wedding here." His tone was resolute; the man expected to be obeyed.

He took more swallows from the bottle, then cut a sideways look at Dylan, forehead creased. "Angie still has yet to give me a grandchild. It's been a year and nothing."

"Pop, stop," Gavin muttered with an apologetic look at Dylan before turning to Sienna. "Go downstairs." He palmed her cheeks and kissed her softly on the mouth, lingering, then whispered, "We'll leave soon. I promise."

With great reluctance, Sienna left the room, but not before sending Murtagh another rigid warning. "Don't forget what I said." The man's roaring laughter followed her out.

Chapter Thirty-seven

"We have to hit back and hit hard."

"Shut up, Eddie, or get out," Gavin bellowed.

"Yeah, Eddie." Dylan shoved him hard in the shoulder. "This shit's not some fucking video game."

"No, it's not. It's war." Murtagh rounded his desk. He sent Bran a nod of dismissal. When the door closed, he said, "Edwin is right." Retrieving a cigar from the mahogany wooden box on his desk, he used the solid gold guillotine cutter birthday gift to clip the tip. "I need to make clear who now rules the southeast. It won't take long before word spreads of McCrae's death. There will be many looking to take control of his territory. A firm message must be sent branding the Kavanagh mark."

There was a knock on the door, and Miser stepped inside. "It was the O'Learys." No preamble. "They were behind it."

"Seriously? The fucking O'Learys?" Dylan jerked his head between them all. "They're southwest territory. What are they doing going after the southeast? McCrae has deals in place with them."

"There's been a lot of infighting according to that lackey I've been questioning out back," Miser commented. "The twin brothers, Declan and Finn, both want control now that their father is dead. Finn chose to take from what he thought was a weak clan to start building his own. He got his intel from a man named Mullen, a low level within McCrae's rank. Seeing that his boss's health was on the decline, Mullen saw an opportunity to rise up."

"He thought wrong." Puffing his cigar, getting it to kindle nicely, Murtagh reared back in his chair. "Get your team in place. Find Mullen. Gavin will be heading this one."

"Like hell I will." Gavin rubbed his aching forehead. "Pop, I said I'm not in this." So much unnecessary violence. All he wanted was to live his life free of it, continue his role as GM at Lucas's company, and live happily with Sienna and any children they might have. Take out the trash. Take his family on vacations and watch his kid open gifts on Christmas morning. Normal shit. His father coming to his feet derailed his thoughts. "Pop, I can't be part of any of it. I have Sienna to think about."

The room went eerily silent for a long moment. The man's green gaze held Gavin in a viper hold as he placed the cigar in the ashtray, came around to the front of the desk, and sat on the edge. "What do you think happened to that bloke you beat to a bloody pulp?" Murtagh cocked his head. "We don't leave loose ends, son. You've been in this whether you want to admit it or not."

Gavin looked at Miser and was sent a Machiavellian grin. Sweat beaded the back of his neck as he imagined Dale's awful demise at the hands of his sick and sadistic cousin. No, at his own hands. The moment he got Kavanagh involved to find Dale, he'd sealed the man's fate. Dale's death was on his hands. His chest constricted with excruciating torment and unrelenting guilt, so tight, he couldn't breathe. Backing away, shaking his head, the room spun on its axis as he digested the horror of his actions. "I can't do this . . . can't be here," he choked out, swung open the door, and fled from the room.

Murtagh rushed to the door. "If you walk away, you keep fucking walking, you hear me! Things are about to get hot, and you'll get no protection from me, boy, understand! Nothing! Banished!" he barked.

Gavin stumbled; his breath hitched. He pivoted, facing his father. Dylan and Eddie stared back at him within the frame of the door.

"Pop, don't! You don't mean that. Tell him you didn't mean it," Dylan pleaded.

"Yeah, Pop, come on, don't banish him," Eddie followed.

"You heard me! He's banished!" Murtagh thundered and pointed a stiff finger across the room. "If I find out that either of you had any contact with him, you'll be granted the same."

Doing his best not to let the anguish of those words affect him, Gavin turned, and headed to the basement.

Chapter Thirty-eight

Sienna came out of the bathroom wearing a towel wrapped around her. She dropped it to the floor, sat on the edge of the bed, and began rubbing moisturizer over her body. "That shower felt fantastic . . . just what I needed."

Giving a look over her shoulder, Gavin lay with his back to her. He hadn't said a word the entire ride home.

When he came to the basement to get her, the weight of the day showed in his weary eyes. He'd kissed his grandmother, hugging her tightly while whispering something in her ear that actually had the crabby woman tearing up. Then, he did the same to both Caren and Abela. Both ladies' expressions mirrored Nana Rue's. His behavior was like that of a man about to go on a long, faraway journey.

The car ride was filled with one word responses to everything she'd said, until he'd finally muttered, "'I'm tired. Please, no more questions.'" She'd let the matter drop. Now that they were home, away from the wackadoo Kavanaghs, her curiosity outweighed her understanding of his need to rest. She wanted to know what took place after she'd left the office.

"Gavin?"

"Hmm?"

She turned off the lamp and slid in beneath the covers. Her bare breasts brushed enticingly at his back. She draped a leg over his hip, intent on grinding against his bare buttocks, but he was in his underwear. That was a surprise. She'd expected he'd be naked and eagerly waiting for her to join him.

Slipping a hand inside his boxer-briefs, stroking his surprisingly flaccid length, while administering kisses on the back of his neck, she asked, "Are you going to share with me what happened in the meeting with your father after I left the room?"

"Nothing happened," he muffled into the pillow.

"Nothing happened, huh? So, for about forty-five minutes I waited in the basement while you, your brothers, and your father just hung out, shooting the shit with one another?" Silence. "Fine, don't tell me." Getting frustrated, she rolled away from him and jerked the comforter up over her shoulder. "You want to shut me out of your little family meeting? Whatever."

Slowly, he turned and got on top of her, settling between her thighs with his legs spread, his knees baring most of his weight. But that was it. His face stayed buried at the side of her neck. Wetness slicked against her skin. He was crying. *Oh god! Oh god! Oh god!* Concern jolted her pulse, pounding rapidly. With both arms, she enveloped them protectively around his back and locked her ankles over his hips, sheltering him tight.

"I love you," she whispered and stroked his body, soothing fingers massaging as more hot tears soaked her flesh. "Babe, what's wrong?" The room was pitch dark. The digital red numbers on the clock its only illumination.

"Babe?" Witnessing this strong, powerful man so broken, worry welled up inside her, so strong that she could hardly breathe. Gathering her nerves, she tried to focus. He'd taken care of her. It was her turn to do the same for him.

As she continued to run a caressing hand up and down his back and threaded fingers in his hair, massaging his scalp, she voiced softly, "Sweetheart, whatever it is, we can get through it together. But we can't do that until you tell me what's wrong."

A heavy, shuddering breath left him. "You deserve better," he said, his tone, a low, plaintive murmur as an unsteady hand palmed her cheek. "When I look at you, I see pure light, goodness, perfection. Me? I'm my father, a thug perpetrating as a business man. A thug, that's what I am. I'm not destined to be anything more than that. I proved it when I went after Dale." His voice shook on those last words.

Sienna reached over and clicked on the table lamp. His head lay cradled within the well of her right neck and shoulder. "Gavin?" she called softly after a stretch of silence. A faint sniffle, then he released another breathy sigh. She palmed his wet cheeks and brought his head up. "Baby, look at me." His eyelids lifted. Tears soaked his blond lashes. "What happened in the office after I left?" Anguish sealed his features down tight. "Please, talk to me."

"I'm not worthy of you, but I love you, and I don't know how to let you go," he said through ragged pulls of his breath.

Fear gripped her. "What do you mean, let me go? What are you saying? Did your father tell you that you had to stop seeing me? He couldn't have checked me out already." She got a puzzled look. "Caren said your father has everyone checked out before they can become part of your family."

"No." It was all he said as he peeled out of his underwear, then captured her left breast in his mouth, nipping and sucking like it was his last meal before kissing a path up her neck to her mouth, tonguing her greedily. His lips trailed a warm path down her body, and lower, licking her inner thighs. A soft moan reverberated against her clit.

"I love your scent, your taste, I love you."

He devoured her pussy with long, tongue-stroking skill, so much so, she was quivering through an amazing orgasm in seconds. With haste, he came up and entered her on a whisper of her name, but kept up a slow rocking, measured and controlled, yet his kisses were feral, rough as if starved, desperate.

Their push and pulls gained the slightest momentum before they pitched over the cliff together. With a final shudder, he eased off her, but remained snug against her body with one leg snaked between hers, the slickness of his semen smearing between their joined thighs. A soft sniffle left him as he placed a gentle kiss upon her shoulder.

Sienna released a long, glorious sigh, slaked beyond coherent reasoning. "Wow, though it was pretty quick, I think that one takes top honors." No playful reply. "Babe, please talk to me." And he finally did. He spilled it all, the impending retaliatory battle his father was about to wage, his banishment from the family, right down to him feeling responsible for Dale's demise. The things she learned rocked her to her core with fear and grief, but the remorse and sorrow she could see in his drowning blue eyes, his guilt over Dale's likely cruel death would be a lifelong punishment for him.

Holding him close, she administered light kisses upon his cheek, forehead, chin, and a gentle peck upon his lips, then reared back to meet his gaze.

"Even after everything Dale did to me, I hurt for how he may have suffered. As for your father, that's his war, not yours. You're not him." Sienna came up and got on top of him; their warm naked bodies pressed tightly together. "You have a great career with Lucas and a wife-to-be who loves you." A tear slid down his right temple that she swept away with her thumb. "Hey, let's get married in Vegas."

He blinked rapidly, then his blue eyes leveled, fixed, tentative. "Really? You still want to marry me even after everything I've told you?"

"Yes, and I'm sure as hell not getting married at the Kavanagh compound." A man died in that house, there was no way she would host her wedding there. Nor did she want to invite the Kavanaghs to her happy day. "Not gonna happen. And no offense, but your people are cray-cray."

"Tell me something I don't know, and I'm banished, so you don't have to worry about inviting any of them."

Hurt and anguish were visible in his gaze. "Give your father time to cool off." No reply. "Are we getting married or not?"

He sat up, taking her with him. "I'll hit up Sean to see if we can borrow his gulfstream." He reached to the nightstand for his cell.

She caught his wrist. "Perfect, but not yet." She took hold of his semi-hard cock, and delivered swift pumps, her hand working his shaft, easily giving it life, then lifted, and guided the length of him along the wet walls of her eagerly clutching channel. "First, I'm going to ride you, Mr. Crane."

A slow smile grazed his lips as firm hands latched onto her bare buttocks. "Oh most definitely."

Chapter Thirty-nine

A quarter past midnight, standing before the officiant, surrounded by his buddies, all of whom came to stand as witnesses, Gavin was about to marry the woman of his dreams, a woman far out of his league, and far more than he deserved.

As it had been at Lucas's wedding, a best man hadn't been chosen. Each one of his buddies that stood at his back, physically and figuratively, held the title. Behind Sienna, Bailey's bright white smile of approval was blinding as she clutched in her hand the platinum band within the black velvet box. Thanks to Lucas's jeweler's impeccable customer service, Gavin picked up the rings before they'd left for Vegas.

"Dearly beloved," the officiant started, "love is an adventure. It cultivates like the universe itself only by perpetual exploration. Love between two people whose passion for one another brings them to this point of sharing a boundless. . ."

As the man went on, Gavin wanted to tell him to speed it up. He held his breath, expecting the roof would cave in, something, anything that would prevent Sienna from saying the two most important words in the world in that moment.

Dressed in a simple white sleeveless dress and white strappy heel sandals, his lady resembled a beautiful angel. She'd picked out his wedding get-up—black button-down, long sleeve shirt over a black suit coat and black slacks. She'd told him it was her day to have him however she wanted. She could've put him in a rainbow beanie, and he wouldn't have objected . . . well, maybe a little. As long as she didn't back out, he didn't care what he wore.

"Please join hands," the officiant finally said after a lengthy speech.

Gavin took her hands in his; his gaze locked with hers. Her smile lit up her beautiful eyes, not appearing the least bit nervous. Yet, he was close to sweating through his tailored shirt.

"Do you, Sienna Grace Keller, take Gavin Rowan Crane to be your lawfully wedded husband, to have, to hold, and to love, in sickness and in health, until death do you part?"

"I do."

Releasing a quiet breath, Gavin lightly stroked his fingers at her palms with a subtle look upward. The roof hadn't caved in on them. *So far, so good.*

"Do you, Gavin Rowan Crane, take Sienna Grace Keller to be your lawfully wedded wife, to have, to hold, and to love, in sickness and in health, until death do you part?"

"I do."

"Do we have the rings?" the officiant asked.

Gavin retrieved the five-carat emerald cut solitaire from his jacket pocket, and Bailey handed Sienna the platinum band.

The officiant turned to Gavin. "Please repeat after me. With—"

"Wait. Let's do this part together." Sienna brought up the wedding band. She stuck out her left hand, fingers splayed. "Cross your arm with mine."

Gavin was a bit confused for a moment but quickly caught up. He extended his arm beneath hers, their wrists crossing. She nodded to the officiant to continue.

"Please place the rings on your fingers and repeat after me. With this . . . these rings, I . . . we thee wed." Gavin heard one of his buddy's soft chuckle behind him at the officiant's confusion from being thrown off script.

Together, they slipped the rings on each other's finger, repeated their vows, and then linked hands, hers squeezing lightly.

"By the state of Nevada, I now pronounce you husband and wife. You may kiss the bride."

Gavin took his wife into his arms and kissed her, unable to stop, unable to let go.

"Uh, bro?" Dax tapped him on the shoulder. "You might want to come up for air sometime soon."

He forced himself to pull away and rested his forehead gently against hers. "I love you."

"I love you, too."

"You love her. She loves you. Great. Let's celebrate." Dax pulled a small toy horn from his inside jacket pocket and blew.

Chapter Forty

Sienna's gasps of pleasure fell in chorus with the delicious pounding Gavin was giving her from behind. On her knees in the middle of the bed, legs spread, his cock slid rapidly in and out of her with precise deftness. She could hardly catch her breath. The nonstop, hard thrusting went on for long minutes as she gripped the sheets for some semblance of purchase, her body caught in a tidal wave of pleasurable sensation.

A sudden, deep guttural moan escaped him. He tensed, gripped her buttocks tight, and took his release, filling her so full that his semen streamed down her inner thighs. He kept pumping his hips, draining his penis to depletion, then blew out a ragged breath and rolled off onto his back. She collapsed to the mattress in exhausted bliss, yet looked forward to being woken later for another round. It had been that way for the past several nights. He'd been fucking her at last count three times a day. He'd said he couldn't get enough of her. The feeling was mutual.

Sucking in much needed air to soothe her parched lungs, she turned her head on the pillow to look at him. Eyes closed, his sweaty chest heaved. She smiled at his weary look of utter gratification. "How would you rate that one?"

"It was off the charts," he breathed and gave her left butt cheek a good smack. "Hand me the remote. Let's see what the weather will be like tomorrow.

"Have you finished packing? The plane is scheduled to depart at 6:35 in the morning."

"I guess I'm as packed as I'm ever going to be. I've always wanted to visit Barcelona."

"We're not just going to Barcelona. I'm taking you on the full Spain experience, Mrs. Crane," he said while aiming the remote at the TV.

Mrs. Crane. She loved the sound of that. "I'm looking forward to it.

"It was nice of Sean to let us use his plane for our honeymoon. He's a really great guy. Maybe we can have him over for dinner when we get back as a small token to say thanks. By the way, he's a hottie. Is he seeing anyone?" She smirked at his wide-eye stare, then he cut her a grin, showing he wasn't at all bothered by the hottie comment.

"That's a plan, and I got your hottie." A firm hand slapped her backside again, the sting reigniting a burst of sexual arousal.

"Sean's got his eye on a lady, but I doubt anything will come of it."

"Why is that?" Sienna snuggled her nude body against his with a sigh of contentment. He switched the remote from his right hand to his left and brought his arm around her shoulders, pulling her into the security of his sweet embrace.

"The woman's sort of seeing someone."

"Oh. Well, he's sexy and sweet . . . and stinking rich, not too many of those with that combination out there. I'm sure he won't have any trouble meeting someone."

"You'd be surprised. Enough talk about my buddy that you apparently find sexy and hot." He rolled over on top of her and settled in between her legs. "Like I said, I got your hot right here."

"You most certainly do." She moaned as he sank his hard shaft deep inside her once more, taking her to exquisite, sexual paradise. Hours after he'd finally gotten his fill, completely spent, sleep crashed down hard upon her. He woke her a short time later. They had a flight to catch.

Chapter Forty-one

Stretched out beneath the covers of her big comfy bed, Sienna could barely keep her eyes open. She and Gavin had returned from their honeymoon in Spain just under three hours ago. An uncontainable smile broke out. *Best honeymoon ever!* Not that she had another to compare it to, but it had to be up there among the top ten many girls dreamed about.

They'd taken the AVE train from Barcelona to Madrid and spent a couple of days there sightseeing. Gavin had been determined to show her every nook and cranny of the beautiful city. He'd visited many times before and said it had been one of his favorite vacation spots.

Three days before had been spent in Lisbon, Portugal. They'd enjoyed a private wine pairing lunch in the vineyards of Requengos de Monsaraz. They visited Seville or what Gavin had called *old town* with its brightly colored stone structures and cobbled streets. He'd taken her on a moonlit canoe ride along Maria Luisa Park. They explored the Triana Market and visited the antique shops of the Santa Cruz Quarter, and ended their three-day stay there with a tour of the Alcázar Palace. From there, they made a three-day stop in Granada simply because she'd mentioned that she'd always wanted to sketch the 16th century Cartuja Monastery.

"Your wish is my command," he'd said. That had been no joke. She carried her sketch pad everywhere they went, capturing details of the scenery with her chalks that she felt could not be conveyed in a smartphone snapshot. Throughout their many destinations, they'd made love virtually every single night . . . and even snuck in a quickie sexcapade in the cramped confines of the railway's bathroom on their way back to Lisbon. Gavin was such a feral, sexual male, and she had no complaints. It had been a honeymoon like none she'd ever dreamed of, all thanks to the beautiful, magnificent man she'd married.

Now back home, after a quiet dinner, she relaxed beneath comfy sheets and aimlessly clicked through the TV channels as she waited for Gavin to join her. Each night she looked forward to curling up in his arms as they drifted off to sleep. It had become a bedtime ritual with them.

She released a yawn. "Babe, I'm going to fall asleep if you don't hurry it up."

He stuck his head out of the bathroom and garbled around the sonic toothbrush, "You had better not."

Through another stretching yawn, Sienna continued to whiz through the channels. She tensed up sharply, coming straight up in bed upon seeing the face of Murtagh Kavanagh displayed on the news reel. The picture switched to images of bodies sprawled out beneath white sheets that were stained in blood. *Dear god!* The TV now showed a split screen of the carnage—the left, Florida—the right, Nevada. Smoke billowed from the rooftops of two estate homes. Her mind flashed briefly back to how Abela's parents had died. Her hand flew to her throat. "Gavin?" she called as she stared at the images.

Gavin stepped out of the bathroom, drying his hands on a wash cloth. "Hey, I was thinking we should—"

"Look." She pointed at the TV. "There was a shooting a few days ago when we were away. They're speculating that your father's alleged," she air quoted, "organization was behind the death of several people down in Florida as well as Nevada, but no concrete evidence has been found to connect him. They mentioned something about a faction in Ireland that is somehow linked to all of it as well. A turf war, sources called it."

Staring at the TV, Gavin sat down on the edge of the bed, distress knotting his features.

"Have you heard from Dylan, from anyone?"

"No, they're not allowed to talk to me. I'm considered dead to them. Basically, I have no family."

"What about Lucas . . . Sean or Dax? They must have heard something. And Bailey hasn't called me. That's odd."

Gavin snatched his phone from the nightstand, scrolled, and tapped the phone, then brought it to his ear.

"Who are you calling?"

"Lucas. Hey," he said when it connected, "did you know about the shooting? I know, but . . . yes, I appreciate that."

"What is he saying?" Sienna whispered.

Gavin turned to her. "He said he knew, but once it had been made clear that no one from the Kavanagh family had been injured, he, Sean, and Dax as well as Bailey made the decision not to tell us. They didn't want to ruin our honeymoon and hoped we didn't catch any of it on the international news while we were away." Gavin exchanged a few more words with Lucas and then ended the call.

Watching the horrific scene on the news, Sienna was glad he was no longer connected to his family. Still, her heart ached for him. Though the Kavanaghs were straight-up criminals, this was his blood. He loved his brothers and sister . . . and Abela a little too much at one point. He even cared about his domineering, mob boss, bully of a father. She understood his feelings.

One might wonder why she'd taken care of her mother financially when the woman had hardly looked after her when she was a child. She'd done it because it was a stark reminder to always be better, do better, that's why.

Sienna gave a light tug at his shoulders from behind. "Babe, lie down." She slid over. He set his phone on the nightstand, got underneath the covers, and stared up at the ceiling, his fingers raking back through his hair, his features somber. She came up on an elbow, palmed his left cheek, and pressed a light kiss on his lips. "The Kavanaghs will always be your family. After everything settles down, maybe your father will come around, lift his stupid ban."

"You don't know my pop. His word is law. The only way he'll lift my banishment is if I agree to come into his organization."

That's not happening. "Try calling or text Dylan to see for yourself that everyone is okay. He might respond." Sienna reached across him to grab his phone from the nightstand and handed it over. "It'll at least give you peace of mind."

As he scrolled through his contacts, his cell phone rang in his hand. Seeing Eddie's name on the display, startled, they stared at one another. "It's Eddie."

She chuckled, stroking a hand across the broad plane of his bare chest. "I can see that. Answer it."

He tapped the phone and put it on speaker. "Hey, Eddie."

"Gav, glad I got you. I called Dax last week or so and heard you got hitched Vegas style and have been in Spain for like a month. Cool. I tried calling you several times, but the line kept falling off. Shouldn't those fancy hotels over there have decent wi-fi or some shit so that doesn't happen?"

"We got back home a few hours ago. Sienna's here. I have you on speaker."

"Oh. Cool. Hey, Sie . . . I can call you Sie, right? I mean since we're fam now. And I can say you have great legs without Gav going ape-shit and threatening to kick my ass, right?"

"It wasn't a threat, Eddie, believe that," Gavin groused.

Sienna grinned at the crinkled brow her husband now displayed. Apparently, Eddie could make his brother anxious, smile, and glower in the same breath. The young man was in a deck all his own. "Sure, Eddie, you can call me Sie if you want."

"Cool."

"I saw the news," Gavin said.

"Bro, that was some precision."

"How's the family?" Gavin cut in, abruptly clamping off any spew of the details.

"Oh right," Eddie was surprisingly quick to understand his near misstep. "Yeah, everyone's cool. Hey, can I come by? I'm not that far from you right now. I need to discuss some things if you know what I mean."

Sienna met Gavin's questioning look, and she nodded.

"It's been a long day," he whispered to her.

"I'm good." She then spoke into the phone. "Sure, Eddie, we're up. I'll put some coffee on."

"Cool. I'll be there in fifteen."

Gavin ended the call. "Sweetness, you really should get some sleep. It was a long flight and a long day."

"Just hear what he has to say." She climbed out of bed and slipped on her robe from the chair, then pinned a hand down firmly on her hip. "If he starts talking about you joining in on whatever is going on—"

"Eddie knows better."

"Good."

Chapter Forty-two

"I'm sure Pop doesn't know you're in touch with me." Gavin took a seat on the barstool next to Eddie.

"Nah, he's got his hands full with what's going on, you know making sure there isn't any sort of retaliatory fallback. I'm not on his radar at the moment. That's what I want to talk to you about."

"Babe?"

Gavin met Sienna's stern stare as she set cups of coffee before him and Eddie. Exchanging a quiet understanding with her, he turned his head back to his brother. "What is it you want from me?"

"Pop has given everyone tasks, except me. Even Miser's crazy ass has been put in charge of shit. But Pop won't give me any assignments, says he wants me to see to the home front, make sure everyone has what they need. Basically, I'm like a goddamn secretary. No, worse than that, I'm a fuc. . ." His eyes met Sienna's across the kitchen island. "I'm a gofer." He frowned. "Hey, should she be listening to any of this?"

Gavin extended his hand out to his wife. She rounded the island and came in between his legs, her back against his chest. He secured his arms around her waist, drawing her in even closer, and looked at Eddie. "We have no secrets."

Eddie shrugged. "Okay, whatever. Pop wouldn't like it, but your shit's your shit. Anyway, I need you to talk to Dylan, convince him that I'm ready to take on assignments. That way he'll speak to

Pop. Dylan would listen to you. Pop would listen to you, too, if you weren't banished, that is."

Gavin read the eagerness in his baby brother's eyes. The young man really wanted to be part of the clan. No reservation. A small part of Gavin admired Eddie's level of devotion to their father and his organization.

Eddie had been given a chance away from the Kavanaghs' lifestyle by living with their mother half the year. But the young man had evidently chosen a side.

"Well, Gav, how about it? Will you talk to Dylan?"

His objection could mean Eddie would be spared that life for at least a little while longer. He looked at Sienna half-seated on his lap, quietly taking it all in, her expression showing no condemnation or approval of Eddie's request.

"You recently received your BA. Why not try to look for a job? You could move back to Ireland and manage the family's whiskey distilleries. Or I could have you come on with me over at MVC and—"

"Eh." A dismissing wave. "I had to finish school. That was one of the divorce conditions Ma put on Pop if I wanted to live here instead of Ireland, you know that. My degree would actually help me in Pop's organization. As for the distilleries, not for me, bro. And why should I go work for someone else when I could keep it in the fam? Come on, Gav, help me out here?"

Gavin could see there was no reasoning with him. His mind was made up on the direction he wanted to take with his life, that young eagerness for big shiny things. "I'll speak with Dylan."

Eddie's grin lit up the room. "Thanks, bro. I—"

Gavin brought up a hand as he came to his feet and Sienna moved to his side. "This is serious shit you want to get into. There are things I'm sure Pop has kept you out of, things that go a lot deeper than what you could imagine."

"Bro, I'm telling you I can handle it."

Gavin nodded. "I'll see what I can do."

Chapter Forty-three

"Thanks for agreeing to meet. I know Pop would be pissed if he knew you were seeing me."

Dylan swallowed his iced tea. "With all the shit he's got going, trust me, my whereabouts are the least of his concerns."

"You sound like Eddie."

"Speaking of, why don't you try to convince him to step away from all of it?" With a look at Dylan seated across from him, Gavin took a bite out of his double-crab-cake sandwich. "Uncle Niall's son, Cousin Remmy, could take over the territory, allowing you to step away as well," he said as he chewed.

Dylan stuck a cluster of fries in his mouth and washed it down with his drink. "Nah, since Pop has agreed to let me manage the southeast, I've convinced him to let me mentor Eddie. Then, in time, when I feel Eddie's ready, I'll step down and hand it over to him."

Gavin frowned. Guilt welled tight in his chest. Dylan wouldn't have to do any of this if only Gavin had stepped up like his father wanted. Now the guy and his wife were moving down to Miami so he could reign over McCrae's territory. This wasn't something his brother wanted, Gavin knew that.

"Dude, it's all good."

Gavin blinked, pulled back to the here and now. "What?"

"I know what you're thinking. No worries, bro. You keep doing what you're doing. You have a beautiful wife, and maybe a kid someday, it makes me happy to see you get the life you've always wanted."

"You deserve it just as much as I do, if not more." Thinking back to the woman at the bar, Gavin said, "Dyl, you've had to sacrifice so damn much. You were in love with Cailin, and Pop made you give her up."

"Cailin is my past. And you don't know the whole story."

Gavin cocked his head. "Are we about to play a guessing game or something?"

Dylan chuckled, then quickly sobered. "Pop wanted me to stop seeing Cailin, but I refused. He said he'd put out an order on her if I didn't. So, I threatened him, said that I'd leave the family, be banished."

Gavin sat back in his chair, stunned. "No shit?"

"Pop came back with a challenge of his own. He'd said if he offered Cailin money to fix up her bar, in exchange that she cut ties with me, she'd choose the bar."

"She chose the bar," Gavin said, and his brother nodded. "I'd hate to see what that hole in the wall looked like before she supposedly fixed it up," he muttered.

"I didn't hold it against Cailin. That bar was all her father had left to give her when he died. And she didn't take the money, not one red cent, but still walked away from me to prevent me from turning away from the family."

Gavin shook his head. "Damn. Sorry, bro." He felt even more to blame for his brother's ill fate. "I'm really sorry that—" Getting a dismissing wave, he asked, "Why didn't she check out with Pop? What did he find out about her that he didn't approve of?"

"Oh, she's the niece of Ennis Whelan, the Midwest head."

Gavin flinched. "Pop's sworn enemy. So that's what he meant when he'd said she would have been a plant, a mole."

"Yep. Anyway, it was a long time ago. I met Angie, and she's perfect. I didn't have to worry about her not checking out with Pop because she grew up in foster care her entire life. Though I know how much she wants a baby, with all that's going on right now, it may be a blessing that she hasn't gotten pregnant. She's been cool about everything." He stretched his arms outward, cracking muscles, unknotting the tension in his shoulders. "Anyway, I got this. I'll take care of the southeast and Eddie. You focus on your wife, your family." Dylan grinned. "I couldn't be happier and more proud of you, bro."

Gavin swallowed down the sudden lump that tightened his throat. "Thanks." Yet, his guilt over all his brother had sacrificed remained.

Epilogue

"I can see he's going to look like his dad." Bailey cooed at the baby nestled in her arms.

"Don't condemn the child," Dax teased as he scooped the baby from her.

"Dax, I won't curse around my son, so I'll just offer you this." Seated in the chair beside the hospital bed, Gavin gave him his customary double salute of his middle fingers.

Sean stepped forward and took the baby from Dax. "He's big, no doubt."

"Tell me something I don't know. I pushed him out." Sienna grinned happily. "I still can't believe he was nearly twelve pounds."

"Kayla was half his size, right, Lucas?" Bailey said.

"It's like birthing a toddler," Lucas joked as he was handed the baby. "Yes, essentially, my daughter was half this baby's weight when she was born."

"When you, Gavin, and Connor get settled at home, I'd still like to throw you that baby shower," Bailey said. "Connor arriving nearly three weeks early ruined my plans."

"He was eleven pounds, fourteen ounces. I'm glad he was early," Sienna returned.

"If you're looking for an event planner, I happen to know of someone who could assist," Sean put in. "She's starting an event planning business. I've been helping her with the process."

"Would she happen to be the woman you've been crushing on for nearly a year?" Dax grinned.

"Dude, shut up." With an awkward smile, Sean looked at Bailey who wore a smirk of her own. "Just let me know, and I'll provide you her information."

"How about the two of you come by for dinner? I can meet her and talk about the details."

"I'll mention it to her."

A knock came at the door, drawing everyone's attention. Murtagh Kavanagh entered. Dressed in a charcoal gray, wool, three-quarter length trench coat over a finely tailored gray suit, his massive presence seemed to swallow up the entire room.

No one moved. Even the air felt stalled around them as the monstrous figure came forward.

Gavin stood up. "Pop, what are you doing here?" His head turned to Sienna when she reached out to Lucas for Connor, and the baby was laid in her arms.

Murtagh stepped over to Dax, Lucas, and Sean, giving each man a firm handshake. "It's been some time since I've seen you boys. How are things?"

Each responded with a few respectable words.

Murtagh turned back to Gavin. "I learned that my lovely daughter in-law delivered my grandson. I knew she would." His proud grin stretched wide. "I thought I'd come get a peek at the wee lad."

Gavin and Sienna exchanged a questioning look, then they looked back at Murtagh. "How would you know that? I haven't spoken to anyone in the family about it." Gavin scowled. "You banished me, remember? How did you find out about the birth of my son?"

Without replying, Murtagh smiled and pulled from his coat pocket a small, perfectly wrapped box. "I wanted to stop by to give my grandson his birthday gift." He handed the box to Gavin.

"It's your sterling silver spoon. I'd given it to you when you were born. Your name is engraved on the front of the handle and there is room to add Connor's name on the back."

Connor. Gavin blinked, not sure what to say. The man knew his son's name. None of it should have come as a surprise, yet it did.

There was nothing soft about his father, all rough edges and stern demands. The mere thought that he'd kept his infant spoon all these years showed a caring, fatherly side of him that Gavin had never seen, hadn't known existed. A sadness crept into his chest, constricting, wishing that he'd grown up with the Murtagh Kavanagh that stood before him now. Mentally shaking himself loose of the what ifs, he set the gift box on the side table. "Thanks." He looked around at everyone, who all stood like statues, staring at his father.

"May I hold him?" Murtagh's tone was surprisingly tentative as he addressed Sienna.

Gavin turned to her. She held Connor nestled in her arms protectively close at her breasts. "Sie-Sie, it's okay." Staring unblinking at his father, she eased her hold. Gavin took his son into his arms and passed him off.

Murtagh smiled down at the baby as he rocked him lightly. "Will you look at that. He has my green eyes." He looked around at everyone, happiness lit bright his stern features. "He's beautiful. Solid, this one. You've done me proud, son, you both have." Connor twitched his little frame. His tawny face scrunched, looking on the verge to let loose a wail. "I think he wants his mam." Murtagh came forward and gently laid the baby in Sienna's arms. "Thank you for this fine boy and for loving my son. You are a lovely addition to the family." He placed a gentle kiss upon her forehead.

Gavin saw the look of utter shock flare in his wife's eyes at the man's surprisingly earnest warmth, then narrowed, displaying blatant objection.

"What about your banishment? You kicked my husband out of your family simply because he didn't want to follow in your footsteps. Now, you show up here as if that never happened."

"Baby, it's okay." Gavin stroked her leg atop the blanket. "I'm cool with it. My family is right here."

"No, it's not okay," she argued and looked Murtagh squarely in the eyes. "Well?"

Murtagh looked around the room. He chuckled. "I really like this woman." He took her hand and kissed the back of it. "You fit right into the family."

Her lips pursed, undoubtedly to hold her ground, but Murtagh brought up his hand. "I also came by to tell my son that I was wrong to banish him. In truth, I've kept eyes on him, on you both, while I settled things following my birthday party last summer. I made sure you all were looked after during my reorganization."

"You mean during your turf war." Sienna didn't mince words, and he merely smiled.

"Now that everything has been ironed out," he said cryptically, but Gavin along with everyone in the room understood it for what it really meant—he'd taken control of the territory by taking out those he felt were a threat. "I'd like to visit my grandson on occasion . . . with his mam present of course." He fiddled with Connor's tiny hand, and the baby latched onto his finger. Smiling, Murtagh straightened to his full height. "He knows his grandpop already. Don't you, my boy." He cooed. "He's a beautiful babe."

Gavin noted his wife held her stern stare upon his father, not allowing his sweet, grandfatherly behavior to sway her.

"Is Gavin out? You won't bother him anymore about succeeding you?"

"He's out."

"And you won't bother us about Connor, because I will tell you right here and right now, he will never become a part of your organization. Do we have an understanding?"

"We do."

"Good. Then I will consider letting you visit your grandson . . . with me or Gavin present."

He nodded. "Much appreciated. Well, I will leave you to enjoy that precious wee one." Murtagh looked around at everyone. "Good day to you." He left the room as smoothly as he'd entered it with the door quietly closing behind him.

Dax was the first to come out of his catatonic state, blowing out a breath. "Damn, bro, that man chills my blood."

"Wow, he's massive," Bailey said.

"Sienna, it appears you're able to put the man in check," Lucas remarked.

"Oh, don't think for one second he doesn't scare me. I know what he's capable of." She gestured a hand between her, the baby, and over to Gavin. "But this right here, I will safeguard against the devil himself . . . believe that." Chuckles broke out at her firm, yet light mocking.

Gavin took a seat in the chair. Looking at his beautiful, strong warrior woman cradling his sleeping son in her protective embrace, how could he have been so fortunate? Ultimately, he'd taken a gamble on opening his heart and won the woman of his dreams.

Smiling, he leaned in, and she met him halfway to accept his kiss. "Believe that, huh?"

She smiled. "You know it."

Author's Note

Though inspired by the northeast region in and around Washington D.C., please note that some events and locations mentioned in this book are fictional and are meant solely for you to escape and enjoy.

Acknowledgments

My heartfelt thank you to my wonderful editor, Jessica Verdi, for her tremendous eye for detail in helping me hone Gavin and Sienna's story. I can't say enough how much I appreciate and enjoy working with you. Also, thank you Julie Sturgeon for working with me in choosing and developing a terrific cover and for responding to my late-night emails. You continue to make the process enjoyable. And many thanks to Tara Gelsomino and the entire Crimson Romance/Simon & Schuster team for the countless hours of hard work to help bring the Tarnished Billionaires series to life.

Many thanks to my agent, Brittany Booker. Your continued cheers are much appreciated.

A huge thank you to my family for riding with me on this journey. I could not do this without your constant support. I'm extremely grateful to have you all by my side.

Finally, I am forever immensely grateful for the support from readers. Thank you from the bottom of my heart for enjoying my stories as much as I love writing them.

About the Author

Michele Arris is a Romance Writers of America Golden Heart®
award-winning author. Her work is edgy and downright steamy
with a melting pot of strong, diverse characters. When she isn't
stationed in front of her laptop spilling her wayward imagination
onto the page, she's jotting scenes in her head. "It's enjoyable to
write stories where two people are guaranteed their happy ending."

Michele loves to hear from readers. To see what happens next
in the Tarnished Billionaires series, please visit her website at
michelearris.com. While there, check out pictures of the settings
where the books are based. Also subscribe to her occasional
newsletter for information about upcoming projects.

Visit her Author Profile page at simonandschuster.com.